# FALSE START

## BROOKLYN KINGS 3

# FELICE STEVENS

False Start (Brooklyn Kings 3)
Copyright © 2025 by Felice Stevens



Published by Good Man Press

Edited by Keren Reed
Copyediting and Proofreading by Flat Earth Editing
Additional Proofreading by Lyrical Lines
Cover Art by Reese Dante
Photographer: Wander Aguiar
Model: Bijan

Digital ISBN: 979-8-88949-075-3
Paperback ISBN: 979-8-88949-083-8
Alternate Paperback ISBN: 979-8-88949-081-4

# DEDICATION

To my children, who make me proud every day.

# ACKNOWLEDGMENTS

Thanks as always to my editor, Keren Reed. To Hope and Jess from Flat Earth Editing, you are the best. To Dianne, from Lyrical Lines, I couldn't do it without you. And to Reese. Thank you for everything and more.

And to the readers, you are the reason and make it all worthwhile.

# PROLOGUE

Patrick

*Ten years earlier*

"I can't believe I'm doing this," I muttered to myself. Nerves, excitement, and a bit of fear all played pinball in my brain as the car approached the club. My team was in the midst of a great winning season, setting records left and right, and I knew my dream of being drafted by the pros was waiting on the horizon if I continued to play at this level and didn't get hurt.

Most of my teammates had used the money from their first endorsement deals to buy cars or jewelry. Some had bought themselves condos. A few had gone on spending sprees, and I could see that they'd end up broke if they didn't rein it in or get a good lawyer and financial manager.

Me? I'd joined an exclusive sex club where anonymity was key. Being the starting quarterback for the college team everyone picked to win the National Championship meant I had girls lined up before, during, and after the games. And yeah, I'd been more than happy to accept what they offered. But it didn't satisfy the itch, the craving I'd had for years, to know what it would be like with a man. So I'd paid the twenty-thousand-dollar fee and joined. Under an assumed name, of course.

Because Patrick "Trick" Sloane had an image to uphold: Football player. Starting quarterback. Macho. Heartthrob with the ladies.

Totally straight.

But what often appeared to be the tallest, strongest tree in the forest most likely had its roots spread in many different directions. And what hid below the surface created the vision above the ground.

I was bisexual. I wanted guys as much as I did girls, and sometimes more.

But getting it on with a guy didn't fit in that nice box I'd put myself into, and there was no going back on the life I'd wanted since I'd thrown my first football. I was on my way to a National Championship and a career that would put every move I made in the spotlight.

So I did the one thing I could think of. Figured out how I could get what I needed on the down-low. And given the number of exclusive clubs I'd found in my search, I wasn't the only one.

I adjusted my mask so it sat straight and tight to my face. I'd gone all out to hide my identity, even getting colored contacts to change my blue-green eyes to gray and temporarily streaking my brown hair with some crap I'd heard the cheerleaders talking about that would wash out in one shampoo. The car slid to a stop in the exclusive Laguna Niguel neighborhood, an imposing iron gate rising high before us. I leaned out of the window and gave the security guard a slip of paper with the number I'd received earlier to grant me entry. The gates swung open, and we accelerated up the curving drive. The house spread out, long and rambling, the windows ablaze with lights.

"You can stop here," I said to the driver as we slid behind an idling Mercedes-Maybach in the large circular drive. I counted several Rolls Royces and a few Ferraris and Maseratis. "Thanks."

The driver grunted and I exited, gazing around me, a little unsure what to do or where to go next. A very large, unsmiling man approached me with an iPad.

"Identification number?"

The pristine collar of his shirt gleamed bright white against the black of his well-fitted suit. He reminded me of the massive tackles I faced every Sunday but without the padding. It wasn't necessary—he was intimidating enough on his own. I repeated the number I'd given to the security guard and waited as he checked.

He nodded. "This way."

I followed him in, side-eyeing the others undergoing the same process. Men of all sizes, shapes, and colors. We were all here for one thing: discreet sex with a man because something in our lives outside these gates forbade us from being ourselves. I wasn't sure about anyone else, but I was slightly freaking out. It would be my first time having sex with a man.

"The first floor is for mixing and mingling. Second and third floors have private rooms. If you wish to use one, let one of the house managers know, and they'll arrange it. They'll be wearing red roses on their lapels." He fixed me with a frown. "No drugs, no smoking. If you get drunk, you're out and your membership will be revoked. Like you, everyone here has been tested and medically screened. There is to be no picture-taking or filming of any kind. No asking names or exchanging any personal information. Again, if you are found to have violated the rules, you'll be asked to leave and barred for life."

I licked my lips, suddenly anxious to get inside. "I understand."

The upward tick of the corner of his lips was gone in a moment. "Enjoy your evening."

I blinked. "That's it? I can go now?"

The man swept a hand in front of him. "Be my guest."

I strode away, touching the mask covering my face from brows to cheeks, and entered the house. Classical music played. A large buffet was set up on one side of the airy room, while several bars occupied the other. I wandered toward the closest, the hum of conversation rising around me. I caught several interested glances from men who looked older than me, but I didn't stop to talk.

"What can I get you, sir?" The bartender, also masked, stood waiting.

"Uh, just a club soda." We couldn't drink during the season, which, thinking about what I was planning to do here, almost made me laugh. I'd bet half my endorsement check that having gay sex for the first time probably wouldn't be sanctioned by Coach either.

"Coming right up."

With a drink in hand, I now felt capable of sizing up who was there. For all the times I'd thought about being with a man, I didn't have a type—I figured it would hit me when I saw him. I sipped my drink, scanning the room, and decided to check out the rest of the house.

As I made my way through the sea of suits, I was stopped numerous times.

"Hi, there. How're you tonight?"

"Why rush away? Let's talk."

"You've got a great ass."

Having finally escaped, I peeked in the other spacious rooms, saw more of the same, and kept moving. Glass sliders framed the glittering waters of the outdoor pool, and I walked outside, where it seemed less crowded and quieter and where more intimate conversations were taking place. My drink finished, I headed over to the bar and got another, and then I spotted him.

Short pale-blond hair framed a face I could tell was beautiful—even with a mask covering half his features—and his strong jaw was dusted with light-gold stubble. He wasn't bulky, had more of a runner's physique—long legs, slim waist, and a taut ass. My mouth dried as our eyes met. His were a clear, pure blue, reflecting wariness, yet I spied a spark of interest. A slow smile crept up my face.

"Hi."

"Hi." He licked his lips, and I could see he was just as nervous. His full mouth fascinated me, and I ached to kiss it. What would it be like to taste a man and feel his scruff against my own? Sweat popped up on my arms and ran down my back while at the same time I shivered as if cold.

God, what was happening? I'd been with plenty of girls in college, yet none had affected me like this masked stranger.

"First time?" I managed to ask.

"Yeah. You?"

I nodded. "I didn't really know these kinds of clubs existed."

His full mouth quirked a smile. "Oh, yeah. They're everywhere. You just have to know how to find them."

He seemed young, around my age, and I wondered how he'd come to be here. Was he closeted because of homophobic parents? Obviously, he had money, as the fee to join this club was steep. "Wanna sit?"

He nodded, and we took seats on one of the couches by the pool. He nibbled on that plump bottom lip I was losing myself in. Would it feel like a woman's? Doubtful, and I didn't care. I wanted him with a hunger that was almost frightening. This was the guy. I knew it in my bones. I went for it, deciding I had nothing to lose—we both knew why we were here. Putting my hand over his, I leaned in close.

"I don't even know what to say."

He laughed. "Me neither."

"Are you from California?"

His eyes dimmed. "No. East Coast. What about you?"

Since he wasn't being more specific, I kept it the same. "Midwest."

His lips curved upward. "Big difference for you, I imagine."

"You know it. But I like it. Hoping to stay if things work out for me."

"Good luck with that, then. I'm not sure. I like it, but I don't like having to take a car everywhere. No one walks here."

"You don't have a car? I thought everyone in California did."

He grimaced. "No. I don't drive." He clasped and unclasped his hands. "So what brings you here?"

Not about to reveal that it was my first time with a man, I gave the easy answer. "I like that the men are vetted. I know that doesn't mean everything and there can still be problems, but it's one less thing to worry about." I took a sip of my drink. "From what I can see, I'm assuming you're a model or maybe in the fashion or entertainment industry. How come you're here?"

Outrageously long lashes hid his eyes for a second. "Same as you."

Another round peg trying to fit into a square mold.

We sat in silence for a few moments, and I liked that he didn't fill the space with nonsensical chatter. My desire for him grew, and I put my arm around him. He was tall but settled into the crook of my shoulder as if the space were custom made for him. I leaned in and whispered in his ear, "Wanna go somewhere more private? Get comfortable?"

Hot breath hit my cheek, and I smelled his sweat and light cologne. His eyelids fluttered. "Yeah."

Before we moved, I kissed those delicious lips that had been teasing me since I'd first seen him, and they did not disappoint. Soft yet firm and definitely mascu-line, they clung to mine. We were panting when we separated and stared at each other. His eyes blew wide with shock, and I imagined mine were the same. Like a live wire, lust burned hot and bright through my blood.

Aching with the need to be naked and alone with him, I pulled him to me again. "I want you so bad."

"We have to look for a person wearing a red rose," he murmured. "Hurry."

I rose to my feet and held out my hand. He took it, and I held him tight, afraid he was an illusion that might slip away.

We returned to the house, I spotted one of the managers, and we approached him. He checked his iPad. "Second floor, Room 5. You'll find everything you need."

Face hot, I glanced at my companion, and his neck was red. "Let's go." I squeezed his fingers and received an answering pressure. We mounted the impressive staircase, passing several couples on their way down, slightly flushed and less immaculate than they'd been at the start of the evening. My blood surged as we approached Room 5. This was actually happening.

We entered the darkened quiet room. I closed the door behind us and pressed him up against it. "I've been dying to be alone with you from the minute I saw you."

His breath stuttered. "Y-you have?"

His hard body molded to mine, and it was like the dreams I'd been having since I was a teenager and had realized I was bi. I'd never thought I'd have the courage to discover what I'd been missing, but Coach always said you'd regret the chances you didn't take in life.

"Yeah. You're so sexy, and your mouth..." I dipped my head to kiss him, and this time he moaned, the husky sound shooting straight to my balls. I cupped his cheeks and attacked, my tongue plundering, and he sucked it hard.

"Oh God, I need...please," he gasped.

I tore off my jacket, and he lost his as well, leaving it on the floor. We undressed, stopping to kiss and fondle each other, and by the time we were naked, I was ready to blow. My dick had never been so hard. His full cock slapped against my stomach, leaving a smear of sticky precome, and I swiped it with my finger. Curious, I sniffed it, then put it to my mouth and licked it.

Salty but interesting. I didn't have a chance to think more as the hottest, wettest mouth I'd ever felt slid over my cock and sucked me to the root. An impressive feat, considering I was eight inches and pretty thick. I groaned and bucked my hips.

"Fuck, yeah. Fuck." I held his head in place as his tongue swirled around my crown. He looked like an angel, but his mouth was pure devilry. "Don't stop, oh God."

To my dismay, he released me. "That's the plan. I'm not wasting this on a blowjob I can get anywhere."

I didn't think I could be any more turned-on, but when he lay on the bed, I almost whimpered at the sight of him spread out naked. I couldn't admit it was my first time with a guy, so I pretended to be cool. "I'm sure they have the stuff in the drawer here." I opened it, and my eyes widened. "Damn," I whispered, eyeing all kinds of dildos and sex toys I'd only heard about.

My partner crawled closer and stared at them, and to my surprise, took one, slathered on lube, and lay back, legs spread wide. "You're really big. Better prep myself."

Fascinated and turned-on, I watched him shove the thick toy past his rim, so nonchalant. Though obviously this wasn't his first time, he still winced at the toy's girth. Dragging it slowly in and out of his passage, he hissed, but I could tell the moment pain turned to pleasure, his hand a blur as his body twitched.

"Whoa. Hold on." I put my hand on top of his. "No offense, but I didn't come here to watch you get off on your own." My hand gripped my rock-hard shaft and stroked it several times, waves of ecstasy rolling through me as I imagined sticking it inside this man. "I need in you. Now."

Shivering, he pulled out the dildo and lay wide open for me. I'd never put a condom on so fast, and I picked his legs up to his shoulders, giving me complete access to him. I squeezed some more lube onto my fingers and coated my dick.

"Do it," he ordered, giving his cock several pulls. "Come on."

At his urging, I pushed past his tight little hole, and holy shit, it was like nothing I'd ever felt before. I'd had hot sex with plenty of girls, but this? This was different. I became part of him. He sucked me into his body, his ass wrapping around my shaft like a tunnel of fire.

"Fuck, this is incredible." I moved a bit, and slid through the silken fist of heaven. My hips took on a life of their own, and we went at each other like wild beasts. I held him, my fingers digging hard into his hips so I could grind my pelvis into his, our groans reverberating in the quiet room. Sweat poured from my face, slicking his chest and abdomen as I continued to pound him. His hand flashed up and down his shaft as I approached the boiling point.

"Oh my God," he cried out and came, spilling over his hand and stomach, his body twitching and shaking. I followed a moment later, my dick squeezing almost painfully, but then pleasure overtook me, and I spun out of control and exploded. My vision grayed, and I collapsed on top of the zoned-out man.

My eyes fluttered shut, and he lay curled in my arms, our legs tangled.

Less than an hour later, I was hard and eager again, and I kissed him to wakefulness.

"Hey," I whispered. "I want you."

His sleepy smile was all the approval I needed, and I found another condom and poured lube, coating my shaft and rubbing my slippery fingers around him rim.

"Oh, yeah...yeah." His mouth fell open, and he panted, clawing at the sheets.

Seeing how wild he was, I pulled out and flipped him on all fours, loving the sight of that firm, hard ass. I spread him wide and thrust in with a grunt.

"God, you're so fucking tight. You're killing me."

"Harder," he moaned, holding on to the headboard and pushing back on me. "Oh fuck, this is it. Fuck me," he yelled, and spurred on by his wild responsiveness, I pumped into him faster, his ass clamping my dick like a vise as he came, and that was it for me.

When I could breathe, I kissed his shoulder. "We'd better get going, or they'll charge us rent."

It took us a while to clean up, and outside the bedroom door I kissed him, reluctant to let him go.

"Will you be here tomorrow?"

Regret filled his eyes. "I can't. What about Saturday night?"

*Shit. That's the one night the team goes out to parties.* But at the thought of those full lips sucking my dick, there was no choice.

"I'll be here."

******

Six months had passed, and my mystery man and I had been meeting at Intensity at least twice a week. With the Rose Bowl championship under my belt and the draft looming, I didn't have much time to myself, but this man was a fever in my blood I couldn't quench. The campus parties no longer held any interest for me—I couldn't do it with some random girl. All I wanted was my guy.

Oh yeah, as far as I was concerned, he was mine. We talked and laughed about anything and everything. When I wasn't with him, I wondered where he was. What he was doing.

Each time we met, I fell harder, and I knew it was becoming a deeper problem, because I thought about violating that confidentiality agreement and meeting him in the real world. Masks off.

*Does he think about me? Care as much as I do? You're an idiot. What do you think you're gonna do—keep him like a sugar daddy? I can't offer him half a life. That's no better than what we're doing now.*

I should walk away and concentrate on football, but the mere thought of never touching him again slowed my heartbeat to a crawl and dimmed the bright sunlight to a foggy gray.

I was in a car on my way to Intensity. The draft was coming, and I'd find out where I'd be going. I'd received interest from San Diego, Austin, and Portland. Portland had the better team, but if I stayed in San Diego, I could keep seeing my guy.

When I entered Intensity and his eyes lit up, my heart pounded. The thought of leaving and never seeing him again was inconceivable. God, was I in love with him? How the hell had this happened?

"Hi." He wrapped his arms around my neck and tilted his face up, our lips meeting in a kiss. He was no light-weight himself, but at six foot five, I towered over most.

"Hi, yourself." Our tongues danced and teased. "*Mmm*, you taste good."

"And you smell good." He buried his face in my neck. "You always do."

His rock-hard body melted into mine, a perfect fit, and I tangled my fingers in that platinum-blond hair. "I missed you."

He smiled against the dip of my collarbone. "You saw me four days ago."

"And?" I growled. "If I could see you every day, I would."

Big, blue eyes met mine. "I don't know what to say. I wish that too, but we both have other commitments."

"Yeah. I'm, uh, looking for a job, and I have three prospects."

Hand in hand, we walked to the man with the red flower, who gave us our room number. Once inside, he sat on the bed and began to undress. "Where are they?" He kicked off his shoes and undid his slacks. He wore a white button-down that accentuated his tan and brought out the startling blue of his eyes, the only spot of color on his face, which was covered—brow to lips—by a tight black mask.

"Here, Austin, and Portland." I took off my shirt and pants and sat by his side. "What do you think? You have to know how much you mean to me."

He held on to my shoulders. "I think I'm not the kind of person you should change your life for."

I cupped his cheek. "What if you already have?"

He froze, his lips parted, his breath catching. "What are you saying?"

"I—I'm crazy about you. I can't stop thinking of you. I just wanna be with you all the time."

A pink flush covered his face. "I feel the same. The times we're together are the happiest I've ever known."

My heart pounded—it sounded like we'd made a promise to each other. And even though I had no idea how we'd manage, I knew we were meant to be together.

We rid ourselves of the rest of our clothes, and I pushed him onto the bed. Everything about him fit me. How could people say that being with a man was wrong when it all felt so damn right?

He took the lead, riding me slowly, twisting me into knots. My hips bucked hard, and I held him by the waist, thrusting into him.

His hair was plastered to his brow in wet ringlets, and those blue eyes blazed fire. "Harder," he gasped. "Come on." His hand flashed over his dick, and I was mesmerized watching him as he came, spilling through his fingers.

My heart thundering, I dug my heels into the bed and slammed up into him. I couldn't catch my breath as fire consumed me and I shattered, my cock throbbing and swelling. I slung an arm around him, holding our sweat-slicked bodies close.

"Stay with me a while," I managed to mumble.

He sighed and slid off me. "I can't walk yet, so yeah."

We lay side by side, and I kissed his cheek. "You never answered me. What should I do?"

"You should make the decision that's best for you."

"Being with you is what's best for me."

He smiled and snuggled in close, his face against my chest. I closed my eyes.

**

I awoke with a start, sitting upright. An empty bed greeted me, and I reached across the sheets, finding them cold. Why had he left? We'd fallen asleep before, and he'd never left me alone.

"Shit." I adjusted my mask, flopped onto the pillow, and stared at the ceiling. How long had I been out? A quick check of my watch showed the time to be almost two hours past when I'd arrived at the mansion. "Dammit."

My clothes were scattered, and I picked them up, dressing in haste, shaky fingers fumbling with the buttons. I glanced in the mirror and winced at the beard burn and messy hair. I took a moment to do a rapid repair, then hightailed it out of the room, my gaze searching as I descended the stairs, but I didn't see my lover.

Throat dry, I headed to the bar, where I gulped two large glasses of water.

"Rough night?" With a leer, an older man with slicked-back hair and a large diamond pinky ring stepped into my personal space. "Wanna go upstairs and play some more?"

"No." I pushed past him and decided I'd had enough for the evening. I called for a car and returned to the university. I had them drop me off outside the gates, where I ditched the mask in a garbage pail, took out my contacts, and returned them to their case.

Head down, hands stuffed in my jacket pockets, I trudged through the quad thinking about what we'd said to each other earlier. I'd have to keep this entire part of my life a secret to follow my dream. I wasn't a scholar by any means—I'd always struggled a little in school—but I excelled at a college football career that, barring injuries, would set me up for life.

None of which could be accomplished if I kept on fucking guys. My eyes burned with shocked tears. Did he even care about me? If so, why would he leave without saying good-bye? It seemed as though the choice had been made for me.

"Trick. Hey, Trick." One of the cheerleaders who was always flirting with me blocked my way. What the hell was her name? Lily? Lexie? "What're you doing all alone out here on a Saturday night?" She licked her lips. "Are you going to the Omegas' party?"

"Nah. Not in the mood."

She flipped her hair and slipped her arm around my waist. I played the game, drawing her closer, allowing her full breasts to nestle against me.

"Oh, too bad," she pouted, and slanted a look up at me through thick lashes. "We can go to my room if you'd like. My roommate is out. We can have our own private party."

She snuggled into my chest, and I sighed, thinking of my mystery lover. "Sure. Lead the way."

******

Three days later, I entered Intensity but didn't see him, though I made sure to walk through each room, scanning every face. I returned the next night and the next, but my mystery lover never showed. After a month, I gave up, coming to terms with the fact that he was gone and I'd never see him again. My lover had made it clear we had no future. I'd been naïve or plain stupid to think we could meet on the sly while I still played pro ball. Life sucked.

With everything good happening for me, I shouldn't be dwelling on a man I barely knew but found impossible to forget. The following month, I was chosen by the San Diego Sharks as their starting quarterback. My mother cried, and my father hugged me.

"We're so proud of you. We're the luckiest parents to have a son like you," Dad said. "Go out there and make your dreams come true."

It had all been for nothing—those months spent with my mystery man were never anything more than a dream of love I'd been foolish enough to believe possible. Time to focus on making other dreams come true.

# CHAPTER ONE

Fallon

*Present day*

I was damn good at keeping secrets. It was what I'd done for years as personal assistant to NFL superstar and future Hall of Famer, Devlin "Devil" Summers. I'd covered for him as he'd hidden being gay in the macho world of football and being in love with his teammate, Brody Martin.

But now that he'd retired and come out, he no longer needed me in the same highly intense capacity as when he'd been an active player. Don't get me wrong. People still loved him as an NFL commentator and sports show host, but it wasn't the same as being the franchise quarterback and face of the Brooklyn Kings. And while I knew he'd keep me, full workload or not, it wasn't enough. I needed my days filled with making appointments and spreadsheets. Being necessary. Busy. Working hard so I didn't have time to think I had nothing else in my life but calendar dates to fill up for other people.

Here I was, thirty-one years old with zero life plan. I'd done the college thing, and nothing called to me as a career. Living away from everyone I knew and everything familiar had been tough—I'd spent most of the four years mourning the death of my older brother, Rory, and my parents' complete erasure of my existence. I wasn't whom they wanted for a son. It was for the best, as it turned out, to be on the West Coast for those years, far away from memories and pain.

Thank God for Dev, who, as Rory's childhood best friend, had stepped in and saved me—paying all my expenses for the four years of college, no questions asked.

*"I know how being away from home can make you do stupid things."*

But I had little time to dwell on my past or any other problems. Dev called, sounding frantic.

"Fallon, dude, I know it's Sunday and your day off, but I forgot my dress shirt and sports jacket in my apartment. Can you grab them and get to the stadium? I'm really sorry. I'll make it up to you."

"Yeah, sure, of course. They don't have extras lying around for hotshots like you?" I joked, already on the move.

"Cute. Trust me, I've gotten my spanking from Shane and JJ."

I smiled to myself. As together and focused as Dev had been in his playing career, he was a bit of a shit show in this new role of television sports announcer.

"I bet. Maybe you still need a personal assistant. Just saying."

"We'll talk when you get here. I owe you one."

Something in his tone stopped me in my tracks. I lived only a few minutes away and had quickly reached Dev and Brody's loft in Tribeca. "What's going on?"

"Nothing, I swear." An edge crept into his voice. "Just get here as fast as you can, please."

"I'm at your place." I used my key to enter the building and another for the private elevator that would take me directly to their apartment.

"Thanks. Sorry to make you do this."

"No worries. You know I'm always here for you."

It was true. I loved working for Dev. He was fun, kind, paid me extremely well, and never treated me like I was the annoying kid brother of his best friend from elementary school. He and Brody had become the family I'd lost.

I entered their apartment and found the shirt and sport jacket hanging on the back of the bedroom door. Within minutes I was retracing my steps and calling for a car. By the time I reached the lobby, I spied it waiting for me at the curb. I sighed and rested my head on the leather seat as we headed to the stadium. Traffic was lousy as usual for a Sunday, and I closed my eyes. Maybe one day I'd get up the nerve and learn to drive, but every time I thought about getting behind the wheel, I got palpitations. Knowing Rory's last moments had been in a car careening out of control kept me a passenger for life.

Fortunately, before I had a chance to get too into my head, I got a call from a headhunter who'd been after me ever since Dev had retired. Instead of ducking his call yet again, I decided to hear what he had to say.

"Hey, Norm, how's it going?"

"I'm good. Did you see I sent three good offers? Have you had any thoughts on them? They're really anxious."

*Hmm.* They might be, but I wasn't. "No, not yet. I'm still working for Devlin Summers—matter of fact, I'm on my way to the stadium now for him."

"You're being foolish." He huffed, his frustration evident. "You've basically been demoted to a gofer, and you know you can handle so much more."

I winced at the truth, but I had my reasons. "Listen, I'll call you next week. Promise."

Forty minutes later, we pulled into the parking lot, and I got out and flashed my pass, allowing me to bypass the crowds. Clothes in hand, I hustled to the media area, holding up my credentials, and found Dev in the *NFL Weekly* booth. His frantic face transformed to relief when he spotted me, and he motioned with his hand.

"Fallon, thank God. You're a lifesaver." He grabbed the button-down and sports jacket, and in the middle of the booth, stripped off his tee and slipped his arms into the shirt. In the adjacent media booth, I spotted Brody joking with his cohosts. He caught my eye and waved, laughing and shaking his head at his husband, obviously knowing why I was there.

"I *am* a lifesaver," I joked. "So why're you trying to get rid of me?" My tone was cheerful, but Dev frowned as he put on the sports jacket.

"Seriously, Fal? You can't mean that. You know I value you as a friend as well as a personal assistant. I just think that with me taking on this new job, everything you were hired to do—and have been doing for all these years—isn't applicable anymore. I don't receive the level of fan mail I once did, and my calendar is pretty minimal since Brody and I have stepped back during the off-season. We're all about relaxing, spending time with his mom, working at the Kings' summer camp, and hanging out in our cabin upstate."

As much as I wanted to argue with Dev and point out he was wrong, I couldn't. My entire day during the off-season had been spent figuring out how to manage where Dev would be at any given moment, sorting his hundreds of fan emails and letters per week, and taking his phone calls and arranging publicity. Now, all that had dwindled to a minimum. Not because Dev wasn't still beloved and popular, but he and Brody had decided to prioritize each other. Unsurprising, as they'd had to hide their relationship and pretend to be apart for so many years. They deserved their time together, open and free. Yet still...I argued my point.

"But maybe one day you'll be in the spotlight again. You're doing television appearances, and maybe you'll want a book deal..."

Dev's brows drew together. "Even if that's true, it would all be years in the making. Nothing I'd expect you to wait for. C'mere." He put an arm around my shoulders and steered me to a quieter corner. "What's going on? I know you've had headhunters knocking at your door trying to hire you—multiple offers, in fact. I'll give you the best reference. But talk to me. Is everything okay?" Big brother Dev had entered the chat, and my throat closed up. I could try and bullshit, but Dev was no fool.

"I guess I don't like change." My smile was weak. "And I'd hate to lose our friendship. Once I don't see you, I figured we'd lose touch and...you know..." Cheeks flaming, I shrugged, unused to sharing emotions.

"So you're gonna dump me?" Dev teased, but seeing I didn't join him, his humorous expression faded and his brows knitted. "Wait, you're serious? Fal, what the hell? We've known each other forever. You're the kid brother I never had..." His face drooped, and his eyes grew shiny. "When Rory died, I tried to take his place, though I knew I could never—"

"Don't. It's...okay." Looking him straight in the eye, I put a hand on his shoulder. "You were there for me. That's what mattered. Still does." I gave him a squeeze. "And it always will." Big, tough, and a ferocious competitor on the field, the real Devlin Summers was a sweet, softhearted man.

"I've gotta go do the opening now, but we'll talk later. I wouldn't let you go to just anyone. You're the best—more than someone who's worked for me. You're family. We're always gonna be in each other's lives. And I might be on to someone for you. Someone who'll need your expertise dealing with the messy life of a football player."

I walked with him to the seating area, where his cohosts were getting ready. "A player? Who? From the Kings?"

"Dev? You ready?" JJ McClain, Hall of Fame running back, gave me a friendly but business-quick smile. "Hey, Fallon."

"Hi. I'll get out of your way."

Dev took his chair and put on his mic. "Yes to all that. We'll talk later."

I moved out of camera range and stood to the rear of the media booth as the intros were made.

Shane Treadway, winner of three Super Bowls, Pro-Bowl MVP, and holder of numerous rushing records, began the show. It was my cue to leave. Much as I loved Dev and Brody, I wasn't that into football. If I watched, it was to see the players in their tight uniforms.

"The Kings haven't lost a game so far this season, Dev. How do you like their chances for the playoffs? Can they go all the way?"

"I believe so, Shane. It's definitely a rebuilding year, but I was just informed this morning that the Kings have finalized a trade for superstar quarterback Patrick Sloane."

At Dev's words, I froze. *What the fuck?*

Instead of exiting the booth, I flattened against the wall, hoping no one would kick me out before I heard more of this monumental news.

"Whoa. That's huge. Trick Sloane coming to the Kings? How'd they manage to hide that?"

I'd have liked to know that myself. Dev hadn't mentioned anything, although to be fair, I didn't pay much attention to the football news side of the job.

Dev chuckled. "You know that's top secret. The Kings have perfected the art of pulling off stellar trades like this under the radar. Sloane will add some much-needed depth to the offensive line. Harte McKinney as backup is good, but he's been injured and might be thinking of retirement soon."

As they delved more into the Kings players, I slipped out of the booth and found a seat. Still processing the news, I rested my head in my hands, inhaling and exhaling, attempting to settle my racing heart.

Patrick "Trick" Sloane. Winner of multiple college records. Rose Bowl and national champion. Two-time MVP of the Pro-Bowl. One Super Bowl appearance. Model good looks.

My first lover.

"No," I muttered. "Not my lover." Could you call someone your lover when he'd never seen your face and didn't know your name? I rubbed my hands together. Ten years later, and I could still feel his mouth on mine, his hands on my body, rough and demanding. I shivered from the memory of those blazing nights of passion.

During the car ride home, I tried to work, checking Dev's email and messages, but aside from the usual rude, homophobic comments about his marriage to Brody and assorted dick pics, there was nothing requiring his time. After announcing their retirement and coming out, he and Brody had done the whirlwind magazine and television tours, but that had died down with the start of the season. Both of them were focused on this new career path, and after so many years spent with them, I could see how happy they were now that they were out and living as they were meant to be.

I made reminder notes to schedule Dev's upcoming appointments and book his hotel room, cross-checking with Lizzie, Brody's part-time PA.

Stuck in traffic and with nothing else to do, I googled Patrick Sloane. His face peered up at me, ten years older and more rugged, which only enhanced his good looks. I read his bio and winced. Married twice, no children, and the tabloids loved him—and he seemed to love them back, giving them ample material. His ex-wives were both underwear models. Both blond and extremely... healthy.

"You sure have a type, Trick," I murmured. "Still love the blonds. Maybe that's why you were so into me." As I grew older, my platinum hair had darkened to more of a golden blond, and once I'd left the heat of California, I'd grown it out to slightly above my shoulders.

The traffic jam unsnarled, and we'd begun to move again. The Kings' stadium was situated at the end of Brooklyn, near the Marine Parkway Bridge, and it was always a haul to the city. Forty-five minutes later and finally in my apartment, I could do more of a deep dive into Patrick, and the news was hopping with the trade. A gossip site had caught him in the airport the previous evening, and I replayed the tape of them following him. Fingers entwined with his latest girlfriend—another long-haired blond—Trick's generous lips kicked up in a sexy, lazy smile.

*"Yeah, I'm excited to play in New York. The fans are the best, and if I don't give them two hundred percent, they'll let me know it."*

"Ain't that the truth." I chewed my burrito. "No matter how many winning seasons Dev gave them, the moment he threw an interception, they booed him." I continued watching the video.

*"What about that ankle? You went down pretty hard last week."*

Trick's eyes narrowed, and he stopped. *"It's fine. I'm ready to get on the field and show my new teammates and the fans."*

*"But it's still taped, isn't it? We saw you a day ago on the beach, and you were favoring it."*

*"I said I'm fine,"* he snapped, hefting the bag on his shoulder. *"I'll talk to you all soon. Have to find my bags and get to my hotel."*

"Are you planning on living in the city now, buying a place?"

Trick's lady friend frowned, and he chuckled. "I think that's a good idea, although Mimi here would rather be in LA. She lives for the beach and the sun."

The interviewer stood with his microphone after Trick walked away.

"That was Patrick—Trick—Sloane, the new quarterback of the Brooklyn Kings. My guess is, we'll be seeing a lot more of him now that he's relocating to the city. Is the wild child of the San Diego Sharks finally ready to live the quiet life with his beautiful lady, or will we see the same hard-partying Trick Sloane on the East Coast? Stay tuned, ladies."

After clicking out of the story, I turned on the television for background noise and decided I might as well look at the emails Norm sent. By telling me he might've found someone I could work with, Dev had made it pretty clear he thought the time had come for me to move on. A wave of sadness rolled over me. Change was going to happen whether I liked it or not.

Norm had sent those three prospectives he'd mentioned. One was PA to a fashion designer, and I immediately passed. From friends in that business, I'd heard stories of their diva behavior, and I had no desire to deal with spoiled brats. I was a PA, not a babysitter. The second was a television reality star, and while working for her could be fun, she wanted me to live in and travel extensively to help promote her new perfume and swimsuit line.

I set that one aside.

The last and most promising was personal assistant to a Broadway star whose name was well-known in the industry. That sounded interesting...until I saw the salary, which was quite a bit less than Dev paid me. I knew Dev paid me better than the norm, and I didn't expect to make the same salary, but halving my yearly income wasn't something I was willing or able to do.

With a heavy sigh, I closed my laptop and stretched out on the couch. A nap sounded pretty good, and to the sound of the Kings scoring a touchdown, I closed my eyes.

The buzzing of my cell woke me. I rubbed my face and peered at the screen. *Damn.* A three-hour nap was more than I'd intended. Dev's name continued to flash across my phone. I hit the speaker as I tried to wake up.

"Hi, sorry," I yawned. "I fell asleep. Do you need something?"

"Yeah. Listen. Do you have plans for dinner?"

"Only with my DoorDash guy," I joked.

"Well, that's about to change. Meet us at Keens at eight thirty."

"Wait, what?" I struggled up to sitting and rubbed my face. "What's this about?"

"I'll tell you when you get here, but trust me, you'll be happy."

"Dev—"

"See you later. Bye."

He ended the call, and I groaned in frustration. Typical Dev. He loved surprises, and I hated them. But my stomach growled, and I couldn't complain about the prospect of a night with two friends and a great steak dinner. I showered and changed into a crisp, blue-and-white button-down and a pair of navy dress pants. A spritz of cologne, and I was ready. Now that I was up and dressed maybe I'd go out after dinner, have a drink, or go to a club. It had been a hell of a dry spell for me, and I wouldn't mind someone to hold for the night.

The ride uptown took less than fifteen minutes, and I was greeted by the hostess.

"Follow me, please. Your party is already here."

The restaurant was about three-quarters full, conversations humming as we passed, and everyone's food looked delicious. I could be a hermit sometimes and I'd admit I was glad Dev had called me to meet them.

At a corner table, I spotted Brody, and he waved to me. Dev grinned and whispered to the third person at the table, who turned to face me. My stomach, only moments before filled with anticipation, flipped over with dread.

"Fallon, meet Patrick Sloane. Remember I told you I had a plan? This is it. Or him. Trick, this is Fallon McKenzie, *the* top sports PA. I think you two are perfect for each other."

With zero recognition in those heavy-lidded, blue-green eyes, Patrick gave me that trademark blinding smile and held out his hand. "Nice to meet you, Fallon."

# CHAPTER TWO

## Patrick

*Damn, Fallon's a hottie. Just my type, too. All that blond hair and big, blue eyes. Mmm-mmm.*

Endorphins flooded me. It had been a long time. Way too long. Not that I hadn't wanted it. I had no problem getting it up for the ladies, but there was something about a hot guy...

*Rein it in, Trick. You're not at your club, and he looks...sweet.*

I studied Fallon as he took my hand. Something about him...I couldn't place it, but he seemed familiar. Maybe it was his eyes. I did love me pretty, big blue ones.

Dev and I had been friendly when he'd played in the NFL. He and Brody were cool, both legends in the league. Definite Hall of Famers. I recalled the game he'd gotten rammed by one of my teammates—unfairly, in my opinion—and I'd apologized for the bad behavior. I'd admired him and Brody, had watched the tape of their coming out and retirement announcement numerous times—wishing I had the courage to admit to being bisexual. The way I saw it, I was a football player, and whom I had sex with had nothing to do with how I played the game. But of course, I knew that wasn't the reality, so I kept my mouth shut.

I had no contacts on the East Coast, and thought it would be nice to have friends, so I'd had no hesitation accepting Dev's dinner invitation. Plus, I'd figured I could pick up some inside tips on the team.

The pretty-as-fuck scenery was a bonus.

But this Fallon guy didn't return my smile and dropped my hand as if it were covered in shit. He backed away a few steps and remained silent.

Unaware of his friend's tension, Dev said, "We just got here a few minutes ago."

"Dev, I—" Fallon began, but Dev cut him off.

"Calling you out late on a Sunday might be unusual, but I'm telling you, there's a method to my madness. You've probably seen that Trick here has just been traded to the Kings, and he doesn't know anyone in the city." His attention shifted to me. "Are you from California?"

I nodded. "I'm from Kansas originally, but I've lived in Southern California since college. So yeah, I'm a tourist here for the most part."

"You want me to be a tour guide?" Fallon asked, his dark-blond brows arched high. "Really, Dev?"

Dev rolled his eyes at Fallon, who sat stiff, a frown pulling down his mouth. "No, don't be ridiculous. You heard what I said." He turned to me. "Fallon is the best of the best. I wouldn't even think of giving him up, but he just doesn't have enough work and he's wasting away doing bullshit tasks for me. He's the only reason I knew the time and place to show up every day and had meetings with my agent, lawyer, or PR teams from whatever company I was working with." His gaze shifted to Fallon, then returned to me. "I think you should hire him as your PA."

Dev hadn't mentioned this earlier. I'd thought we'd gotten together for a little postgame recap, but the more I thought about what he said, the more it made sense.

"Oh, wow, that would be great." Although I might end up walking around with a perpetual case of blue balls, I did need someone to help me coordinate my life. My agent wasn't my PA, and the first time I'd asked Mimi to take messages for me while I was busy at training camp, she'd balked, saying she was my girlfriend, not my secretary. I'd given in and hadn't pushed it because I never wanted to make her angry. Happy girl, happy world.

Fallon's startled eyes met mine. "What? No way."

*Ouch.* This guy disliked me on sight for no reason. "Why not? I need someone, and from what Dev's said, sounds like you're efficient and the most organized person he knows."

If I thought the praise would butter him up, I was wrong.

"Because...because I don't know," Fallon protested, his expression uncomfortable. "I feel like I'm being ambushed."

"If you want, I'll interview you formally."

Brody chimed in. "That sounds fair, Fallon. Lizzie had a ton of offers after I retired but decided she'd stay and earn some extra money managing my socials while she goes to school."

Dev took Brody's hand and squeezed it. "Which, of course, my husband is paying for in full." He lifted Brody's hand and kissed each knuckle. "Because he's the nicest person alive."

Brody's cheeks pinked, and I couldn't help wondering what would it be like to be out and proud and an active player. My gut tensed as I imagined the guys in the locker room suddenly eyeing me as if I were different. They'd think I was checking out their asses and dicks. All because I liked being with men as well as women.

"You guys are cute." I chuckled, but the truth? I was envious of their openness and curious about some things. "Does anyone give you shit about your relationship?"

Brody's face tightened. "I still get nasty hate mail, and though I won't swear to it, some of the sportscasters I work with and some of the players seem less than thrilled."

That reasoning was why I frequented the exclusive clubs. Anonymity. Discretion was my middle name, but it had been years since I'd been able to get it on with a guy, the last time proving to be a massive disappointment.

It had nothing to do with the man I'd been with—he'd tried everything, but I'd kept comparing him to my first, which wasn't fair. My mystery man had taken me apart and put me back together, and without him I remained unfinished, like a puzzle with a missing piece. Regret had taken up residence in my soul once he'd disappeared.

Fallon studied me, and if I didn't know better, I'd have sworn there was contempt in those narrowed blue eyes. I was an acquired taste for sure, but damn, this guy wasn't even giving me a chance.

I put on my most winning grin. "C'mon, Fallon. Why not try it out for a month? I need someone, and I definitely have more work than Dev can give you. For starters, I've got lots to do with moving here that I'll need help with."

Fallon, for all his outrageous good looks, had a backbone of steel and wasn't a pushover. "I'm not sure."

"One month. Then you can see if you love me or hate me," I joked, but Fallon didn't smile.

*What is this guy's problem?*

Perhaps sensing the bizarre tension, Dev said, "Why don't we order dinner, and then Trick can tell us about himself and what he expects." He frowned at Fallon, who didn't meet his eyes but lifted a shoulder.

"Sure."

I had no idea why it was so important that I prove myself to this person. He should've been regaling me with his work and what he could do for me—I shouldn't have been begging him. Throughout dinner, he remained mostly silent, eating his steak and drinking his beer, speaking only if asked a direct question.

We were having our coffee when he finally turned to me. "I have to ask you something."

Catching Dev's eye, he shrugged, and I folded my hands on the tabletop. "Sure. Ask away."

"How do you feel about an openly gay man working for you? Would that be a problem?"

It felt like he was challenging me. That the question was a test I needed to pass.

The only problem would be keeping boundaries, but I'd manage, like I had all my life. And I admired the hell out of Fallon for laying it on the line.

"Listen. I respect everyone. And frankly, I don't give a damn whether some prejudiced asshole has an issue with whom I hire." I paused and tipped my head toward Dev and Brody. "Or whom I'm friends with. Is that enough for you?"

I couldn't tell if my impassioned statement had made an impact. Fallon's brow remained furrowed, his eyes clouded with indecision and mistrust.

Dev nudged his shoulder. "C'mon, Fallon. Give it a try. And none of this one-month BS, 'cause you know that won't be enough time. The rest of the season would be better. It's end of September now. Give it until after the postseason, and then make a decision. Brody and I are gonna take off after the Super Bowl for three months, so there really won't be anything for you to do."

Fallon glanced at me again, his white teeth chewing his full bottom lip. It was silly to be so concerned about why some random guy was hesitating about working for me, but surliness aside, he intrigued me. I wanted him.

"I guess...all right. Until January, when the season ends."

I couldn't help grinning. "The season ends in February with the Super Bowl, and I intend for the Kings to be there."

"That's what I'm talking about," Dev crowed. "Let's get a bottle of champagne to celebrate." He raised a hand to our server, and I took the opportunity to lean closer to Fallon.

"Let me give you my personal cell. I'll text you my address—right now I'm staying at The Baccarat Hotel, but I need to find a place. I'd like you to help with things like getting a PO Box, setting up appointments with real estate agents to look at apartments, stuff like that."

Fallon gave me a sharp nod, pulled out his phone, and we exchanged information. The champagne was brought and popped, and I held up the flute.

"Here's to new beginnings and new friendships." I held Fallon's gaze. "Fallon, I'll catch up with you tomorrow. And now I'd better get back to the hotel. I left Mimi alone all day, and she was not happy about it." I didn't relish returning to the suite and hearing her complain, but I planned to take her to all the sights of the city in the morning, which I was sure would include a shopping spree.

"Go home and make your lady feel better." Dev took out his wallet. "We've got this. Talk to you soon."

"Thanks, guys. See ya. Tomorrow, Fallon? We'll talk."

"Yeah, sure. Just give me a call or text to let me know when."

Outside the restaurant, a couple of people asked for photos, and I obliged before my car arrived. It was close to eleven, and I didn't want to call Mimi because she liked to go to bed early when we didn't have plans. I'd told her not to wait up as I'd be late.

I exited the elevator and saw two people, a man and a woman, walking out of my suite. They were giggling, flushed and disheveled, and it didn't take a scholar to figure out what had been going on while I was gone. I waited for them to get into the elevator, then knocked on the door.

I heard quick footsteps. The door opened. "Did you come back for a quickie...oh, shit." Mimi stood naked under a tiny, see-through silk robe, her hair tangled and face roughened from beard burn, red marks on her neck.

"Oh, shit? What's wrong, *lover*?" I strode inside, glancing at the empty champagne bottles on the dining-room table. "Did I come home too early? Didn't have time to get rid of the evidence?"

"Baby, it's not–"

I raised my hands and stomped into the bedroom, where the sheets were rumpled and the aroma of sweat and sex hung like a fog in the air. "Don't tell me it's not what I think. I'm not thinking anything. I know you were getting it on in *my* bed, with two other people."

Mimi flung her arms around me. "Baby, I was so lonely. You were gone all day, and I missed you so much. They got me drunk, and I don't know what came over me."

The smell of her turned my stomach, and I pulled her clinging arms from my neck. "I know what came all over you. Or should I say who?" I quirked a brow. "You were so lonely that you picked up two strangers and brought them to my hotel suite to fuck them in my bed. Don't deny it. Just leave."

"Leave?" she shrieked, blond hair waving over her shoulders. "Where am I supposed to go at this time of night? I'm not from here. I don't know this damn city."

"Not a problem." I pulled out my phone. "I'll book you on the earliest flight to LA. But you'll have to leave here tonight. I'll help you pack."

If she thought standing there almost naked was a turn-on for me, she was dead wrong. We'd had a lot of fun in bed, and she was pretty to look at, but we weren't a love story. I'd met her during the off-season.

Some of the guys and I had been invited to a magazine party with all the swimsuit models who'd been on their covers. Of course we'd said yes, and I'd spotted Mimi immediately as she'd been featured on the most recent issue. She was my type—blond, with lips that spoke of wicked pleasure. We'd hooked up that night and had started seeing each other. We'd now known each other for about six months, and it was more her idea than mine to come with me to New York. Since I didn't like being alone, I'd figured it would be nice to have someone familiar to come home to.

I watched dispassionately as she pulled on her clothing and took out her suitcase. She threw her things inside—the designer bags, clothes, and shoes I'd bought for her or she'd been given by the companies she sponsored—and zipped it up. I'd told her to pack light and that we'd send for her things after I found an apartment. Turned out to be fortuitous for her.

Finally finished, she stood, chest heaving, breathing heavily. "I can't believe you're doing this to me."

I busted out laughing. "Sweetheart, I think you've got it mixed up. You were the one cheating on me. Now, I booked you on a five thirty a.m. flight to LAX. You won't have long to wait at JFK." I checked my phone. "And the car should be downstairs in about five minutes."

I walked to the front of the suite and waited. With a huff and a pout to her lips—and I had to admit I was going to miss those luscious beauties wrapped around my dick—she flounced past me, suitcase in tow. I opened the door, then slammed it shut behind her.

*Another one bites the dust.*

I should've felt sadness at her departure, but I didn't. Fact was, we'd been nothing more than enthusiastic bed partners. I couldn't remember a single conversation we'd shared outside of where we'd go for dinner or what club she wanted to go to. Thinking of Dev and Brody and how their eyes spoke a language no one else needed to learn, I wanted something like that. Something that would last forever. Something evergreen.

From memory, I believed Intensity had a branch in New York. It should be easy to transfer my membership from West to East Coast. Sure enough, when I pulled up their private web page, I found the information. My eyes burned with fatigue.

"Plenty of time to do this tomorrow."

I undressed and went to sleep.

**

The next morning, I sipped my coffee while eating breakfast, but my attention was on my laptop. I had to fill out some information, and I received an approval and ID number. Both clubs operated the same. They sent you a welcome kit via personal delivery, which included a mask and three pins—red for not participating, yellow for there to look, and green signaling you were up for anything. I signed their confidentiality agreement and hit Send. That was it. The membership transferred seamlessly.

That done, I texted Fallon.

*Wanna come by around noon and have lunch and we can discuss? I'm in Room 1550.*

The message went to *Read* status, and I waited.

*Sure. See you then.*

I called the front desk to tell them to allow Fallon up automatically and went to take a shower. I couldn't explain why I felt this overwhelming sense of relief, but I found myself smiling as I stood under the spray. It might be temptation to have someone as gorgeous as Fallon with me all the time, but it would be a good willpower test. Fallon piqued my curiosity—maybe it was his reluctance to take the job. Was it about working for me, or was it something else?

I spent the rest of the morning reading through the playbook Coach Jackson had sent me and viewing old Kings' games. I couldn't wait to get on the field.

At noon exactly there was a single rap on the door. I jumped up, heartbeat inexplicably accelerating. Fallon stood waiting, blue eyes wary, hair in a messy bun. He wore a white button-down tucked into slim trousers. Effortless and gorgeous.

"Come on in."

I closed the door behind him and watched him walk away. Damn, he had a fabulous ass. High and round and firm...I blinked and pinched my eyes.

*Lord, give me strength.*

# CHAPTER THREE

Fallon

I really didn't want to be here. In fact, all morning I'd debated texting Patrick and canceling. How was I supposed to work with the man who'd taken my virginity but didn't know it?

In high school I'd always been too afraid to hook up, though I'd known guys who did. Rory had told me not to rush, that I should wait until I cared about the person before I had sex.

Dev had known I was gay, had come out to me after he'd graduated and signed his contract with the Kings. He'd said he wanted me to have someone I could talk to who understood what I was going through. I admired him so much. It was Dev, not my parents, who'd given me the sex talk, teaching me about protection and not to go wild simply because I was living on my own. We'd had long conversations about respecting myself as a gay man. How I deserved to live a free and open life. Ironic, coming from a man who'd hidden who he was, but he'd made the choice to follow his dream. Plus, he had Brody.

*"I want you to be happy, Fallon. I'm always available if you need me—I don't care if we're in the postseason or what. It's what Rory would've expected of me. Just promise me you'll be safe. I don't like the thought of you out there, all alone. That can lead to bad decisions with worse consequences."*

For my twenty-first birthday, Dev had bought me a membership to an exclusive sex club.

*"It sounds weird, but these people have at least been vetted. I know you're going to have sex, but I don't like thinking you might end up in trouble because you'll meet someone who might hurt you. The world is filled with strange people who are looking to take advantage of someone innocent."*

*"Hey,"* I *protested, laughing. "I'm a city guy. I know what's what."*

*But Dev didn't find it funny. "I worry about you, Fallon."*

And then I'd met Patrick. It was a first time I'd never forget that had turned into an affair to remember. Nights of incredible, heart-stealing passion with a man who'd brought me to a paradise I hadn't known existed and had never reached again. He'd made me feel wanted, and though we'd been anonymous, I'd had a connection with him. How could I not, when he'd been the first person inside me?

Our months together had woven a bond between us, and despite knowing it was foolish, I'd fallen hard for him. It had gone so far beyond sex—he'd made me laugh, and we'd shared similar world views. I'd thought long about it and had decided that maybe it was time to take it to the next level, see if he wanted to leave Intensity and make things work in the real world. With his hints of asking if I was staying in California and his job prospects, I'd believed he was thinking the same.

*We made love as had become our custom and fell asleep for a little while. I awoke before him and used the bathroom, then returned to the bed, thinking it might be a good time to have that talk. The sex that night had been hard and desperate, and his mask had loosened in his sleep, slipping to the side. His face revealed, I froze, my heart skipping a beat.*

*I knew him. Hell, everyone in Southern California who followed college football knew that face. Patrick Sloane, superstar quarterback of the Laguna University Sea Lions. His team had won the Rose Bowl, and he was headed for the pros.*

*Holy shit. My brain could barely process this. Patrick Sloane was into guys? No question about it as my ass was sore and bruises had already begun to spring up over my hips and thighs where he'd gripped me hard. Patrick "Trick" Sloane had fucked me like his life depended on it.*

*It made sense he'd come to a place where his identity would be protected. It saddened and upset me that people had to hide who they were. I got dressed and studied the sleeping man, all muscle and beauty stretched out on the bed, committing him to memory. I fled, tears sliding down my cheeks, knowing it had been the last time he'd touched me, heartbroken that it had to end this way.*

I'd spent the rest of the night sleepless and empty, feeling as though I'd left part of myself—the best part—in that room with Patrick Sloane.

In the intervening years, I'd had lovers but never love. Seeing how Dev and Brody completed each other, how they went through so much to be together and fought for their relationship despite their hardships, I didn't want indiscriminate sex with someone I'd never see again. I wanted that fairy tale. An all-encompassing, forever love. I wanted to lose my breath every time he walked into the room. I wanted my lips to tingle and my balls to ache. I wanted not to be able to keep my hands off him and for him to give me those special looks reserved only for me. I wanted laughter over inside jokes and feet tangled under blankets. I wanted... *Dammit.* I wanted the man I'd left sleeping in bed, dark hair spread on the pillow. The only man who'd made me come alive.

The man I could never have.

Now here we were, a decade later, and by some strange twist of fate we'd been thrown together again. I figured I'd see how the lunch went, and if I still had reservations, tell him I'd decided to go with another offer. He had no idea who I was, so it wouldn't be a problem.

"Sit, please," he said, pointing to the couch. Instead, I sat in the club chair. "Can I ask you something?"

I clasped my hands. "Yeah, of course."

"Why do I get the feeling you don't like me?" His lips quirked. "I always joke that people need to know me before they hate me."

"I don't dislike you. I don't even know you."

*Except how your dick feels in my ass.* I mentally slapped myself. *Shut up, Fallon.*

His eyes warmed. "I hear a 'but.' Talk to me," he urged. "Maybe I can make it right."

*Damn the man's charm.* Despite everything, I responded with a smile. "I'm naturally cautious, that's all. Why don't you tell me what you see the job entailing?"

"I made a list. Let me get my phone."

Funnily, that made me feel better. Knowing he'd taken the time to think about my job meant he wasn't all flash and about the party life, like I'd read. Because yeah, I'd done my homework on him as well.

His dark brows pulled together, Patrick studied the screen. "Okay. Obviously, someone to answer my fan mail and manage my social media, but I wanna make sure I see everything that comes in from the kids. Especially the ones who are sick. I'm a sponsor for Hearts and Hands, so that's really important to me."

"Oh, wow, I didn't know...I saw that when–"

"You looked me up," he finished, and my cheeks warmed.

"I mean, yeah." Did I sound defensive? "I'm sure you did the same for me."

He leaned back, those powerful arms stretched out over the couch frame. "Of course. We went to college not far from each other."

*We sure did.*

"Yeah. I might've seen that."

"But you're originally from New York?"

The rush of imminent tears startled me, and I blinked furiously. Patrick didn't need to hear the sad story of my life. He was my boss–potentially–not my friend. "Yeah. I needed a change of scenery."

Those penetrating eyes burned into mine, and I felt probed to my damaged soul. "Okay, let's talk about the job. Aside from social media, I need someone proficient in scheduling, for both my promotional appointments and the personal ones. I can easily lose track of where

I'm supposed to be and when, especially in the off-season. I have a lot of endorsements."

"Not a problem. Dev had his days filled with that kind of stuff, too." I chewed my lip. "What about your personal life? Are you going to want me to coordinate with your girlfriend?" Curiosity had been eating away at me. She obviously wasn't in the suite, and I wondered why.

"No. She and I have parted ways."

I waited to see if he'd explain further, but he just stared into space, and I figured I'd let it lie. "All right. How do you want to handle my access?"

He steepled his fingers under that strong jaw, and I couldn't help admiring his muscles. He'd grown into his body since the last night we'd spent together.

"Well...I know you and Dev were close friends before you started working for him, but how did you work it with him?"

I explained our system and how Dev had given me a separate email to answer his messages but would always check his fan mail himself, or I'd make sure to bring to his attention anything I thought important.

"I had full log-in rights to his personal calendar, and he'd give me his passwords for his social media. Anything personal between him and Brody or anyone else they wanted to keep private, they had a separate account I didn't have access to."

"That works."

I had to ask. "You didn't have someone working for you in San Diego, when you were on the Sharks?"

"I did." His eyes crinkled shut with laughter. "Multiple people, in fact. I never found the right fit. Or if I did, they were poached or got married and moved away..." He shrugged. "So, new move, new beginning."

"New you?" It slipped out of my mouth before I realized it. "Sorry. I didn't mean that the way it sounded."

"Nah, it's okay. You might be right. I think I should stop with the ladies and concentrate more on the game. I'm filling some pretty big shoes, replacing Dev, and I need to show the fans and my new team I can do it."

"I'm sure you can do whatever you put your mind to," I murmured. *And whomever*, but I bit my tongue on that one.

"How about we order lunch and go over what I need from you?"

He handed me the room-service menu, but all I could think of was our time together when he'd had everything I could give. I found it impossible to forget what for him, I was certain, was a mere blip in his outrageously healthy sex life.

"Uh, yeah." I scanned the booklet. "Turkey burger with fries."

"Sounds good. I'll make it two."

He placed the order, and I forced myself to relax. I had to let go of the past and move on.

Again he sat opposite me, but this time I was ready. "Here's a sample of my average day with Dev." I showed him a redacted calendar, and he studied it carefully.

"You're efficient as hell. And just what I need." He held out a big hand. "So? Do we have a deal? Are you willing to come work with me?"

I might be making the biggest mistake of my life, but I nodded. "Yeah. I am." The fact that he said I'd be working *with* him, not *for* him, meant he'd treat me as someone valuable.

Our food came, and we dug in and talked about life in New York City. I gave him tips on where I thought he should live, he entertained me with stories of his career, and I finally relaxed and was able to separate the past from the present. This was going to work out fine. All my worrying was for nothing. Patrick Sloane was a professional. An adult. Not the twenty-one-year-old guy I'd had sex with.

He opened his laptop. "I'll set you up as an admin, and you can start now. If you want to," he added quickly, as if thinking he was pushing.

"Yes, why not? You need to find a place and get things set up. As luxurious as this suite is, I'm sure you don't want to live in a hotel any longer than you have to."

"Yeah, I'm already sick of it. But since I don't know the city at all, I'm in your hands."

"Don't worry," I reassured him. "I'll find you the right place. Do you want to be downtown, near Dev and Brody, or you don't care?"

Crossing his big arms, he reclined on the sofa. "At this point, it doesn't matter all that much since I'm away so often during the season. But yeah, I'd like to be nearby so I'll know at least two people I can meet for a beer."

"That narrows it down." I typed away. "One or two bedrooms?"

"At least two. My parents and I are real close, and they come to stay with me a lot. So they need their own space."

"Got it." Waiting for the page to load, I let my mind wander. Did my parents think about me at all? I'd stopped contacting them years ago—every holiday I'd call but they never reciprocated or asked about me or my life, and they made no attempt to see me despite living less than two miles away, on the Upper East Side.

I knew I was a disappointment to them—I didn't measure up to Rory. They'd lost the one son they'd loved. But Rory loved me and always told me to be myself because there was no one else like me. And though Dev had tried his best and I loved him and would forever be grateful for all he'd done, I really missed my brother. I blinked at the tears burning my eyes and concentrated on this new chapter of my life.

"How much do you want to spend? The median price for a two-bedroom in Tribeca ranges from between three to four million dollars."

Trick whistled. "Damn. Dorothy, we are not in Kansas anymore."

"I'm sure you're used to prices like that, living in Southern California."

"I grew up in a little house—we didn't have much money. Part of the fights that broke up me and both my ex-wives was that I didn't want to live in a huge mansion with all the luxuries. I wasn't home much, so it didn't make sense to me. There were no kids yet, so why bother? A small, two-bedroom condo was enough for me."

"But not them?" This painted such a different picture of whom I believed Patrick to be.

His smile was wistful. "No. Not them. They thought the life of a football player's wife meant going to events, premieres, and partying. They didn't want to travel with me or even come to my games unless it was postseason. Neither lasted more than a season."

"Guess they tried to play you."

His brows shot up, and my stomach flip-flopped.

*Shit, what the hell did I just say?*

"I'm sorry. I didn't mean—"

"Don't worry about it." He chuckled. "You're right. But I've settled down now. Fact is, Dev's been a great role model. He's not that much older than me, but I look up to him. He's the toughest competitor on the field and no drama off it."

"He's a great guy." Dev truly was, but I wanted to hear more about Patrick's personal life. "So you've gotten rid of your properties in California?"

"Yeah. Each ex got the condo we lived in when we were married—I sure as hell didn't want the apartments, but funnily enough, in the end they did. I kept a small place by the beach I bought years ago, before I got married. It was a dump, but I fixed it up. It's quiet, and I go there just to get away from it all. Or to lick my wounds after a loss."

"And you're from Kansas?"

"Yeah. Small town about fifty miles from Kansas City. Nothing like this, that's for sure." He tipped the bottle of beer to his lips, and through lowered lashes, I watched his Adam's apple bob as he swallowed. His neck rose up thick, tanned, and strong, and I could see the faint blue vein running up the side. I remembered licking it, tasting him.

*Concentrate, idiot.*

I bit my tongue and listened to Patrick speak.

"After a game, we'd head out to the lake and hang out. Fool around...you know, stuff like that."

No, I didn't, but I listened. Sports didn't dominate our high school culture. We would hang out in the park, or at someone's house, playing video games. Maybe one of the guys' older brothers would buy us beer. Inevitably, guys and girls would pair up and sneak off to make out. I'd kissed a few girls so no one would guess my secret.

"Where do you live?" Trick asked. "Do you have a partner—a boyfriend?"

My fingers fumbled. "I, uh, live a few minutes away from Dev and Brody. It made it easy if he needed me in a hurry. And no, I'm not dating anyone, so you don't have to worry about my personal life taking precedence over work."

Trick frowned. "Hey, that's not what I was asking. You can find out all about my private life from the news." His eyes glimmered with amusement.

"That's not reality, though. The tabloids love to make up stuff."

He rubbed his jaw. "For the most part. I was a bit of a bad boy, though."

For some reason that made me happy. "Well, New Yorkers love a shit-talker, but only if they're a winner."

A fierce light entered his eyes. "I intend to win. I didn't come here to lose."

At his husky growl, a tiny thrill ran through me. As if it were yesterday, I remembered it purring in my ear. "Then you'll have nothing to worry about."

He focused those intense blue-green eyes on me. "I'm serious, Fallon. You need to make sure I know if you have something going on that's important, and that includes a boyfriend. I'd never ask you to put yourself second to me. If there was ever a conflict, I'd want you to come to me and talk it out. I look at this as a partnership. Both of us should be happy."

"Sounds good. It's never been an issue in the past, and it won't be now." Time to get it out of the way. "I'm pretty much a loner anyway. So...you and, uh, are you and your girlfriend really broken up, or is it one of those fights and she'll be back soon? Just so I know what to expect."

"Nah, we're done." There wasn't a shred of regret or resignation in his voice. "Mimi and I were never gonna be anything more than surface. I knew she was with me because I'm a football star, and I'm not gonna pretend I was attracted to her scintillating conversation about politics and the economy."

My lips twitched. "I have no doubts about that."

"I'm already O for 2 in relationships and just stopped paying alimony on my last ex-wife, since she remarried last year. I'm not planning on getting involved with anyone for the time being. I've decided it's too much for me to concentrate on both football and women. And football wins every time."

"Got it." I plugged his information in to a real estate database and came up with at least six apartments. "I have two places you can look at right away. Check the photos, see what you think. I can make you appointments—"

"Can you do it?" Trick waved a hand, and I gaped at him.

"You want me to pick out an apartment for you? Trick, that's...this is going to be your place."

"Yeah, but realistically, I'm barely gonna be in it almost half the year. Fact is, you could even stay there when I'm on the road."

I burst out laughing. "Yeah, okay, sure. I have an apartment, you know." A shoebox of a studio that even with the excellent salary Dev paid me was all I could afford in the neighborhood. But it sufficed for now.

"I bet mine would be nicer."

I couldn't help matching his grin.

"No kidding. But I can't pick out your apartment."

"Why not?"

This wasn't him teasing me. "You're serious."

He scooted forward on the couch. "Dead serious. Look. Go see the places, take real pictures—not the bullshit ones they put online—and send them to me with your honest opinions."

Not even Dev, whom I'd known almost my whole life, had ever entrusted me with something this personal. But then he had Brody, plus the city born-and-bred street smarts.

"If you really want..." I responded, still uncertain.

He knocked my foot with his. "I want."

That gravelly voice hit a chord straight to my balls, and I pressed my lips together to keep them from trembling.

*If only...*

"I'll get on it right away."

"Great, thanks. I have to meet my agent and go over stuff. Could you...would you mind hanging around here today? I'm waiting for a delivery of the rest of my stuff from California, and I want someone I trust to accept it."

"Not a problem. I work from your place, not mine. I'll start calling realtors to see apartments. Do you need me to make you any dinner reservations?"

A knock at the door prevented him from responding. "Hold that thought," he said and left to answer the door. I overheard murmured voices, and Trick returned with a large, sealed envelope in his hand.

"No need for dinner reservations, but thanks. I'm gonna go get ready now. See you in a few."

"Sure." I began the process of contacting real estate agents.

"Hello, this is Fallon McKenzie calling on behalf of Patrick Sloane of the Brooklyn Kings. I'd like to arrange an appointment to see the apartment at 30 Warren."

"Of course, Mr. McKenzie. I can have someone meet him at the apartment this afternoon. Say, two thirty? Would that work? We'd be thrilled to show him this property, or any others he might be interested in."

I knew not to say that Patrick wouldn't be coming with me—they'd automatically push me off until he could make time for them personally. They only wanted to meet the main attraction. I'd make up an excuse as to why he had to cancel at the last minute.

"Sounds good. We'll meet you at the residence."

"We can send a car for you if you'd like."

I held back a laugh at the agent's eagerness. "That won't be necessary. Thank you and see you then."

I made a second appointment for a showing on Washington Street and was met with the same barely restrained enthusiasm. I put the appointments in my calendar and was continuing my search for suitable apartments when Trick emerged from the bedroom. He wore a button-down shirt with the sleeves rolled up, and I couldn't help eyeing all that dark hair on his strong forearms. A pair of dress slacks stretched over his powerful thighs, showcasing the outline of that impressive dick. The whole package made me slightly weak. If sex on a stick was a picture, it would be Patrick Sloane.

"What?" He grabbed the suit jacket and glanced at me. "Is something wrong?"

Busted. I blinked, shaking my head. "No, sorry, I was running through the appointments I'd made."

"Oh, good. I thought I was dressed all wrong."

*Oh, no. You're perfect. Just fucking perfect.*

He slipped his phone and wallet into his pockets. "I'll see you later or tomorrow."

"I have appointments for two places—both sound like what you're looking for. I'll send you pictures."

"Okay. I, uh, I might go out later, so if I don't answer, I'll catch up with you in the morning. What time do you start?"

I grinned. "When I wake up—around six. I start by checking emails and socials."

His jaw fell open. "Okay, well...that's a little early for me. Let's say, eight thirty? I'll have breakfast ready for us."

Even though it was during the season, it seemed like Trick didn't play by the rules and was planning on hooking up during the week between games. I'd never had to worry about that with Dev, since he and Brody were together. Guess he wasn't *that* done with women yet.

I merely nodded. "See you tomorrow. I'll be ready in a few minutes, and I'll leave with you."

"Don't rush. Stay and finish whatever you're doing. I'm late, and the car's already waiting. The door locks behind you. I'll have the front desk make you a key card."

"Thanks."

He left, and I found several more apartments to check for tomorrow and made some notes, then decided to hit the bathroom before leaving. As I passed through the bedroom, I stopped short when I saw on the bed the contents of the envelope Patrick had received earlier that afternoon. I sank to the bed and stared at the familiar logo on the letterhead.

Intensity.

The West Coast club we'd met at in college had a New York branch. I knew because I was still a member. I was out but frequented the discreet club. Why? Dev continued to pay for my membership as part of my yearly Christmas present. He still thought it would be safer than hooking up with random strangers, but I rarely went more than once a month, if that. Occasionally I'd meet someone, but it was only ever a one-night thing. I had no room for a relationship—I'd spent so many years managing the drama of Dev's.

But this was totally unexpected. What if I saw Patrick there with another man? My stomach lurched, and my hand curled into a fist.

He'd be there later. I'd bet on it.

Good thing I had no plans to go. I was definitely staying home.

# CHAPTER FOUR

### Patrick

I adjusted the mask, anxiety spiking that I might be recognized, but a scan in the full-length bathroom mirror at Intensity disproved my fears. With my hair slicked back and the mask skintight, I was unrecognizable even to myself. Besides, I wasn't there to have sex, just watch and get the lay of the land.

It had been well over a year since I'd been to a club. Every once in a while I'd get the itch, but sometimes it would be when we were on the road, where I couldn't do much to scratch it. If I was home, I'd go, and though I got off, it left me empty. Hollow. Maybe because I knew the sex would never lead to anything.

My heart pounding, I walked out of the restroom, eyes and ears adjusting to the sights and sounds of the club. Intensity was housed in a large brownstone in Manhattan, innocuous from the outside and indistinguishable from the other grand homes on the block. Your irises were scanned upon entry, and then the interior door opened as if into another world.

Three floors of decadence awaited. The top floor held the private rooms reserved for people who wanted their intimate times...intimate, only witnessed by the two of them. The second floor showcased open rooms for couples who enjoyed their sexy times in public and, if they chose, with audience participation.

The main floor salon was for mingling—no open sexual activity, although I'd spied kissing and light fondling among some couples. A dining room in the rear held an opulent buffet. Below the stairs on the lower floor was the kitchen, which kept up a steady replenishment of refreshments. And, I remembered reading in the brochure, the basement held playrooms, where anything went and people lived out their secret fantasies. I was way too vanilla for that.

For my first visit, I wore a yellow pin, which meant I would have to give permission to be touched or kissed. I took a glass of champagne from a passing waiter and sipped, stepping fully into the parlor and taking in the scene. Classical music played softly in the background, and I leaned against the fireplace mantel, seeing if anyone caught my eye. Which someone did. He stood at the far end of the spacious room, staring up at a magnificent oil painting of a soldier riding on a horse. The stranger, well-built but not overly muscular, filled out a pair of sleek navy pants, the gorgeous curve of his ass like a peach, ripe for the plucking.

The sight of him, with his thick dark hair curling past his ears, sent my stomach into free fall. Strange because I'd always been more attracted to blonds, but the pull to meet him was strong. I couldn't allow anyone else to get to him first. I crossed the room to stand by his side.

"Beautiful painting, isn't it?"

The man blinked, outrageously long lashes framing pretty eyes of deep, rich brown. They might be his natural color, or they could be contact lenses. I couldn't blame him. I also wore colored lenses, turning my blue-green eyes a slate gray.

"It is," he murmured, his voice smooth and subdued. "I'm not surprised, though. The entire house is like a museum. It's stunning."

"Not your first time?" I asked, enjoying the dance. My nerves buzzed with an excitement I hadn't felt in years, and my belly fluttered. His lips, full and soft, enticed. I wanted to kiss him.

"No, but it's been a while."

"Ah. You were...involved?"

He dipped his head in answer.

I touched my mask. "I'm new to the city but not to this scene."

"Oh? So you know how it works?" A smile creased his cheek. "I see you do, as you're wearing your pin. Yellow, like me."

His fingers caressed the small piece of metal on his lapel, and my pants grew tighter, wishing those elegant fingers were wrapped around my aching dick.

"Yeah. I wasn't sure what to expect, so I figured I'd take it slow."

"Slow can be good." His tongue swiped over his full lower lip. "I personally prefer getting to know someone before...." He bowed his head, a red flush creeping up his neck. I had a crazy urge to press my lips to the place where that sweet curve to his shoulder began. Jesus, this wild, uncontrollable desire hadn't happened to me since my mystery man in California.

"Yeah. Is that what we're doing here? Getting to know each other?" I took a chance, leaned in closer, and watched his eyes widen. Heard his breath hitch. My fingertip played along his clean-shaven jaw, and he swayed toward me. "Can I kiss you?" Anticipation fluttered in my belly, and my lips tingled.

Like a frightened deer, the man jumped away. "No, I'm sorry. I-I can't." To my shock, he fled the room.

*Dammit.* I'd moved too fast. I'd broken my rule of taking things slow.

Hoping to catch him and apologize, I took several steps, when someone planted himself in front of me.

"Hello. You're new here, aren't you?"

His face was all angles and planes, shiny black hair setting off large blue eyes. If the way he filled out his Italian suit was any indication, he matched me in weight. Heat poured off him, and he reached out and ran a finger over my button.

"I am," I answered.

"And you're yellow. Are you sure you want to just watch and wait? Or can I persuade you otherwise?"

I gently moved his hand away. "Not tonight."

"Too bad," he said with true regret. "I'd really love to taste your ass."

Startled by his boldness, I shook my head. "Sorry to disappoint."

After I left him, I walked through the rooms but didn't see the man who'd intrigued me. I even ventured upstairs, where couples were into public play, though I doubted he'd be there. I peeked into the first interactive room.

"Whoa," I muttered, my feet rooted to the floor. One guy was lying spread-eagle on the bed, taking it up the ass, while another man's cock was being fed into his gasping mouth. The smell of sweat and sex was overwhelming, and I wasn't the only one viewing. Several people were riveted to the scene, and from their audible breathing, into it.

Not my scene at all. I backed out and glanced into the other rooms, where much more vanilla sex was occurring. My guy was nowhere to be found, and I gave up, figuring he'd left for the evening. I should return to the main salon, find the big dark-haired guy, and rid myself of this unsettling tension that had been twisting inside me all day. I knew what it was from but was reluctant to admit it.

Fallon.

God, he turned me on. That tight butt and sexy smile. Blue eyes the color of the sky. But he was off-limits. Aside from being my PA, he was a good friend to Dev, and the last thing I wanted was to mess up that dynamic. Fallon seemed to keep parts of his life closed off, but not his sexuality. He was out and had all the opportunities open to him. I wasn't and couldn't offer him anything but a back-door affair, which wasn't fair. He'd want a boyfriend he could go out to dinner with and hold hands with on the street.

To find an outlet, I'd have to continue to come to Intensity, but in the meantime, I guessed I'd have one hell of a fantasy life with Fallon playing the starring role. Coach Jackson didn't expressly forbid sex between games—he'd only given us the usual warning about no partying, drugs, excess alcohol, and smoking. No worries on my part. I had no intention of putting on a display like those guys did upstairs in the viewing rooms.

Downstairs again, I spied the man who'd made his outrageous overture earlier, and he arched a brow, giving me a look that left no doubt what he wanted. I kept walking.

I returned to my hotel suite to find it empty and laughed at my disappointment that Fallon wasn't there.

*Idiot. What did you expect?*

It was close to midnight, and with a sigh, I sat on the couch to unwind before taking a shower. Texts I'd ignored all afternoon popped up, and I read Fallon's first.

*Saw two condos I think you'd like, one more than the other because it had an en suite in the bedroom for your parents. Not far from me or Dev.*

I enlarged the attached photos and whistled. Yeah, the place was gorgeous. Super modern and sleek, with two large bedrooms and three bathrooms. Floor-to-ceiling windows overlooked the river, and I could picture myself sitting on the balcony, watching the boats sail past while the lights came up in the buildings surrounding me.

As much as I traveled for games, one thing I'd always looked forward to was coming home. And though I'd kept the beach house, that was for getaways, not permanent living. I was ready to put down roots, and with this five-year contract from the Kings, it was likely my career would end here, in this city. I wanted to go out on top, not be forced out because I was too old or injured.

The first thing I'd done when I'd gotten to New York was ask Dev about a gym. I had no intention of getting lazy. Coach hadn't said I'd be starting this Sunday, but as far as I was concerned, I was. No offense to Harte McKinney, the backup they'd been using this season, but I wasn't here to twiddle my thumbs.

As I stripped in the bedroom, I noticed with a start that I'd left the envelope from Intensity on the bed. I wondered if Fallon had seen it and immediately dismissed the thought.

"No way. He worked for Dev all those years and knows to be discreet. He'd never snoop in my personal stuff." Still, I made sure to slip it into my underwear drawer, then climbed into bed. My thoughts turned to the man I'd met earlier—not the one who'd made his intentions known that he was down to fuck. No, it was the skittish, dark-haired stranger who stuck in my mind. Oh, the dirty things I'd like to do to that sweet, sweet mouth.

I turned over and sighed. So many years I'd been living this double life. I remembered being a college student and discovering these clubs existed, after joining an online chat room and seeing the listing. The anonymity was what had drawn me to it, and then I'd met him, the man who'd given me the most intense sexual experience of my life. Even now, after so many years, so many one-night stands and lovers, I remembered every detail of our months together. The talks we'd shared. The searching kisses, his moans of passion, the hot clasp of him as I'd buried myself deep within his willing body—all were forever burned into my memory.

I'd been willing to take the chance with him, but he'd never given me that opportunity.

**

The next morning, Fallon met me on Washington Street in front of the high-rise, and I liked the vibe of the area. People recognized me but in that New York way, they simply gave me a side-eye and kept on walking, respecting my privacy. The expansive lobby was filled with greenery, and we were met by the real estate agent, who sported a bright smile when he saw me.

"Good to meet you, Mr. Sloane. I'm sorry you couldn't join us yesterday. Now, your assistant seemed to think this apartment was the better of the two for you to see first. What do you think? Beautiful, yes?" The agent pointed to the bright, open space. "The building is barely five years old. The unit we're viewing has a private elevator that opens to your apartment only. There's a gym, swimming pool, and entertainment rooms. Everything you can possibly want under your roof."

"It all sounds great." I walked to the center of the lobby, where sunbeams from the atrium slanted across the creamy marble floor. "And I have a view of the river?"

"Let's check it out."

Fallon followed us into the elevator and it gave me an opportunity to appreciate the broad sweep of his shoulders narrowing to slim hips and that perfect ass. His golden hair waved around his neck, and I smelled the spice of his cologne. Why was it so difficult to control my urges with him? I'd never felt this intense pull to any of the men I'd hooked up with over the past ten years.

Yesterday at Intensity was the first time I'd felt a spark of attraction to a man that came close to rivaling my mystery man from California, but who knew if I'd ever meet him again. I sure as hell did plan to return and see.

The moment we entered the apartment, the agent started his spiel on the marvelous European cabinetry and Italian marble, but I ignored him and walked toward the floor-to-ceiling windows in the living area, showcasing the river. Leaving him and Fallon behind, I opened the glass doors and stepped outside. Thirty stories up, I could barely hear the traffic. The gray swells of the waves in the choppy, windswept water were as beautiful to me as the blue whitecaps of the Pacific Ocean.

"It's mesmerizing, isn't it?" Fallon stood by the door, and I faced him with a smile. Strands of hair blew across his face as a sharp breeze passed by, and several caught on his full bottom lip.

*So are you.*

"I guess I should see the rest of the apartment since I won't be living out here."

Amusement glimmered in Fallon's eyes. "It's just as beautiful."

"I'm sure it is. Let's go see."

Together, we followed the agent from room to room. Everything looked perfect.

"I'll take it," I stated when he'd finished, and the shock on his face told me this wasn't how it normally worked.

"Oh, uh, sure. What offer would you like to put in?"

"Whatever you think will get me in here as soon as possible."

"So you don't want to see the other one I found? You might like it better," Fallon said, clearly surprised at my snap decision.

I grinned. "I like this one. That's good enough. Great job, Fallon."

Pink suffused his face. "Thanks. I—uh, so I guess I'd better cancel the showing for the other condo."

"Yeah. And then we have to go furniture shopping."

"I-I can do that for you. I'm sure you have more important things to take care of. Just tell me what you like."

"I'm sure you can, but I'm very particular about the bed I sleep in. I usually get them custom made. At my height, I have a hard time finding a comfortable mattress."

"You didn't need to see the apartment, but you have to try out your mattress?"

I snickered. "That's the one piece of furniture that gets the most action."

Now fire-engine red, Fallon ducked his head and mumbled something about needing to make a call. He practically ran to the other side of the room.

"Mr. Sloane, I think this would be a fair offer." The agent droned on about paperwork, and I nodded along, but I couldn't get the picture of Fallon in my bed and under me out of my mind.

# CHAPTER FIVE

## Fallon

Early morning workouts were never my thing. Actually, workouts in general weren't, but I did find they cleared my head when I could think of nothing else but the blood pumping through my veins and the sweat slicking my skin. Plus, sitting all day meant I didn't get much physical activity, so here I was, at five thirty, at SportsLab NYC, the number-one gym for athletes in the city, pumping iron.

With my set finished, I wiped my face and arms and got on the treadmill. Earbuds in, I started running, which gave me a chance to think about what had happened at Intensity.

I'd wrestled with myself over whether to go or not, but who was I kidding? I had to know if he'd show up.

I'd put in my colored contacts and had even pulled out a high-end wig Dev had gotten me for a Brooklyn Kings costume party he'd invited me to. I'd wanted there to be no chance of Patrick recognizing me.

I'd known it was Patrick from the suit he'd worn—the same custom-tailored one he'd left the hotel suite in for his earlier meetings. Plus, he had a starburst of freckles on the right side of his neck I'd memorized from our time together. Funny how I remembered such a small detail from so many years ago.

And when he'd touched me…God, I'd fucking burned for him. In the years since we'd been together, no one had caused my bones to melt like this man.

He'd wanted to kiss me, and I'd imagined the silky sweep of his tongue parting my lips. The soft yet demanding pressure of his mouth on mine. My whole body had become one pulsing core of hungry need, and that was why I'd run. I'd thought I was over him, but if I'd stayed, I would've ended up under Patrick Sloane.

My feet pounded the treadmill, the miles piling up. If I could run him out of my system, I would, and I cursed my weakness. This had been my fear—that working so closely with Trick would have me thinking of nothing but sex. Sex with him.

Someone got on the treadmill next to me, and my annoyance spiked. By now it was six in the morning, and while the gym was filling up, there were plenty of empty machines they could've picked. I turned my head to glare at the person and met Trick's smirk.

"Surprise."

Breathing heavily, I slowed my steps to a walk and grabbed my towel to wipe my face. "What're you doing here?" I questioned when I stopped panting.

He glanced around the room. "I think I'm exercising."

I rolled my eyes. "Ha-ha. Yeah. I didn't know you were a member here."

"I asked Dev about a gym and got my agent to arrange it. I intend to be on the field this Sunday." His jaw hardened.

There was the fierce competitor I'd read up on, and without thinking, I blurted out, "You look perfectly fit to me."

A dark brow rose, and he flashed me his trademark cocky grin. "Thanks for noticing. Just gonna go for a quick run, now that I finished my lifting."

*Dammit.* Why did my blush meter work overdrive whenever I was close to this man? I needed to work on that.

"Anyway..." My cooldown complete, I hopped off the treadmill. "I'm gonna hit the shower and go home. I'll be at your hotel by eight thirty, after breakfast."

"No, don't do that." He frowned, and I squinted at him in confusion.

"Don't do what? Shower or eat?" I sniffed myself. "Trust me, you do not want me sitting next to you and your eggs smelling like this."

"Ha-ha. Look, I'll be here for about another half hour. Come to the suite, and we'll have breakfast. We can go over the day's schedule. I have to be at training camp by ten." Those turquoise eyes twinkled at me. "Looks like you'll be furniture shopping on your own after all."

I wanted to be annoyed but couldn't. More often than not, I'd shared breakfast with Dev and Brody, which I was sure Patrick Sloane knew. As a matter of fact, I was sure he knew everything about how I worked with Dev. No way I could refuse in good faith.

Besides, I kind of didn't want to. Much as I hated to admit it, I had no complaints so far. I'd made something out of nothing, arising from my past with him and what I'd read on social media. I should've known better. Everything I'd anticipated was in my head. He didn't know who I was. Patrick had been nothing but professional, and my decision to go to Intensity had stemmed from my own curiosity to see him. He was a free man and could do whatever he wanted with whomever.

"I think I have an idea of what you'll like, and I promise I won't get you anything you'll hate."

Serious now, Patrick nodded. "I trust you. Don't forget to stop at the front desk and get your key card." He turned on the machine and started to run in earnest. "See you later."

Leaving him, I walked home. I felt...good. Almost happy. It took me a while to recognize the emotion, as I tended to shoulder other people's emotions to the extent of ignoring my own.

I showered and put on work clothes–a button-down shirt and slacks–then checked Patrick's emails. It was the usual requests for interviews, gushing fan mail, and junk. Realizing I was going to be late, I grabbed my iPad, phone, keys, and wallet and took a car uptown.

I stopped at the front desk, and the clerk smiled and handed me an envelope with a key card. "Mr. Sloane asked us to make sure you have this."

"Thanks."

I took the elevator up to the suite and entered, but he wasn't in the living room.

"Patrick? It's Fallon. I'm here."

"Be right out."

I set up my iPad and read through Patrick's social media, checking first to see if there was any negative press that would require him to make a statement. While technically my job was personal assistant, it tended to merge with the role of public relations, and I would refer any media stories to the Kings organization for them to handle.

"Hey, sorry. I was on the phone." When Patrick entered the room, I'd have sworn it was as if a switch was flipped, and the energy soared. He wore a pair of sweats and a Brooklyn Kings T-shirt. His thick biceps bulged, and I had to bite down on my tongue.

"No worries. I was just checking your socials."

He grinned. "What trouble am I getting into today?"

I laughed, sharing his good mood. "Surprisingly, nothing."

"Well, the day is young." He stretched, and I had to look away from the enticing peek of tanned, ripped abs as his shirt hiked up, revealing a dark treasure trail.

*God, the things I could do with that...to that...*

"Fallon?"

I blinked away from my fantasy of licking a wet path past the waistband and dipping my tongue into his navel.

"Sorry. What is it?"

Amused, he handed me the room-service menu. "I asked what you wanted for breakfast."

Face hot, I studied the booklet. "Uh, the American is fine. Eggs scrambled and whole-wheat toast."

"Okay."

He placed the order, and I returned to stalking his socials. "Mimi seems to have moved on."

"Yeah? Lemme see." The cushion beside me dipped from his weight, and he leaned in close.

God, he smelled so good. Like the air after a cool spring rain and fresh laundry detergent, plus the hot natural scent of his skin. His body heat must run higher than normal because the man was a damn inferno. All that warmth soaked into me.

"I'm not surprised," he murmured, studying the picture on the screen. Mimi was on the beach, in a tiny bikini, and hanging on to the arm of a big, tall, buff guy. "She dislikes being alone. And that's Alexander Monk, the Texas Stars basketball player. He's more her type."

"What's that?"

"Hard partier, hits the clubs every night. Likes to be in the news. Runs his mouth like he plays, fast and dirty. That's not me."

"That sounds like how the press reports on you."

"Like what? Playing dirty? I've never been accused of that. I never deliberately set out to hurt anyone on the opposing team. Shit like that pisses me off." His annoyance was palpable. I could feel him shaking. "It ruins the whole spirit of the game."

Seeing how upset he was, I rushed to apologize. "No, I meant the partying. I'm—I'm sorry. I just know what I read in the papers. I wasn't agreeing with it."

He ran a hand through his thick hair. "As stupid as I've behaved in my private life, I've never let it interfere with my professional life. And the personal mistakes I made were years ago. I'll admit to the partying in the off-season." He shrugged. "I like my company. But the reality is, playing football is all I've ever wanted to do. It's all I know how to do."

This was a completely different side of Patrick I hadn't known existed. "I'm sure you did well in school. You had to pass your classes."

"Barely. I didn't take school seriously—you know how it is. You're from a small town, and you get plunked in the middle of a huge university where you don't know anyone. I went a little wild." He rubbed his jaw, his eyes distant.

*Yeah, I remember.*

"Wild how? I thought you weren't allowed to do that during the season. At least that's what I learned from Dev and Brody."

A slight twitch of his lips. "Well, there's always ways around that. And I was a smartass those days."

"Was? Or have some things never changed?" I razzed.

"Hey," he protested. "I resemble that remark."

We shared a laugh, but I found him staring at my mouth and...I froze. Those blue-green eyes darkened. I recognized that glint in a man's eye.

Lust.

I couldn't look away.

Could he sense my desire? How bad I wanted him?

Panic whirled through me. My heartbeat accelerated, and I watched his chest rise and fall rapidly. A flush suffused his cheeks, and his lips parted. The air crackled between us, and I knew if he made even one move, I'd give him everything.

The doorbell rang, startling us.

"I'll get it." Grateful for the distraction, I jumped up and practically ran to the door. I let in the man wheeling the cart. "Thanks."

Patrick had his wallet out and handed the guy a couple of twenties. "Thank you. I'll call when it needs to be picked up."

The man smiled. "Thank you very much, sir." The door closed behind him.

"Okay, let's dig in. I don't wanna be late for training camp." As if nothing odd had occurred only moments before, Patrick began to eat. Obviously, he could turn his emotions on and off easier than I could. I nibbled on a piece of toast, still tangled up in what had almost happened.

Foolish as it was, my brain couldn't shut off. I couldn't slip, no matter how badly I wanted Patrick. It had been a while since I'd had the urge for sex—months, in fact. My libido, like my life, had been stuck in neutral. Maybe it was time to find someone to fuck Patrick Sloane out of my head.

We finished our breakfast, and Patrick collected his stuff. I crunched the last of my bacon, wiped my hands, and returned to the iPad.

"I'll stay here and look at furniture—did you hear anything about your offer? Maybe I should hold off until you know it's accepted and you get the apartment."

He shook his head. "I'll call the agent today. But I want it, so you can go ahead and order what you think will look best in the space. I don't have time, and I don't care that much. I'm not into anything fancy. Plain, neutral stuff. Except like I said before, my bed."

"Got it." I clicked on the sites I used helping Dev with his apartment. "You're pretty sure you'll get it, even though other people might be bidding against you?"

He winked and slung his duffel over his shoulder. "Something else you'll find out working for me—I always get what I want."

He left, and I alternated between wondering what the hell he meant and smiling at his absolute confidence. You had to be born with that. Self-worth and that slight arrogance wasn't something you could learn. Patrick Sloane had that enviable "it" quality I wished I possessed but didn't. Ever. My parents had made certain of that with the subtle putdowns and comparisons between me and Rory, which had only increased after I'd come out to them.

As if my gayness had explained everything to them.

Rory had told me to brush it off, but I'd found it impossible. Being the golden child, he hadn't understood. And I didn't hold it against him because he loved me for who I was. No matter what, losing my brother, the only person who'd loved me unconditionally, had irrevocably changed me. Knowing there wasn't another person who understood me completely—someone I used to cry to about never finding someone to love who would love me as well—was the loneliest feeling in the world. It was why I chose to use sex clubs. Love wasn't going to happen for someone like me. I'd settle for an escape.

With the floor plans of the co-op downloaded, I ventured out to the stores and spent someone else's money. I got Patrick squared away and even had them hold the delivery date, none of which could've been accomplished without using Patrick Sloane's name.

Back at the suite, I waited for Patrick, but around six my phone buzzed with a text from him.

*Having dinner with Dev and Brody. I'll see you tomorrow.*

I sent him a thumbs-up and left, my plan for the evening decided.

*Intensity, I'm ready for you.*

# CHAPTER SIX

Patrick

"A podcast? What's the focus, football?" I stabbed at my steak. I had no desire to bring the mood down, but I was pissed. After a full day of practice, Coach had pulled me aside and told me he wanted to give it another week before starting me. He promised I'd get some playing time, but I was a starter, not a backup. Two weeks of forced inactivity was making me restless, and when I got restless, I did stupid things.

"Yeah. We're calling it *The Huddle*. We'll talk about football, of course, but also focus on the needs of LGBTQ students who want to participate in sports. Plus, we're hoping out athletes will want to come speak on the show. And anyone else," Brody answered.

"Sounds good. I'll be listening for sure."

"If you want to come on and talk about your dating life, feel free. It's not only about us gays." Dev chuckled.

I chewed, imagining what the guys would say about me going to a sex club to get my rocks off with a guy. While I was friendly with them, I didn't feel the need to spout off about something so personal, although I had a feeling Dev wouldn't mind. He'd probably enjoy hearing about it.

"I'll pass. At this point, I just want to play football. What I'm doing on the side to get a little action isn't all that interesting."

"Doubtful. You know people love to hear about people's sex lives, especially hot football players." Dev popped a shrimp into his mouth. "But we'll let it slide this time."

"Thanks." I smirked, then became serious. "Really, though. I think it's a great idea. People should see that they can be anything they want, no matter who they choose to sleep with. But let me ask you something. Do you think it's necessary for a professional athlete to come out? You've been there. Did you feel pressure?"

Dev and Brody exchanged glances. Brody nodded. "Every single day. We hated having to hide for the sake of the game."

"And you never thought about coming out while you were playing?"

Sadness darkened Dev's green eyes. "I struggled with it every damn day, but I didn't think the fans or our teammates would be ready to hear that."

"That sucks, guys. I'm sorry you had to deal with that." I finished my meal, and the server whisked the plate away. "It's not fair."

"I believe sooner rather than later, the tide will change," Brody said, his usually mild face surprisingly fierce. "All it needs is for someone to take that first step."

"We came close many times." Dev put a hand over Brody's. "But with both of us on the field, on the same team...we decided to wait until we retired. It would've turned the games we played into a circus. Maybe we were wrong, but what's done is done. Now tell us about practice. How're you liking the team? Are you nervous about starting?"

I'd hoped they wouldn't ask. Embarrassed, I ducked my head. "I'm not starting."

Shocked, they both stared at me. "What?" Brody sputtered. "Why not?"

My sigh came out as a growl. "Because Coach feels I'm still not ready or in top form. He wants to make sure my ankle is a hundred percent, even though it is. Dammit, I wanna get in there and show them what I've got."

"Piece of advice?" Dev set his fork on the table.

"I'm all ears." Dev had been in almost the same position after his backup stepped into his place and played way beyond anyone's imagination. If anyone knew how to handle the situation, it was him.

"Coach knows what's what. Use the time to study the films, learn the playbook, and think outside the box. The Kings are very much a family organization and value teamwork and players getting along. It's why I always wanted to play for them. They stood behind us and me anytime we needed them."

Dev's explanation made sense. "I hear you. I just hate feeling useless."

"You're not. Watch and learn how the team meshes. Be the bigger man to match the big salary. Congratulate Harte and encourage him—guy's got all the experience in the world. He's a good backup for you."

Wise words. I'd known Dev would give me the perspective I needed. "Thanks. I remember you doing that for Fontaine when you were injured. I appreciate the advice."

"We've all been there. Anytime you wanna talk, we're here for you. And I'm serious. Think about coming on the podcast. Fans would love hearing about your life in the big city as a single guy."

In the car on my way home, I wondered if I would ever be able to do what others had done and come out as bisexual. Coward that I was, I knew it would be easier if I ended up with a woman, but the truth remained that lately my thoughts had revolved around being with a man. Like the beautiful man from Intensity.

Which was why, like the evening before last, I found myself in the salon, mask on, sipping a Scotch and scanning the room. *Fuck it*, I thought. If I wasn't going to play on the field, I might as well play in the sheets.

A knot of excitement tightened in my belly when I saw him across the room, standing by the fireplace. The beautiful man with the dark-brown waves, dressed in a sleek suit. Our eyes met, and his widened, flaring hot with recognition.

Determined this time not to move too fast, I strode over. "We meet again."

"So I see." His generous mouth curved upward.

"Your glass is about empty. Can I get you a refill?"

"I think I'd rather have a clear head to talk with you."

Hoping his words meant what I thought they did, I needed to make sure not to overstep and scare him away a second time. "So you're not planning on running?"

He set the glass on the mantel and took a step closer. "Not this time."

My glass joined his. "I was hoping you'd say that. Why don't we find a more private spot?" He opened his mouth, and I shook my head. "Not upstairs. Here." I held out my hand, and after hesitating, he took it. I led him to a corner in an adjoining room, where couples were engaged in more intimate conversations. Something I hoped for with my new friend. I positioned myself catty-corner to face him. "I thought I'd frightened you away the other night."

"Yet here I am."

"In the very awesome flesh." I grinned, wondering what he looked like under his well-fitted suit. Usually, I didn't spend this much time talking to a potential bed partner, especially a man. There was always someone willing and eager to get naked quickly.

"Are you sure you don't want to go upstairs?" I turned on the charm, giving him my most wicked smile.

He gazed up at me, wary and a bit tense. "I think this is good enough, don't you?"

About to disagree, I held my tongue. Why was I rushing it?

"All right. Would you like another drink?"

He nodded, and together we walked to the bar, where he got a beer and I ordered another Scotch. We returned to our private corner.

"I know enough not to ask for specifics," he said, "but what brings you here?"

I stared into the tumbler of amber liquid in my hand. "Probably the same as most everyone else. With my job, I'm not in the position to be out. It's been... hard."

As I spoke the words, I realized how truly sad it was. I'd spent my life hiding because of other people's beliefs. On the field I was willing to take any and all risks to win. But when it came to my heart, I was...afraid. Not an emotion I'd ever thought to hear, and I didn't like it. I wondered if I'd ever have the courage to be myself.

"I'm sorry," the man whispered. "I should go."

"No, please don't." I didn't want him to disappear again. I couldn't let that happen. "Did I say something wrong? Most likely you have similar issues. Sometimes it helps to talk it out with a stranger, even if we can't get into specifics."

Those deep brown eyes filled and glistened. "I'm not the right person for you to confide in."

"I've upset you." Perhaps my story hit too close to home. "We can talk about something else. The weather. Sports. Anything."

"I don't really follow sports much."

Conversation wasn't normally my strong suit, but I grasped for the first thing that came to mind. Anything to keep him with me. "Are you from New York? I've only recently moved here." He nodded, and relieved that he seemed to have abandoned the idea of leaving, I pushed on. "So you probably know all the best restaurants that aren't on the must-lists that change every week."

Laughing, he took another drink of his beer. "Yeah, that's pretty silly, isn't it? I like to go to the ones that aren't trendy and crowded. Nothing's worse than being squashed into a table, elbow to elbow with strangers, while you're trying to have a conversation with someone, and instead of hearing them talk, you hear the person at the next table chewing." He shuddered, and I laughed.

"Oh God, that's my worst nightmare."

"And if they talk with their mouth full…"

Dancing eyes met mine, and something strange shifted inside me. Fuck it, I was so attracted to him. I wished…I wished we could rip off these damn masks and go find one of those out-of-the-way places and be ourselves. I knew it would be breaking the rules, but I was nothing if not a risk-taker, and sometimes a rule was made to be bent. Or broken.

"Can I ask you something?"

Instantly his guard went up, those walls slamming down. "Sure."

"Would you ever consider…maybe getting together outside of here?"

He frowned. "That's against the club's rules."

I nibbled on my lip. "Maybe, maybe not. It says we're not allowed to take off our masks while we're here, and we're not allowed to divulge personal information—while on the premises." In a bold move, I took his hand. He shivered, and I wondered if he'd ever been hurt and that was why he was so reluctant to get closer. In my years of experience at these clubs, I'd never met a man so jumpy. "It can't control us once we leave. I just want to be alone with you for a little while. Nothing more. I promise."

"I can't." And I heard the agony in his voice. Frustration swelled inside me, knowing he wanted to but something prevented him. "We're having a really nice time. Please don't force me into something I can't give you."

My thumb played with his fingers, and he trembled. Knowing I affected him was a win for me. I couldn't let the night end without knowing what he tasted like. His proximity enflamed my already burning desire, and I couldn't help myself. I picked up his hand and kissed each knuckle. "I won't. But before I go, can I ask you for one thing?"

Wary, he nodded. "If I can give it, sure."

"A kiss?" Instant refusal sprang up in his eyes, and I rushed to squash it. "Please? Only a kiss." His hand, still held in mine, trembled. "My lips on yours. Imagine it." His eyes blew wide, and I teased my tongue over his fingertips. One by one. His breath grew short, then stuttered. "Please," I whispered again. At his slow nod, my heart surged with the same adrenaline jolt as if I'd thrown a winning touchdown.

In our private corner, I leaned in and dipped my head. The moment my mouth hit his, I was lost. The way he'd been so nervous during our time together, I'd believed he'd be shy, timid, but the fierce, fiery push of his tongue past my lips drove that thought from my mind. My man was in full control, and damned if I didn't fucking love it. I sucked his tongue, and then we traded places, his tangling with mine. The world reeled under my feet, and I held on to him for balance. This wasn't a kiss. This was ownership, and I willingly gave myself up, body and soul. The memories of another kiss like this set me reeling. My first lover...first love...that same desire, the all-encompassing hunger to hold on to him and never let go.

Needing air, we finally parted and stared at each other, chests heaving. His eyes glowed, and I was sure my face was as flushed as his. I leaned in close, ran my nose down his cheek, and he swayed toward me.

"I have to go," he murmured.

I wanted to clutch him tight and make him promise he'd see me another time, but like sand through my fingers, he slipped away and was out of the room before I could speak.

With my mystery man gone, nothing remained of interest, so I ducked out of the room and stepped into the private bathroom to remove my mask. A separate entrance led to the street, and I ducked my head as I left. The night air played around me, cool and fresh, and I walked for several blocks, enjoying it. Eventually I called for a car to take me to the hotel. I checked my messages and saw one from the real estate agent that they'd made a counteroffer on the condo. I texted him.

*Accept it and get the deal done.*

We drove past crowded streets and I wondered where my mystery man lived. Still itchy from the mask, I rubbed my face. Obsessing over someone whose name I didn't know, whose only connection to me was a sex club, was a story for the gossip column and proved I had way too much time on my hands. Sex could wait. It would always be there. Dev was right. It was time to concentrate on football and what I was getting paid to do.

# CHAPTER SEVEN

## Fallon

I didn't like what I'd done. Pretending was never right no matter the reason, and kissing Patrick without him knowing who it was left me sad and angry.

The rest of the week I kept busy with arranging everything he'd need to move. I needed the distraction because there were too many times I'd catch myself staring at the wall, thinking of our kiss. The passion that had shimmered between us as he'd touched my face. Emotions I'd thought I'd buried a decade earlier burst free, and I ached not only from desire but with the loss of what we'd had. And what might've been.

Patrick had spent the week studying the playbook, talking on the phone with Dev, and watching training films. I might not know him well, but I could sense his nerves and tried to keep out of his way, only coming to him when absolutely necessary. He was polite but quick, with little time for joking.

He also stayed home and didn't go to Intensity, which for some stupid reason made me happy. Trying to prove that I wasn't hung up on Patrick, I went out to a club one night after work.

The space was small and the music loud. I vowed not to send out don't-touch-me vibes and stood by the edge of the dance floor with a beer in my hand.

"I don't think I've heard this song in five years," a voice at my shoulder said, and I turned to see who'd spoken. He was about my height, with short, curling hair. Dark-rimmed glasses framed an earnest yet nervous face.

"I'll see that five and raise you at least eight," I responded with a smile.

He tipped his glass of clear liquid with a floating wedge of lime. "Nathan."

"Fallon. Nice to meet you."

A twitch of his lips. "I guess my next line should be, 'Come here often?' But for some reason, you don't look the type."

Amused, I turned my back to the dance floor to face him. "No? What type do I look like?"

He took my answer to heart, serious brown eyes meeting mine. "A guy who's been hurt. Someone who doesn't really want to be here." His gaze skittered away from mine for a second. "Like me."

"So why are you, then?"

He tipped his head toward the dance floor. "My friends told me the best way to get past a breakup is to surround yourself with people. They've been together since college, though, so I'm not sure why they're the dating-advice experts."

In the crush of bodies, I spotted two men dancing together while not very subtly checking us out, and I smiled to myself. That would be Dev and Brody for sure if the three of us ever went out together. They'd be pushing me to talk to someone.

"I have friends like that, too. Because they're a couple, they want everyone around them to be as well."

"Yeah. I've tried the apps, but nothing's clicked. So I decided what the hell. It's Friday night in the city. Might as well be here rather than sitting at home, you know?"

Boy, did I ever relate. "I guess so because here I am." My beer finished, I raised the empty glass. "Want to come get another drink?"

He ducked his head. "Sure." We made it to the bar and found a space to lean against it. Talking to someone as nice as Nathan was far more interesting than getting sweaty on a dance floor.

"So what happened with your ex?" I was curious.

His mouth drooped. "He cheated. But I should've known. Bryant was super successful, gorgeous...you know how it goes. We worked together on a case—he's an entertainment lawyer, and I'm a forensic accountant. He was charming and funny, and I fell for him head over heels. Stupid, right?" He huffed out a fake laugh, and my heart squeezed at his pain.

"No, I don't think it's stupid. At all. Sometimes someone comes into your life and turns it upside down, and there's nothing you can do about it."

"Is that what happened to you?" Nathan asked.

About to deny it, the words died on my lips. "Yeah." I took a long drink before continuing. "I—it was my first time, and we were together only six months, but I've never been able to recreate how he made me feel. It's been about ten years." Now that I'd said it, I couldn't stop the words flowing. "And the craziest thing is, he's come back into my life, and he has no idea who I am."

"Oh, wow," Nathan breathed, his own story of woe forgotten for the moment. "Are you gonna say something to him?"

No way I'd reveal the details of how Patrick and I had met, but speaking about it with a total stranger made me curious as to what they'd think. "I'm not sure. I want to because it doesn't feel right that I remember and he doesn't. I, uh, look a lot different now than I did when we were together." I wasn't about to reveal that I belonged to a sex club. Nathan seemed like the kind of guy who might not understand.

"Yeah, why not? I mean, maybe the two of you can get together after all these years." A dreamy smile lifted his lips. "My friends call me a hopeless romantic, but I don't mind. What's wrong with that?"

"Nothing. It's just...we can't be together." I gnawed on my lip. "He's not out, and I am."

"Maybe he'll be more willing now. You might not think so, but the world is more accepting."

"In some ways." Nathan was truly the eternal optimist. "Not in his profession. I really can't say any more. But why do you think you should've known your ex would cheat? Because he's good-looking and successful? 'Cause the guy I'm looking at meets those criteria as well."

Even in the dim light, I could see Nathan's cheeks turn scarlet. But I wasn't lying. Nathan had a fit, trim body, an adorable face, plus the whole clean-cut image, complete with glasses, was hot. Not my type because I obviously fell hard for a bad boy with a big ego and a dick to match. Nathan needed to find someone who'd appreciate him.

"Come on. You're saying that to be nice. I'm just an average guy."

Someone had fucked with this man's self-esteem. I knew all about that—the subtle putdowns and any accomplishment brushed off as nothing special or worthy of praise. Being tossed out and forced to grow up at eighteen had given me an inner strength I hadn't known I possessed.

"Fuck whoever told you that. You *are* special. Everyone is. Sometimes we learn that the hard way. Your ex sounds like a tool. You're better off without him."

Still unconvinced, Nathan shrugged a shoulder and had another sip of his drink. "Maybe."

Nathan wasn't the type of guy you could take home, fuck, and walk away from the next day. He was the dating kind. And I wasn't about to lead him on to think it would be me sitting across from him at brunch on Sunday morning.

We stood watching the scene in front of us, and as I scanned the room, I caught a guy checking us out. Or checking Nathan out, to be exact. He was a little older, late thirties, dressed well in a suit, and alone.

*Nothing ventured, nothing gained.*

"I'll be right back. Gotta use the bathroom."

Nathan nodded, but from his sad expression, he must've thought I was ditching him. And maybe I was, but for a good reason. I set my bottle on the bar and weaved my way through the crowd until I came to the man in the suit, whose gaze remained fixed on Nathan.

"He's free, and I suggest you make your move before someone else does."

Startled light eyes met mine. "What?" But he peered over my shoulder. "I don't—"

"Yes, you do. Trust me, he's a nice guy."

He touched his tie, his eyes narrowing with suspicion. "Yeah? So why aren't you with him?"

Fair enough. "Because I'm hung up on someone else."

His mouth drooped. "I-I lost my partner two years ago, and this is my first time out."

"Don't hurt him," I warned. I might not have my own life sorted out, but here I was playing matchmaker for two strangers.

"I wouldn't."

"He's the real thing." I nudged his shoulder as I passed him. "Don't be like me."

I did use the restroom and by the time I returned, Nathan and the stranger were in conversation, smiling and laughing. I watched them for a moment, and when I saw them take out their phones, obviously exchanging numbers, I laughed to myself.

*My work is done.*

On the way out, I paused by Nathan. His new friend had gone to the bar. "Good luck." I winked.

"Oh, hi." He blinked and pushed his glasses up. "Thanks for...well. You know." And then he blushed. Nathan really was a sweet guy.

"Have a great rest of the night."

But Nathan wasn't finished. "You know, sometimes you think things are impossible, but they're not. I came tonight only to get my friends off my back, and now I met Blair and you. Maybe try again with that guy?"

I gave his shoulder a squeeze. "Yeah, sure."

My walk home took me across several avenue blocks, past strolling happy couples and groups of friends. As a lonely teen pretending to be someone he wasn't just to fit in, I was present but never seen, unwilling to open myself to the possibility that I'd be laughed at or, even worse, ostracized. I chose to hide for the sake of popularity and having friends. Rory told me to be proud of who I was and never conceal my light.

And when he died, he'd taken that brightness with him, and I'd yet to find my way out of the darkness. Coming out to Dev hadn't erased the pain of my loss—nothing could.

**

By the next morning, my mood hadn't shifted. Dev was my cheerleader, and sometimes you needed to listen to someone list your positives instead of taking the negative punches on the chin, over and over. I hadn't had much time to speak to him since I began my new job, as he and Brody had been out of town, covering games on the West Coast. After the shocking kiss with Patrick and the talk with Nathan, I was contemplating doing the impossible, but I needed to talk it out before I took the step.

Dev's calendar—which I continued to monitor in case he needed me for something—indicated he didn't have anything on his schedule, so I texted him to see if he and Brody wanted to have lunch. Patrick was at training camp. He was starting the following Sunday and would be leaving on a two-week road trip. I had a mountain of things to do, but I needed my friend to give me advice.

Dev called me instead of texting back. "How's the job going? It's working out, isn't it?" he asked with a hopeful yet cautious note in his voice.

"Yeah, it's good. I'm glad to say you were right and I was wrong. Patrick is a professional, and I'm busy from morning to night."

"I knew it. You were being a pain in the ass about it."

"Okay, no need to sound so smug. So? Are you and Brody up for lunch?"

"Brody's got a commitment—he's doing an interview with *Out in Sports*—but I'm free."

"I guess I can deal with you one-on-one."

"Cute. Where should we go? I'm not much into the restaurant scene. We order in a lot."

I thought for a second. Nothing too trendy as Dev liked simple foods and wasn't a huge drinker. Low key was best, especially for the frank discussion I was contemplating.

"How about Walker's on North Moore? It's close, and they don't get a huge crowd."

"Sounds like a plan. See you at one o'clock?"

"Yep." I ended the call and paced my apartment in an effort to think things out, which didn't accomplish much since I could barely turn around without bumping into myself. I could get more for my money if I moved away, but I liked the area and being close to my friends.

A few minutes before the hour, I entered the restaurant. "Hi. I have a reservation for Summers?"

The hostess checked the screen. "Yes, Mr. Summers is waiting. Follow me, please."

I spotted him at a corner table, and of course, he'd already been approached by several fans and was chatting away. He and Brody never said no to anyone who wanted their attention, and I waited patiently while he signed autographs and took pictures.

I slid into the seat across from him. "Looking good. I guess you don't really need me after all," I joked.

"To keep a bare-bones schedule, no. But as a friend, always." He put a large hand over mine and squeezed. "What's doing? Is this just a catch-up meal, or is it something else?"

I shifted. *Damn.* Dev had always possessed uncanny insight. Luck was with me when the server approached, and I ordered a bellini. Dev ordered a beer.

"Now that I'm not playing, I'm going to indulge." He scanned the menu. "Let's get some chicken tenders for the table to start." He smiled at the server, a tall, thin woman who'd introduced herself as Katelyn. "We'll order the mains in a few."

"I'll be back with your drinks and put your order in."

She left, and Dev picked right up. "So? What is it?"

Suddenly, I didn't know what to do with my hands. I drummed my fingers on the table. "I...I wanted your opinion."

He sipped from his water glass. "Of course. Shoot."

Never having discussed my personal life much, aside from quickie recaps of meaningless dates that had gone nowhere, I chewed my lip, knowing I had to choose my words carefully.

"A long time ago, I met a guy. We were together."

His brows shot up. "For how long?"

"Almost six months, but it wasn't...I don't know. It was just a hookup."

"Doubtful, if we're having a conversation about him so many years later, but go on." He thanked Katelyn as she placed his beer in front of him. I barely noticed my glass.

"I mean, yeah, whatever. Like I said. It was a long time ago. Thing is, now I've seen him recently. I recognize him, but he has no idea it's me. I know it sounds weird, but I look totally different now."

"Must be the hair. When you left you had it buzzed pretty short."

I shrugged, and Dev's lips curved up in a slow smile.

"Lemme guess. You want to see if you can recreate the magic." Dev slapped a hand on the table. "I say go for it. That's fantastic. About damn time, too."

I rolled my eyes. "Okay, lover boy. Rein it in. Because it's not as easy as all that."

"Why? Because he doesn't remember you? It's no big deal. Just remind him. I'm sure if it was as memorable as you say, it'll be fine."

"That's not it."

"So what is it? He's married?"

"No. Not married and not seeing anyone."

The chicken tenders arrived, and we ordered our mains. Dev dipped a piece into the sauce. "I'm confused. I'm not seeing a problem."

"No. You wouldn't. It's, uh, he's not out."

Dev's brows drew together. "*Hmm.* That's problematic." Nibbling on a tender, he thought for a moment, and his face brightened. "Wait. You said you haven't spoken in years. Maybe he—"

"No," I cut him off. "He's definitely not out and not about to come out either." I drank a little of my bellini. "So there's the problem. Or not. Maybe I should just forget about it. He's not going to change for me." I dipped a piece of chicken into the honey mustard and ate without tasting, the thought of never kissing Patrick again depressing as hell.

"How do you know?"

I set the food on my plate. "Trust me. I know."

"That sucks. But you're not going to be in a relationship where you have to hide everything, are you? You can't. It's not fair to you."

"You're right." I traced the stem of my glass with my fingers, unable to forget how one kiss from Patrick had awoken everything dead inside me. "But...what if I'm okay with it? For a while," I added hastily, seeing the storm brewing in Dev's eyes.

"Fucking hell, Fallon. Why would you do that? I won't let you."

I winced, but I understood his anger. It wasn't directed at me but at a world that made it necessary. Dev and Brody had walked that path, and he'd always chafed at living a lie.

"Last time I checked, I was over the age of consent," I responded mildly. "I don't need your permission, Dev. I'm asking you as a friend."

The anger in his eyes faded, and he sighed. "I understand. And I'm not telling you to give someone an ultimatum, because that's not fair to him either." He pushed his hands through his dark hair. "Dammit, Fal. Why the hell do we have to live like this?"

"It's all premature, because I haven't decided whether I want to tell him who I am."

"Any man would be lucky to have you as a friend. I know I am."

Our food came, but neither of us made a move to eat it. I was too emotional. Once again, I wanted what I couldn't have—my brother, parents who loved me, and now the man who couldn't come out.

# CHAPTER EIGHT

Patrick

"So we're heading to Birmingham first, then Austin."

I was going over my schedule with Fallon. He was an organizational wizard and had my days color-coded by personal and professional appointments, and drilled down even further, dividing my time between things I had to finish by day's end and things that could wait.

"Yep. I have you scheduled for press interviews in both cities. Both are Saturday at your hotel and should be quickies. Plus, an interview with a sports radio station in Birmingham. That's on Saturday before dinner. I have the questions he's asked previous guests, but you should expect him to push you about replacing

Dev and the rivalry between the two teams. I emailed you everything."

"Damn," I swore, and his gaze flicked to mine.

"What? Is something wrong?"

"Hell, no. I'm just amazed how you stepped right in and took control like you've always been here. I wish I'd found you years ago. My ex-wives got annoyed when they had to answer the phone."

"Thanks, but it's my job." He ducked his head, concentrating on the screen in front of him, a pink blush creeping up his cheeks. I had to wonder. A man like him—young, great-looking, intelligent—why was he alone? I decided to push a little.

"Now that I'll be away for a couple of weeks, you'll have some time to yourself."

His smile was wry. "The work doesn't stop simply because you're not here."

"No, but I want you to relax and have a break. Go hang out with your friends. Meet a guy and have some fun."

His color deepened. "I'm fine," he mumbled. "Okay, so I have an email from *NFL in Motion*. They want an interview."

"Yeah, sure." Frankly, I was more interested in being the one asking questions. "Have you dated anyone lately?"

He shook his head, blond strands escaping the messy short bun he favored. And which I loved. I wished I could run my hands through that thick mane of golden hair and... *Ahh, fuck.* So not happening. Funny how I was always into blonds, yet my mystery man from Intensity had brown hair and generated the same surge of lust I felt sitting here with Fallon.

"Dude, you need to go out and have some fun."

"I have. Just the other night, in fact." Uncharacteristically snappish, he huffed. "Sorry, but I don't like talking about my personal life."

I wondered if he knew about a club like Intensity, but I couldn't mention it without giving away my secret. With the steep initiation fee, I doubted he could afford it anyway. Plus, something inside me didn't like the thought of one of those rich assholes putting his hands on Fallon. He wasn't soft or weak by any means—at the gym I'd seen his rock-hard abs and broad shoulders—but his skittishness suggested he'd suffered some kind of pain or trauma, which could easily be exploited. Instinctively, my fingers curled into fists. I'd never been a possessive guy—the women came and went without a second thought. The only exception was my first lover, the beautiful blond man who'd kissed me breathless and left an indelible mark on my heart. I eyed Fallon, wondering...he'd be the right age and had been at school in the area... *Nah.* I dismissed my speculation as far-fetched. No way could they be the same person. Not like there wasn't more than one blond, blue-eyed man in Southern California. My guy's hair had been lighter, and he was leaner. My thoughts turned to the man I'd kissed at Intensity. For days, his taste had stayed on my tongue, and I ached to see him again and explore his luscious mouth. Not meant to be, as I was leaving tonight with the team.

"I don't mean to pry...well, yeah, I do 'cause I'm a nosy bastard, but I'll respect your privacy." I caught his eye. "Even though I think you deserve more than sitting in front of a screen, working on my calendars and appearances every night."

"I'm not that pathetic, don't worry. I go out and have fun."

Which, for some reason, didn't make me feel any better.

"Good. I'll check in when I land. I've got to go pack."

"I've got your travel kit filled and your carry-on ready with the stuff you like on the plane." He grinned. "Gummy bears and M&M's."

I met his smile with one of my own. "I'm a kid at heart, what can I say?"

"Well, you'll have enough to share with all your little friends." He snickered. "And I set out a few outfits, so tell me yes or no, and I'll have them steamed. I have the black-and-white Prada or the blue-and-white Dior."

Travel days used to be track pants and T-shirts, but lately the league had stepped it up, and the guys were sporting designer labels and looking fresh. I had an image to uphold, so yeah, I might've indulged at a few high-end boutiques.

Without even needing to see, I made my choice. "Let's do the Prada for today, and I'll have the Dior for coming home."

"Sounds good. I'll have them come up and steam it while you get ready."

******

I came out from the shower in my briefs, towel-drying my hair. Fallon had stayed on the computer.

"Whatcha doing there?" I peered over his shoulder.

He jumped a little. "Jesus. You scared me. I'm finalizing the last of the deliveries for your apartment—namely your bed, since it was special order. I have furniture set for delivery all next week, then the household items for this week. I meant to ask, do you want a housekeeper to come in once a week? I don't think you'll need more than that. I already have an account set up with a laundry service."

My head spun. "Yeah, sure, whatever. I forgot what goes into setting up a house."

"You don't have to know. That's why I'm here. I'll make sure everything's the way you like it."

*You in my bed, that's what I'd like.*

The room grew very quiet. I could hear his breathing, and mine wasn't too steady either. If Fallon turned his head...God, his mouth would be on my very hard, aching dick. The tension in the air thickened, and my heart pounded.

What if Fallon and I hooked up? Who would need to know?

The knock on the door brought me to my senses. Was I out of my fucking mind? Fallon was my employee, and a good friend to Dev, who'd helped me out. That would be a terrible betrayal on my part.

"That'll be housekeeping to steam your outfit."

Fallon rushed by me.

But damn, a man could dream.

**

Two weeks of inactivity had left me with tingling nerves, and I hated to admit it, but a little anxiety too. Yeah, I'd been a starting quarterback for more than five years, and I'd played in the Super Bowl once, but stepping into Devlin Summers' shoes as the new franchise quarterback was a lot to handle even for someone with a big ego, like me. I knew I had to earn every dollar of the thirty million per year they were paying me.

I left New York for Birmingham with my teammates, and Fallon assured me that upon my return, it would be to a fully furnished apartment. I had little time to think about my condo or Fallon—we left on a Friday, and then it was a whirlwind of practice, media interviews, and downtime, which I used to stay in my hotel room and study the playbook, even though I knew it by heart. Saturday was more of the same.

Game day finally arrived, and we won the coin toss and elected to receive. Coach gave the signals, and the crowd was rocking already, as we were playing the Birmingham Comets, divisional rivals. The bad blood between the two teams had begun the time their tackles had taken Dev out with a post-play cheap hit. The players had been fined, and they'd lost the game, but Dev had ended up in the hospital with a bad concussion that had eventually led to his retirement. Since then, the on-field shit-talking had only increased, but I was prepared.

Coach caught me by the arm before I joined the guys. "Sloane. I don't want any crap on the field. We're here to win a football game, not a street fight. Don't let them goad you into anything that'll cause penalties, lose us yardage, and ultimately the game."

"Got it, Coach. I won't."

We took to the line of scrimmage, and I blocked out all the garbage talk I heard from the Comets tackles and linemen. My guys got into position, and I had the play memorized. We were set.

"Blue 42, Blue 42, hut, hut."

Troy Watkins, one of the league's top receivers, eluded the linebackers and was open downfield. I passed a beautiful spiral to him and grunted in satisfaction as he not only made the catch but zipped downfield for a gain of thirty yards.

"Yeah, baby, that's it." I whistled and clapped, and the fans roared their disapproval, but that only spurred us on. And our winning plays continued throughout the game. I connected for two touchdowns, and my teammates rushed for two more. I threw for over two hundred yards, and we beat the cleats off those fuckers with a final score of 31-10.

"Trick, Trick," the broadcasters called out as we made our way to the locker room. "How does it feel to play for the Kings? Any predictions for the rest of the season?"

"It feels awesome." I fist-pumped. "I'm not jinxing it. One game at a time."

In the locker room, music blared, and we were all in a good mood with the big win. The team was on top of the division. Coach came in, and we all stopped and listened.

"Good game. Trick, I like how you connected and didn't let their smack talk affect you. Troy and Rio, you made the big catches. Defense, I liked what I saw, but I thought we missed a couple of opportunities for interceptions. A Super Bowl championship team is one that capitalizes on every single one of their opponents' mistakes. Let's level up for next week. Go get your massages and treatments, and I'll see you all tomorrow to go over the films."

I was already half-undressed, and my body screamed for a massage. The ice pack on my shoulder could only do so much. The music was turned up, and I rolled my shoulders. I felt a presence behind me and turned to see Rio Durant.

"What's up? Good catch there."

His teeth flashed white beneath the dark scruff. "Thanks, bro. Good to have you here. A bunch of us gonna have dinner at the hotel restaurant. You up for it?"

"Sure thing."

"Catch you there around eight?" His eyes crinkled with laughter. "Troy spotted some hotties when we checked in. They might be up for some fun."

I snorted. "Man, you must be tougher than me. Or younger. I'm usually dead on my feet by eleven. Midnight at the latest."

A lazy grin kicked up Rio's lips. "Depends on what they're offering up to give me a second wind."

Bunch of the guys groaned, and Milo Masterson, the huge All-Pro receiver, megaphoned his hands. "Don't listen to him, Trick. Rio's got a mouth like the river he's named after—big and dirty."

"Aw, come on, Candyman." Eyes sparkling, Rio teased Milo. "You're just jealous 'cause you're an old married man who's gotta go home every night to the same lady."

"And damn happy about it." Milo stripped off his team jersey.

"What's with Candyman?" I asked.

Clearly exasperated, Milo rolled his eyes. " 'Cause my initials are M and M."

Troy jumped on his back. "And he's the sweetest, aintcha?" Troy leaned in as if he were going to kiss Milo, and Rio winced.

"Aw, come on, man. I don't wanna see that kinda shit." Rio made a face.

My jaw hardened. "What shit?"

"You know. Men-kissing-men stuff. I know you're friends with Dev and Brody, but I still can't believe they're gay."

"Because?"

"I dunno." Rio's gaze shifted away.

"Lemme guess. 'Cause they're big and tough and played football."

"I mean, yeah."

Rio Durant was a bit younger than me, small for a tight end but quick on his feet. He'd come to the Kings from the Bisons in the Fontaine trade. He had great skills, but his shit-talking on the field and his off-season antics got him numerous warnings from his coaches and the league.

He continued to run his mouth. "Guy-on-guy gay shit...not into it."

"Then it's good you're not gay. Some people are. Fucking learn to deal with it. I'll be lucky to be as great a player as Dev was, and you too if you racked up as many catches as Brody did. They're future first-ballot Hall of Famers."

The locker room grew quiet.

"And you're right. I *am* friends with them, so I'm setting a rule right now. No shit-talking about anyone's personal life. Married, single, straight, gay. Whatever the fuck you are. It's no one's goddamn business. Got it?" I scanned the locker room, and everyone nodded and shrugged.

"Don't matter to me."

"I don't care."

"Dev and Brody are cool."

"Legends, man."

Perhaps realizing he'd overplayed his hand, Rio cast his eyes downward. "Sorry, bro. I guess I was outta line."

"You guess?" There was little I had less patience with than bullies. "We're here to win. That's the only thing we should be talking about."

He gave me a quick nod. "See you later?"

"Yeah. Sure."

Rio walked away, and I finished getting undressed. I took a shower and checked for any bruising or swelling from the hits I'd taken but found none. I entered the physical therapy room, and the masseur, personally recommended by Dev, welcomed me.

"Come, come. Lie down. I have all the magic potions waiting for you."

I'd been looking forward to this all game—I closed my eyes while his fingers worked their magic. When he probed my shoulder and arm, he tsked.

"You're very tight."

"Probably because I haven't played in two weeks."

"Okay. I'll put some heat on it, then in the whirlpool you go for ten minutes." He fixed the pad on me. "Let me look at the ankle now. That gave you trouble, yes?"

"Not anymore," I stated, but allowed him to flex my foot. "I have no pain."

"Good. Sit there for a few minutes and tell me how my friend Devlin is."

We chatted, and Enzo's smile was sad. "All those years we worked together, he never said anything to me despite knowing I was gay. I would've kept his secret. It's terrible if you feel you can't trust even the people closest to you."

"It's the nature of the game and the fact that every-thing we do is publicized. No matter what people say out loud, most still don't believe gay men can play professional sports, even though that's a steaming pile of horseshit. Dev and Brody are two of the best to have played the game, yet them being gay is going to take up as much space in the record books as their stats. That's BS."

"I'm happy for him. I know the awards don't matter to him as much as being with Brody. And I believe we are closer than ever to accepting players, no matter who they love." He checked the pad and took it off, to manipulate my shoulder. "Better?"

"Yeah. Feels great."

"And you? No girlfriend or wife to keep you in line?"

I grinned. "Nope."

Enzo helped me off the table and over to the whirlpool. I settled in with a gusty sigh. Instead of leaving me, he folded his arms.

"Some of these men run a little wild," he warned. "Parties with the groupies and spending money like they print it. Make sure you stay out of trouble."

I laughed out loud. "I know. I've already heard it from my parents and Dev. I've given up women for the season. I'm here to win a Super Bowl. Sex can wait."

# CHAPTER NINE

## Fallon

I had to admit, it was strange to be in Patrick's suite so often without him, but I kept myself busy from morning to night, answering his social media and with all the details of his move, as well as monitoring him with reminder texts to make sure he showed up for his appointments and interviews. Because they had two away games, the team was traveling straight to Austin and using the in-between time to rest and practice.

We FaceTimed every morning, with me giving him a rundown of what I'd accomplished, and that set off a back-and-forth between us, Patrick telling me how his practice was going and his insights into the team dynamics. Sometimes he asked me for advice, and I gave him my opinions. Dev hadn't needed a sounding board–he'd had Brody to talk to and bounce things off of. No doubt Patrick spoke to Dev as well, but it was nice to know he trusted me to discuss important personal matters. He shared with me the conversation he'd had with his teammates about sexuality.

"I got so pissed, you know? It would hurt Dev and Brody to hear the guys talking about them like that." He drank from a water bottle. "And you too. I shut it down real quick."

"Yeah. It would. I'm glad, Patrick. Standing up to those guys takes a lot of courage."

"It was Rio. He talks out of his ass, but I think I set him and everyone else straight."

"Good for you."

"I don't deserve credit for doing what's right." He frowned. "Who someone sleeps with shouldn't matter to anybody but them. I'm sorry if you've ever been made to feel uncomfortable."

"It's okay. I appreciate knowing how you feel."

"Don't worry. I'm on your side."

Patrick held my gaze, and my heart beat faster, doing a little tap dance in my chest.

I cleared my throat. "You have a lunch interview with *Sports Today*, a call with your attorney at five p.m., and most importantly, it's your mother's birthday tomorrow."

He smacked a hand over his face. "Shit. Between the move and the traveling, I forgot about it. Thanks. I'll call her as soon as I get off with you."

"Do you want me to send her a present? Tell me what she likes, and I'll get it for her." I pulled the laptop closer.

"No, listen. I have a better idea."

"Okay. Shoot." I pulled up my Notes app and waited.

"I want them at this upcoming game. Afterward, they can fly to New York and see my new place. Do you think you can arrange that? I'll let them know the details once you arrange everything."

"Yeah, of course, that won't be a problem. Where would they sit in the stadium? Do you have a box or something?"

"I'll have to let you know. I'll talk to Coach about it. I don't know how they handle that here."

"Sounds good. And I'll try to have them arrive in New York around the same time you do."

"I dunno what time we're flying out. Get them a flight in the morning—they're early risers. And I'm gonna want to have dinner with them, so could you get us reservations?"

My fingers flew on the laptop. "Will do. You want them to come to the suite, or should I bring them directly to your place?"

"I think...I think I wanna show them the place myself. Bring them to the hotel, please. After I land, I'll come there and bring them to the apartment."

"You got it. Don't worry. I'll get it all squared away."

"Thanks, Fallon. How's it all going otherwise?"

My eyes were on the laptop screen, pulling up my list of favorite florists—I figured I'd fill the condo with flowers for his mother. "Everything's fine."

"Fine is such a blah word."

I had to laugh. "Would you prefer fantastic?"

"Yes. Because I'm still feeling pretty damn good about how the game went."

"As you should. You were terrific. No interceptions, and you connected for lots of yards."

I'd hardly ever watched the games when Dev and Brody played, but then again, I wasn't salivating over

Dev's physique in those skintight game pants. Patrick was two hundred and thirty pounds of pure muscle, and I was there for it.

"I'd better go. Gotta get to practice. Thanks."

"Talk to you."

As promised, he was quick to get back to me about timing and gave me his parents' info. Within an hour, I'd arranged for a car to pick them up and take them to the airport, and another would meet them upon their arrival in Austin. They were booked in first class, and I reserved them a suite at a hotel near Patrick's, with champagne and flowers. I'd tried for the same hotel, but it was fully booked. I made dinner reservations for them, had a car ready to drive them to the stadium and security to bring them to the luxury box the Kings rented at the game.

By that time I was ready for lunch, and instead of going out, I ordered from room service and checked Patrick's social media. I had alerts set up to be notified of any online mentions, and several articles popped up that tied my stomach into knots. I set my turkey sandwich aside to read.

*Is Patrick Sloane up to his old tricks?*

*After last week's win over Birmingham, the superstar quarterback and several team members were spotted at a popular hot spot with some local beauties. Has Trick Sloane brought his partying ways to the Kings, or will Coach Jackson, known for his strict rules, rein him in?*

I clicked on the picture to see Patrick with his arm around a gorgeous blond sitting in his lap. The next picture showed them holding hands and sharing drinks. I didn't care about the other pictures of the team, and who they were with. Only a week ago, he was kissing me and asking if we could get closer. Was

Patrick only after as much sex as he could get? I hadn't wanted to believe the rumors about him, but maybe there was more truth there than I'd thought. It shouldn't have affected me as much as it did. Patrick wasn't about to come out as bisexual and start dating men. Standing up for what was right in private was one thing. Living it was another.

With a vicious stab, I closed the article and rubbed my eyes. I was damn glad I hadn't opened up to Patrick like I'd contemplated. It was obvious the guy was still a player and had zero intention of changing. I was here to do a job, and that was what I planned to do. If I wanted sex, I'd find it somewhere else. Maybe tonight.

******

At ten p.m., I wandered into Currents, a gay club in the Meatpacking District. Armed with a tequila and soda, I leaned against the bar, half listening to snippets of conversations while scanning the crowd. It was a younger group than I usually went for, but maybe that was what I needed. Something to shake me out of the funk reading that gossip piece had put me in.

"Wanna dance?" a twentysomething dressed in a tight black T-shirt and sleek jeans asked. Dark-red hair tumbled over his brow, and reddish scruff covered his jaw.

"Sure." I gulped down my drink and let him lead me to the crowded dance floor, where he held my hips and ground into my ass.

I hadn't intended to let anyone touch me, but damn, it felt so fucking good, and before I knew what I was doing, I was pushing back on him, letting him kiss my neck.

"You're so fucking hot," he whispered.

I turned to face him, and he crushed his mouth to mine while his hands grew demanding. Instead of turning me on, it had the opposite effect. I pulled away, and he grabbed my ass again. That proved to be the final straw, and I wiped my lips.

"Not happening."

"Fucking cock tease," he spat out, and without another word, left me standing on the floor.

I walked to the bar and ordered another drink.

"Did he think you were gonna get on your knees right there?" A low voice at my shoulder chuckled.

"Looks like it. But it takes more than a dance for me." I sipped my drink. "If you're looking for something like that, I'm gonna have to disappoint you."

"I'm not. I'm here to unwind after a stressful day at work."

I raised my glass. "Same."

"Ethan," he said.

"Fallon."

"I can't blame the guy for trying. You're pretty gorgeous."

Ethan's admiration rolled off me. He was damn gorgeous—black hair sprinkled with a bit of silver and scruff offsetting light-blue eyes, but I wasn't into throwing out compliments. Frankly, the whole scene depressed me.

When I didn't answer, his brow rose. "I guess you hear that a lot and you're tired of it."

"I'm sure the same can be said of you."

Ethan downed his drink. "Okay, now that we've finished our meeting of the mutual admiration society,

I wouldn't mind blowing this place off and getting a cup of coffee. Care to join me?"

I lifted a shoulder. "I'm not going to go home with you, if that's your ultimate goal for the evening."

"I wasn't planning on asking, but good to know." His lips kicked up in a grin, and I laughed.

"Sorry, I'm just over this whole scene."

"Me too. Come on."

We walked to a diner two blocks away, and I appreciated that he didn't try and fill the silence with small talk. Once we settled in a booth and ordered our coffees, he folded his hands on top of the table.

"So, Fallon, what do you do in our fair city?"

Never one to give away too much, I sipped my water. "I'm a personal assistant."

Ethan studied me for a moment. "I'm assuming it's for someone famous, or you would've given a little more info. Good for you, keeping your boss's privacy."

Our coffees came, and I stirred in the milk. "I've been at this a while. What about you?"

"I'm an attorney."

"I should've known. What's your specialty?"

"Sports and entertainment." Maybe my face wasn't as neutral as I'd hoped because Ethan's face brightened. "And your work is in one of those fields."

"No comment." I fidgeted with the handle of the cup.

"Understood. But now it makes sense why someone like you is at a club during the week. You must be busy morning to night."

"I have my hands full. And so must you. I've seen enough of what goes on to know you deal with temperamental clients."

"The worst." His eyes danced. "Some of the things they ask for in their contracts are too funny—specific coffee drinks to always be available, In-N-Out if they're from the West, bagels from their favorite place in the city if they're from here…" Ethan shook his head.

"The list is endless, isn't it?" I couldn't help but commiserate. "I know someone who made sure they picked out all the yellow Skittles from his candy bowl."

"Dante Williams from the Brooklyn Kings," Ethan stated, and my stomach dropped. "He's a client. Don't worry, Fallon. I know you used to work for Devlin Summers. I've seen you at enough Super Bowl celebrations—I recognized you right away. You're kind of hard to miss." His attempt at a compliment went over my head. My throat seized up, and I didn't answer. "You're working for someone else now?"

I remained silent, and he nodded. "Okay. I'm not one of the bad guys, you know. We're on the same side. I represent a number of players on the Kings. Active as well as retired, like Dante."

"I don't talk about my job. I pride myself on discretion."

"And I'm sure whomever you work for appreciates that." He checked his phone and made a face. "I've got to run. One of my clients just got arrested. I swear, sometimes I'm more of a babysitter than a lawyer."

I'd recovered enough and couldn't help laughing. "Trust me, I get it. But I've been lucky."

He tossed a twenty-dollar bill onto the table. "Yeah, you have been. Dev and Brody Martin are both class acts. Listen, it was nice talking to you. Our jobs can be isolating, with people wanting to be our friends because they think they can get something from us. It's why most of the people in my life are either family or longtime clients." He pulled out a business card. "This has my personal cell and email. If you ever need to talk or just step away from the crazy, contact me."

I watched him stride out of the diner, fairly certain I'd never see him again, but I pocketed his card anyway. I finished my coffee and left for home, already preparing for the following day. Everything had to be perfect for Patrick's parents, especially for his mother's birthday.

**

The next day I checked with the driver to make sure Patrick's parents had been picked up on time and had arrived safely at the stadium. Satisfied that everything had gone off without a hitch, I allowed myself the few hours to watch the game. Patrick looked flawless, and the Kings rolled to a 24-10 victory. Eating my dinner, I watched the postgame interviews, only turning up the volume when Patrick appeared. Even sweaty and tired, he was still the most gorgeous man I'd ever seen.

"I knew I had to win this game. Today's my mother's birthday. She's always been my biggest cheerleader and supporter. My parents sacrificed everything to make my dreams come true. They never missed a high school game, and she and my dad are here tonight, so I made sure to win." His smile beamed big and bright. "This one's for you, Mommy."

Hearing a big, tough guy like Patrick call his mother *Mommy* turned me to mush, and I brushed wetness from my eyes. Emotional, I took out my phone, hoping maybe I could use it as a sign.

"Mom? It's Fallon."

"I know. Your number came up. Is everything all right? You're not sick, are you?"

"No. I-I just thought maybe it would be nice to talk. It's been years."

"Are you back living in New York City?"

Encouraged that she hadn't hung up on me, I took the crumbs she gave me. "Yeah. In Tribeca. I was working for Devlin—you remember him, he was Rory's best friend."

"It's very cruel, you know."

"Cruel, how?"

"Bringing up Rory's name. Thirteen years he's gone, and I miss him every day."

Tears overflowed. "You think I don't remember? But couldn't that be a new start for us? You're right, Mom. It's been thirteen years. Haven't I paid enough of a price yet?"

As if she didn't even hear me, she said, "I'm sure he would've been married and I'd have had grandchildren. I've lost out on so much."

It was always about her. "He was my best friend."

"You can make other friends. I can't make another son."

"You already have another son. Me. Why can't you love me as much as you did Rory?"

In the background, I heard a commotion. "Fallon? Why are you upsetting your mother?"

My father always had a way of putting me in the wrong. "I wasn't. I didn't mean—"

"I know what you mean. All these years of silence, and then you call and make your mother cry?"

I couldn't help it and snapped. "You could've called me, you know. I'm still alive. I'm your son, too."

"Call us when you're more rational. You people are always so emotional. Good-bye, Fallon."

Holding the dead phone in my hand, I squeezed my eyes shut.

*You people.*

No matter what, I'd never be good enough for my parents.

**

The next morning, in the car to the airport to pick up Patrick's parents, I was still trying to put that whole disastrous conversation out of my mind. I spotted Patrick's parents the moment they walked into the arrivals area, each wheeling a bag. Patrick's father was a big, stocky man with a shock of thick silver hair, and his mother wore her dark-brown hair in a simple ponytail. Both were dressed in joggers and sneakers. Patrick's mother wore a puffer vest over a Kings' hoodie, while Patrick's father had on a Kings' jersey with Patrick's number and cap. They held hands, and I smiled to myself because they looked so cute.

"Mr. and Mrs. Sloane. Hi, I'm Fallon, Patrick's personal assistant. Please follow me. I have a car waiting to take you to his suite."

Patrick's mother gave me a big hug. "Fallon, hi. Patrick told us all about you. So nice to meet you. I'm Lori, and this is Don. No Mr. and Mrs., please."

Don stuck out his hand. "Good to meet you. I have to say I'm looking forward to keeping my boots on the ground for a while. All this running around's got me tired as hell."

I laughed as we approached the Mercedes I'd hired. The driver opened the door for us. "Patrick texted me and said he should be in later this afternoon. It won't take us longer than half an hour to get to the hotel."

We got settled, and Lori said, "This is our first time in New York City. I hope we get to see the sights. I know Patrick has training camp, but maybe you could tell us how to get places?" She had that open, friendly Midwestern smile, and inwardly I cringed, thinking of them walking by themselves through the city. Plus, Patrick would probably cut my balls off if I left his parents alone.

"I'll be happy to take you anywhere you'd like to go. I've lived here all my life."

Her eyes, that same blue-green as Patrick's, lit up. "You're the sweetest. That would be wonderful, thank you. Patrick told us you're so incredibly helpful to him. He's very lucky to have someone like you."

They peered out of the window as we drove on the highway, and I wondered how it was possible for two complete strangers I'd met only moments ago to show me more warmth and affection than my own parents ever had.

# CHAPTER TEN

Patrick

I fucking hated traveling. Especially with time-zone changes, it screwed with my sleep pattern and always made me sluggish at training camp the day after. It was the one downside of playing football. But this time I didn't mind, as I was going to see my parents. I'd talked to them plenty since my trade and move to New York City, but this would be the first time I'd seen them in close to six months.

I stepped off the jet, and of course the press was there to take our pictures because who doesn't look fucking fresh as a daisy after a flight? But I did my best and kept walking fast until some fans recognized us and called out our names. One kid yelled out, "Trick, you're the best. Can I take your picture?"

I waved to him and slowed my stride. Yeah, we were tired and wanted to get home as fast as possible, but these were fans. Lots of players kept walking, but it didn't feel right to me. I spent fifteen minutes of my life with the fans but gave them memories for a lifetime.

God bless Fallon for having a car waiting for me. I sank into the soft leather of the back seat with a sigh. I thought I'd catch a nap, but I was too wound up and bounced out of the car without giving the driver a chance to take my bag out of the trunk.

"Thanks, man."

"You're welcome, sir. Great game."

I flashed him a grin and hurried away, anxious to see my parents, but the suite was empty when I opened the door.

"Where the hell are they?" Annoyed, I pulled out my phone, only to have the door open and my parents, accompanied by Fallon, walk in. All three were laughing.

"Oh, rats. You got here first." My mom dropped her bag on the couch and ran to me. "You look tired." She held my face between her hands, concern marring her normally cheerful expression.

"Happy birthday. I love you. And yeah, I never like flying. But I'm glad you're here." Every time I'd see my parents after a long absence, I'd watch them carefully for signs of aging, but from what I'd seen so far, they appeared the same. My parents had married in their midtwenties, but it had taken my mother almost eight years to get pregnant the first time, and she'd had four miscarriages before having me. She called me her "one-and-done miracle baby."

"The trade agrees with you," Dad said. "You're playing better than ever." He hugged me, and I put my arm around Mom.

"I think so. And yeah, the trade's been great. Where were you?"

My mom threw Fallon a sweet smile. "Fallon's been so wonderful. He took us for breakfast at a real New York City diner. Then we went for a ride all over to see some of the sites–the 9/11 Memorial, Rockefeller Center, the Public Library, Central Park. He's been the absolute best tour guide."

"Yeah, he's pretty perfect. Thanks for taking care of my parents."

Red-faced, he waved us off. "It was no problem at all. Your parents are sweet." He hovered by the door. "I'll leave now and let you visit. I'll go to the condo and check that everything's ready."

He met my eyes, and I nodded. "Thanks." Fallon had assured me he'd make my mother's birthday special, and from the way she was glowing from a little sight-seeing, I had no doubts.

"It was nice to meet you both. Happy birthday again."

"Bye, Fallon." My dad shook his hand, and my mother gave him a hug.

"I hope we'll see you very soon. Thank you so much for giving us such a wonderful New York morning."

He left, and I sank onto the couch. "Feels good to be home. Such as it is. I can't wait to show you my new place."

"Fallon said it's a beautiful apartment." Mom sat next to me while my six-foot-three Dad took the big club chair so he could stretch his legs. "Two or three bedrooms?"

"Two, but there's an office I can convert to a bedroom if I ever need to."

"Well, eventually you'll get married, I hope."

After two flops, marriage and kids was the furthest thing from my mind. "Maybe. At the moment, I'm not thinking about anything but football."

"You broke it off with that girl you were seeing? The model?"

"Mimi? Yeah. She's back in California. Right now, all I want is to win the Super Bowl. I have too much going on to get serious with anyone." Mom gave me the *You don't think I'm falling for that, do you?* look I recognized from when I was a kid. "I'm serious, Mom. I mean, yeah, I'll go out sometimes, but I'm not looking for a relationship." I jumped to my feet. "Fallon should have everything set up in the new apartment, and I can finally move in."

"He's such a nice man. How did you find him?" Mom asked.

"He worked for another player who retired, and they thought we'd get along."

"Is he married? Have a girlfriend? I'll need to put him on our Christmas card list."

"No, he's gay. No boyfriend or husband."

"Oh. I didn't know."

"I guess announcing your sexuality isn't something that comes up in conversation when you first meet people."

"Wise guy." She swatted me, and I snickered. "Well, I hope he meets someone. He seems like such a sweetheart. And very good-looking."

I wondered what my parents would say if they knew I agreed with them.

"I'm gonna shower and change, then take you over to see the condo."

"We can't wait," Dad said.

I hustled to the bathroom and got ready in less than twenty minutes. As exhausted as I was, having my parents here and seeing my new place energized me as if I'd downed three large coffees. Mom and Dad were on the couch but jumped up at my return.

"Ready to rock and roll?" I pulled out my phone. "I'll get us a car."

"This is so exciting," Mom exclaimed, and I put my arm around her. "I have a good feeling."

"Oh, yeah? I've bought apartments before." We left the suite and headed to the elevator.

"I know, but something's different. I can't put a finger on it, but I think this is going to be your forever home."

Dad chuckled. "Better listen to her. You know your mother's never wrong about one of her feelings."

It was a family joke but true. She'd warned me about marrying my exes, and had encouraged me to accept the offer to sign with the Kings.

"I'm so glad you're here." I gave her shoulder a squeeze. "It makes it even more special to share it with you."

The ride was relatively quick, and we stood on the sidewalk, heads tipped back to admire the sheer height of the building.

"Wow. This is really tall." Dad shaded his eyes. "How many stories?"

"Thirty. And I'm on the top floor. As soon as I saw it, I knew it was the one."

Mom linked her arm with mine. "One of those feelings, huh?"

We all laughed and went inside, where the concierge greeted me.

"Mr. Sloane, your assistant is upstairs. He left the key for you. Welcome to the building."

I took it from him. "Thanks. These are my parents. They're allowed access at any time."

"Very good. I'll write their names down, and if they could just step over here, I'll take their pictures and enter them in the building directory."

Once that was done, I led the way to the elevator, and my anticipation ramped up as the elevator rose. I'd texted Fallon that we were almost there, and he'd replied with a smile emoji. As I remembered, the doors opened to the apartment and the wall of windows overlooking the glistening river.

"Oh, my. This is absolutely beautiful, Patrick." Mom walked in first, and I spied Fallon waiting off to the side. An explosion of flowers greeted my eyes. All my mother's favorites–peonies, lilacs, gardenias, and roses. "And these flowers. I've never seen anything so incredible. Thank you so much."

The kitchen island held a spread of chocolates and pastries of every kind, a huge birthday cake, and a large salver with several bottles of champagne on ice and crystal flutes beside it.

"Let's go out on the balcony and see the view." I led my parents across the spacious living room, which Fallon had decorated in neutral tones of gray, beige, and sea green. A huge flat-screen dominated one wall, and I could see myself and some buddies kicking back in the off-season, watching games and movies. I hadn't seen the rest of the apartment, but I knew everything would be perfect because Fallon had arranged it.

While my parents were admiring the sweep of the river and my spectacular view of the Statue of Liberty,

I left them to find Fallon. He'd remained in the kitchen and was taking the wrappings off a charcuterie board.

"I hope you like it. I've made reservations for you all at La Grand Boucherie. It's a pretty restaurant and has something for everyone. They know it's her birthday and promised to do something special for her."

"Damn, Fallon. How the hell did you manage to do this all with only a few days' notice?"

He grinned. "That's why you pay me the big bucks."

"Not enough, I'm thinking."

My parents reentered the apartment, and Mom set her purse on a barstool.

"This is the most gorgeous apartment. I can see why you fell in love with it. And Fallon, you did all this for me? Thank you, honey."

His cheeks turned pink. "It was my pleasure. Now that you're here, I'll get out of your way and let you have your family celebration. I've told Patrick about your dinner plans. Enjoy the rest of your night." He reached for his cross-body bag on the counter.

Why did that upset me? I didn't want him to leave. Mom must've read my mind, because she tried to stop him.

"No, Fallon, please. You have to stay. Patrick, tell him, please."

"I think so." My eyes met Fallon's, which were filled with confusion.

"But this is your time with your family."

Mom smiled at him. "You're Patrick's friend, which makes you one of ours. And I had such a good time with you today. I'd love it if you could join us for dinner. Don't you agree, Patrick?"

I didn't hesitate. "Yeah. I do. Please stay."

He chewed his lip and tucked a strand of hair behind his ear. "I'll have to see if they can change the reservation to four."

I folded my arms. "I don't think I've ever seen a table for three, so I think we're safe. It's only a matter of adding another place setting."

"Then it's settled," Mom declared. "And it's my birthday, so you can't say no."

"Don't try and argue, Fallon. Neither of us has ever been able to say no to her, birthday or not." Dad patted him on the shoulder while Mom nodded. "But we would love to get to know you better, since you're working so closely with Patrick now."

"Uh, okay, if that's what you really want. I'll need to go home first to change. I can't wear this to the restaurant."

*Too damn bad.* Fallon was wearing dark-washed jeans and a white Henley that brought out the startling ice blue of his eyes and clung to every dip and curve of his muscled physique. I blinked because he was still talking and I needed to pay attention.

"I had all your clothes and personal items you'd kept in storage since your move brought over. I didn't want to unpack it for you, so it's waiting in your bedroom."

"You could've. I've got nothing to hide." I meant it as a joke, but Fallon didn't laugh, and something in his face set my heart pounding. It was as if he'd penetrated my facade to the very core of who I was. Who I'd hidden.

"I didn't want to presume anything without getting your go-ahead."

"And now you have it."

"Let's open the champagne," Dad said, and the curious tension between Fallon and me broke.

Fallon handed me the bottle and a dish towel, and I opened it without spilling a drop. I filled three glasses and pointed to him. "Get yourself one. No arguing."

He huffed and took one out from the cabinet. When I'd finished pouring his, I held my flute up. "To you, Mom. I love you and thank you for always being there to support me no matter what. I'm the person I am today because of you. I'm so glad you're here with me to celebrate."

The three of us clinked glasses, and Fallon smiled faintly and raised his glass, took a sip, then set it on the island. "I'd better go get ready. I'll see you all later. Patrick, can I talk to you for a sec?"

"Sure." I followed him to the door. "What's up?"

"I really don't think I belong with your family celebration."

"But my mother thinks you do, so that's that. Anything else?"

His full mouth tightened, and he looked so damn adorable I wanted to swoop in and kiss the crankiness out of him. *Shit. I'd better get control of myself.*

"Yeah. Your mother's present. I had Tiffany's send it over. Dev once gave something like it to Brody's mom for her birthday, so I think she'll like it."

"I'm sure it will be perfect. If I haven't already said it, thank you. You've made the day extra special for my parents."

He nodded and pressed the button. After a minute, the doors opened, and he left. My parents were enjoying some cheese and fruit from the board. Mom handed me a plate, and I took a few things without paying much attention, my mind still on Fallon. My former assistants had always jumped at the chance for a free dinner, or to get tickets for a premiere or a sold-out show or concert. Fallon didn't ask for any of that. He deliberately held back from revealing too much of his personal life, which only made me want to know more about him.

"Fallon's such a lovely man. So different from the other assistants you've had who never tried to get to know us."

"Yeah. He helped me find this place and got me settled without me even being here."

Dad popped a piece of cheese into his mouth. "How did you find him, again?"

"You remember Devlin Summers? The quarterback who retired and came out?" They nodded. "Fallon worked for Dev—seems they've known each other since they were kids. Dev retired and he didn't need him as much, so he recommended him to me."

Mom sipped from her glass. "That's good—being able to help the people who were with you all your life. I'm glad he's coming to dinner with us. But why did he look so sad when we said he's like one of the family?"

"No idea." But I planned to find out.

# CHAPTER ELEVEN

### Fallon

I debated calling Patrick and canceling, claiming a sudden onset of stomach pains, but that sounded fake as fuck even to me. Plus, Lori was a nice lady. She'd invited me, and I didn't want to hurt her feelings. Against my better judgment, I put on a suit, sprayed on a little cologne, and called for a car to take me uptown.

To my surprise, I was the first one there. Before sitting at the table, I talked with the manager, ordered a bottle of champagne, and made sure the cake I'd chosen for dessert was there and decorated. I'd also arranged for a beautiful bouquet to be delivered to the table when Lori arrived, and it was already waiting. Assured everything was ready, I finally sat and took a sip of my sparkling water.

The day spent with Patrick's parents played in stark contrast to the recent conversation with my mother and father. Where they kept a laundry list of my faults and deficiencies, never hesitating to point out my shortcomings, Lori and Don lavished praise on Patrick, showing him all the love and affection I'd always hoped to receive.

"Fallon?"

Lori and Don stood across the table from me, Patrick behind them. I jumped to my feet.

"Hi. I'm sorry. Welcome to your birthday dinner." The *maître d'* appeared with the flowers and presented them to Lori. I saw she wore the present I'd ordered for her from Patrick—a diamond heart necklace.

"This is such a beautiful place." They took the flowers to hold them for her while we ate, and we were seated—Lori and Don next to each other and Patrick next to me. The man radiated heat, and he wore a delicious cologne that invaded my senses. Great. Here I sat, turned-on beyond belief, and I had to make nice with his mother.

"It's one of my favorite restaurants—not super trendy, but always perfect."

Patrick gazed around the dining room. "I sure don't know any of the spots. This was perfect. Thank you."

The server presented us with the menus.

"Steak is a must," I joked. "In case you didn't realize."

"What have you had, Fallon?" Lori asked. "It all looks so delicious."

"Well, you can never go wrong with the filet, in my opinion. I've had the ribeye, which is excellent as well. One day I'll order the Chateaubriand for two because I've heard it's incredible and I've always wanted to try it. And I suggest we order some sides for the table—the fries are a must, the gouda mac and cheese is delicious, and if we want to pretend to be healthy, green beans."

Everyone laughed. The sommelier stopped by and opened the champagne, and Patrick raised his glass.

"I know we did this earlier, but I want to wish you a happy birthday again. I'm so glad you're here and that we got to spend the day together."

"Thank you for my beautiful necklace. I love it."

"I'm so glad."

Everyone toasted, and the server approached.

"Are you ready to place your orders?"

"Thank you," Patrick murmured in my ear while his parents talked to the server. "Everything's been perfect because of you."

"My pleasure."

Lori went first and ordered the onion soup and filet, and Don chose mussels for an appetizer and the *entrecôte*. Patrick was next.

"I'll do the onion soup as well, and Fallon and I are gonna share the Chateaubriand."

I blinked. "We are?"

Those penetrating eyes met mine. "You said you always wanted to try it. And so do I."

I licked my lips. "Uh, okay. Sure. That would be great. Thanks."

"And bring us some sides too—fries, mac and cheese, and green beans."

I grabbed my water glass and gulped down the cold liquid, but it did little to quench the fire burning me up. The table was large enough to accommodate the four of us easily, but Patrick was so big, his thick thigh pressed up against mine, and it was as if his bare skin seared me through the wool of his pants. This night might prove to be the death of me.

"Fallon, tell us something about yourself. Patrick hasn't told us much, except what an incredible worker you are." Lori smiled at me, and my heart sank.

I had no desire to talk about myself, but I could hardly refuse, so I decided to keep it superficial.

"I'm a New Yorker, born and bred—I actually grew up not far from here. I went to school out West and then decided to come home and work for Devlin Summers as his personal assistant. I've known him almost my whole life."

"How did you two meet? He's older than you by about five years or so, isn't he?" Patrick asked. The appetizers came, and I'd hoped that would end the questions, but no such luck. They all waited for me to answer.

"My older brother and Dev were very close friends. I was that annoying tagalong little kid. But they were great to me."

Lori and Don began to eat, but Patrick cast a confused look in my direction. "I didn't know you have a brother. Does he live in New York too?"

I couldn't do this. "No. I-I'm sorry. Will you excuse me for a minute? I'll be right back." I escaped to the men's room, where I stood, head down, arms braced on the sink. My chest hurt as I tried to force air into my lungs.

The door burst open. "Fallon, what's wrong?" Patrick loomed over me, and I couldn't answer, only shake my head.

His hand rested on my nape, gently massaging, and after a moment or two I could breathe. "I'm okay. Thanks. You should go to your parents."

"They're the ones who insisted I make sure you're okay, although I had every intention of coming in here anyway."

"I don't want to ruin your mom's birthday."

"Fuck that, Fallon. You made her birthday," he snapped, then gentled his tone. "Please talk to me. What's the matter?"

"It's nothing. I guess I didn't eat much today, and the champagne got to my head. I just needed to splash some cold water on my face." To prove my point, I turned on the faucet and doused my face.

"You're really a terrible liar, you know? I'm not gonna push you, but I'll wait here until you're ready to return to the table."

"Pain in the ass," I mumbled.

"Yep." He grinned, and I knew there was no getting out of it.

I patted my face dry and tossed the paper towel. "I'm fine. Let's go."

I trailed behind him, doing my best to ignore the curve of Patrick's ass and the way the fabric clung to those thick thighs. I sat facing Lori and Don and clasped my hands in front of me. "I apologize for leaving the table."

"There's no need, please. Are you okay? Did something we said upset you?" Lori's soft eyes and kind face sent the words tumbling from my mouth.

"No, of course not. It wasn't you." They waited, expectant, and speaking directly to Lori made it easier. "I lost my brother right before I turned eighteen. Rory died in a car accident—he was in college and was going back to the dorm from an off-campus party. He and I were very close—best friends. Since then..." I shook my head. "It's been hard. I never learned to drive because of that. Silly, isn't it?" I forced a smile, but Lori's eyes filled with tears.

"Oh, honey, I'm so sorry. How awful for you. And your poor parents. Thank goodness they had you to lean on. Was it just you two boys?"

"Yeah. The two of us. But my parents...we're not close. And please. This is your birthday celebration. You don't need to waste your time on my life." I gathered myself. "Tell me about Patrick when he was growing up and when you knew he'd become a football player."

Don launched into the story of how he'd brought Patrick to a Kansas City Chiefs game, and Patrick had pointed to the goalpost after Trent Green threw a touchdown pass, and said, *"I'm gonna do that one day."*

Patrick chuckled. "I remember that. I've never wanted to do anything else besides play football. I've been very lucky and blessed to be able to follow my dream and end up where I have. I don't think many people are able to say that."

"Most people, I'd wager," I muttered.

Our food came, and I'd hoped that would change the course of the conversation. And for a while, it did. The Chateaubriand was everything I'd imagined–the meat juicy and flavorful, the potatoes creamy and delicious. It felt oddly intimate to be sharing the platter of food with Patrick, and during the meal, I could've sworn I caught him staring at me strangely, but I brushed it off as my imagination. Wishful thinking on my part. Lori and Don mentioned several times how impressed they were with the meal, and I breathed a sigh of relief, happy they'd moved on from dissecting my life.

I should've known better. After all, Patrick was a tenacious bulldog on and off the field. He'd obviously inherited it from someone.

"How did you decide to become a personal assistant, Fallon? What was your college major?"

"I honestly had no idea what I wanted to do," I admitted. "But I kept in touch with Dev all throughout school. We...we helped each other deal with losing Rory. When I graduated, he told me to come home and work for him." The condensed, less messy version.

"It's nice to have friends like that." Patrick cut a sharp glance toward me. "Dev's good people."

"He is." Hoping to shift the conversation away from me, I pointed to Lori's and Don's plates with my fork. "It looks like you're enjoying your meals. I can recommend other restaurants you might like for the next time you visit and are able to stay longer. I'm sorry you won't be here for Sunday's game."

A look of regret clouded Lori's eyes. "We would've loved to, but we're going on a cruise. Don surprised me for my birthday." She squeezed his arm. "We have to get home by tomorrow night so we can pack and leave Wednesday."

"But you'll be back for the postseason, of course."

"Wouldn't miss it, especially now."

Patrick knocked my elbow. "You barely ate anything."

He was right, and I'd hoped no one would notice. Once Rory's name came up, my appetite had vanished.

"I did."

"No, you didn't. I hate wasting food. So eat up."

The man was frustrating, but I cut a slice of meat and shoved it into my mouth, chewing with exaggeration. "Okay?"

"No. More. And the potatoes, too."

With a huff, I scooped some up and ate them, aware of the slightly amused but somewhat curious expressions on Lori and Don's faces. I attempted to make light of it. "I guess since he's my boss, he thinks he can make me eat."

The cake came, a confection of lemon and vanilla, and Lori's eyes sparkled. "I've never had a more wonderful birthday. Patrick, I think this move to New York has not only been the best thing for your career, but also personally. It looks like you've found good friends to have in your corner, and that, more than anything, makes me happy."

I could feel the weight of Patrick's eyes. "I think so too."

With the dinner finished, the time had arrived for me to make my escape.

"I'm going to let you all go home now and have some private family time. It was wonderful to meet you. And if you ever need anything, please reach out to me."

I shook Don's hand, but Lori held out her arms for a hug. "Thank you for making this trip so special. And honey, trust me, it'll get better."

She held me until I detached myself. "It's all good. Have a safe flight home."

I escaped and hailed a cab, not bothering to wait for a car. At home, I showered and lay in bed. My phone buzzed with a text from Patrick.

*If you don't tell me what the hell is going on, I'm coming over.*

Brow furrowed, I answered: *What're you talking about? Nothing's going on.*

He called me. "Dude. You left and didn't even say good-bye."

"Yes, I did. I even told your mom to contact me if she needs anything."

"To me. You didn't say good-bye to me. Now what's up? Did I do something?"

I flopped on my back and stared at the ceiling. God, how could I answer that? *You do something to me every time I see you? Ten years ago, you were my first lover and I've never forgotten you?*

"No, you didn't do anything. Not everything's about you, Patrick."

"I know that. Right now it's about you. Listen, my parents are exhausted, and they've gone to sleep. I told them I'm probably going out. Can I come by?"

I shut him down immediately. "What? No way. That's silly. You have training camp tomorrow."

"I know, but that's not until ten o'clock. I can be there in less than twenty."

"Patrick, wait—" But he'd already ended the call. "Damn him."

I jumped out of bed. No one came to my apartment, not even Dev. I didn't need my friends to see how ugly the one room was and how bare I kept it. Like my life. It was too late to stop him, because if there was one thing I'd learned in the short time I'd worked for Patrick Sloane, it was that he didn't take no for an answer.

# CHAPTER TWELVE

## Patrick

Something was definitely off with Fallon, and as I made my way to his place, I grew anxious that he'd bail on me before I got there. Maybe even quit and go dark. When I arrived at his building, I hit his buzzer, and his voice came through the little tin box.

"Yes?"

"It's me, Patrick."

"Please, not now. I just want to go to sleep, and so should you."

"I want to talk to you. Let me up."

"Go home, Patrick."

And the intercom went dead. Well, *damn*. That only made me dig my heels in more. A man with a dog approached, and as he got closer, his eyes grew wide, so I knew he recognized me.

"Hey," I said with a smile. "How's it goin'?"

"Are you...Patrick Sloane?"

"I am. Nice to meet you." I bent to pet his dog, a mutt with floppy ears. "Cute puppy."

"Thanks. He's Waffles, and my name's Josh. Wow. I can't believe it's you. Would you..."

"Take a picture? Sure." We took several selfies, after which I felt it was appropriate to ask. "Do you live here? My friend invited me over, and he must've fallen asleep or something. Mind letting me in?"

"Yeah, of course." The man opened the door, and I followed him in. He lived on the first floor, and I saw from the number on the intercom outside that Fallon was on the third. "Have a great night, and thanks again for the pictures. Great game last week."

"Thanks a lot, Josh." Figuring it never hurt to be nice to a fan, especially one who'd helped me, I pointed at his phone. "Give me your number, and I'll see about getting you seats for this Sunday's game."

"No way! Thank you. Damn, I'm glad Waffles needed that extra walk tonight." He recited his number, and I put it in my phone with a reminder to have Fallon send the guy some merch as well as the promised tickets.

"Take it easy."

"Go Kingdom!" He fist-pumped.

Not seeing an elevator, I took the stairs and stood at the top of the landing. This building looked nothing like where I'd pictured Fallon living—the hallways were dingy and the carpeting old, with dark spots reminiscent of decades-old stains. A musty odor filled the air. I found his apartment and rang the bell. Several times. When he still didn't answer, I knocked on the door.

"I'm not going anywhere, Fallon, so open the door. Otherwise your neighbors are gonna get very angry with you."

I heard the stomping of feet, and then the door was flung open, revealing a shirtless Fallon, hair loose and still damp from a shower. A pair of sweats hung on his hips, revealing he wasn't wearing underwear.

"I thought I told you to leave and that I didn't want to see you."

Fucking hell, he was gorgeous. Those big blue eyes spit fire, and color rose high on his cheeks. A hazy cloud of blond hair waved around his face, and I itched to grab a hank of it, haul him to me, and kiss that angry mouth.

"I don't always do what I'm told. Can I please come in, or are we going to have this conversation out in the hall?"

He narrowed his eyes, straightened his shoulders, and stepped aside. I passed by him and entered a room that was about three hundred square feet. In one corner was a small, narrow refrigerator, and next to it, a stovetop and a sink. Above them, old cabinets with the doors slightly off-kilter. Tucked in behind the kitchen was a door I presumed led to a bathroom. A couch that at the moment was pulled out to a full-sized bed, a mounted television, and there was a desk by a wall, with a desktop as well as a laptop computer. And that was fucking it.

"Welcome to my palace." The sarcasm dripped from his words, and he folded his arms. "Happy now that you've seen my crappy little apartment?"

"This wasn't about seeing where you lived. I'm concerned about you. You've been acting strangely all night."

"I've been running around the city trying to get things perfect for your family and have your apartment ready. I'm tired. That's it." He turned his back to me and walked away.

"I don't think so." I followed him to the opposite side of the tiny room, where he stood looking out the grimy window, which most likely hadn't been cleaned since the middle of the twentieth century. "It started when you told us about your brother." He stiffened. "I didn't know about him. I'm really sorry. That must've been rough."

He shrugged but didn't turn around. "It was years ago."

"So what? You're hurting now. Still." As hard as he tried to push me away, I held on. God knew why, but I needed him to tell me everything. "Is that why you and your family aren't close? Do they think you're responsible somehow?" He shook his head, and I put a tentative hand on his shoulder. "So what is it, then?"

He knocked my hand away. "Why is it so important for you to know? I'm your employee. I work for you. That doesn't give you a free pass to know about my life."

That hurt.

"I thought we were getting to be friends."

"I don't have friends," he answered with a bitter laugh. "I have business associates."

I kept pressing him. "Dev's your friend."

"That—he's different." His lashes lowered, sweeping against his cheeks. "I've known him forever. If it wasn't for Dev..." A shake of his head sent a chill through me.

"Fallon." This time he allowed me to lead him to the sofa bed and pull him down to sit next to me. He still refused to meet my eyes, and his head hung low, that fabulous hair like a curtain, shielding his face. "If we're not friends now, I hope we will be soon enough. It hasn't been that long, but I can't imagine being in this city and not having you with me. I trust you with everything important in my life. Dev and Brody have been helpful, but you're closer to me than anyone else."

It was the truth. The guys I'd come up with in college all had their own lives—kids, wives. We barely kept in touch aside from Christmas cards. And maybe subconsciously I'd held myself back from forming deep, lasting friendships because of my bisexuality.

Fallon tucked a swath of shining hair behind his ear. "From when he was a teenager, Rory had his life planned out. He wanted to go to law school, join the family firm…and of course, my father loved every moment of it. I was the son who never measured up, the one in the background, good but not great in school. The one who hadn't figured anything out yet."

"You were a kid, Fallon. Who knew what they wanted when they were that age?"

"You and Dev. Rory. I wasn't the smart one they could be proud of and brag about. I was just…Fallon. The second son. The gay son. And as it turned out, the one they didn't want."

Dread crept through me. "What're you talking about, didn't want you?"

He lifted a shoulder. "For lack of a better word, after I came out, they disowned me. Told me I'd have to make it on my own. About a month before I was supposed to start college, they cut me off financially and said I'd have to find another way to pay my way."

"Son of a bitch." As someone who'd only known love all his life, hearing Fallon's story sounded almost unbelievable, except I knew he wasn't exaggerating. Fallon was a straight shooter, no bullshit. "What the hell did you do?"

For the first time since I walked in, his lips twitched. "That's where Dev came in, like a white knight. When he heard what my parents had done and that I was going to have to drop out of school, he paid all my tuition and living expenses, without asking for any repayment. He'd come out to me, and I kept his secret for years. And after I graduated, he gave me the job as his personal assistant."

I was stunned, my jaw hanging open. "Whoa. That's...wow. I don't even know what to say to that."

Fallon wiped at his eyes. "I owe Dev everything."

"You owe him a lot. But you took your job to the next level. I know other PAs, and they're nothing like you."

"I'm just doing my job."

"Keeping a secret like that about Dev and Brody... Fallon, that goes way beyond your job description, I think."

"I'm an expert at keeping secrets."

My heart kicked up. "I'm sure you have to be."

Shadows ruled his eyes, and somber-faced, he said, "I've been lying to you."

I laughed, hoping to lighten the mood. "About what? You don't think I'm the best quarterback in the league?"

"That's not it." He chewed on his lip. "If I tell you this, it's going to change how you feel about me."

"Impossible. I already told you I think you're the best, and that's not gonna change."

He rose to his feet and began to pace. "I've been debating whether or not to say something for a while now, and it's gotten to the point where it's not fair to either of us."

Totally confused, I shrugged. "All right. I'm listening." Clearly, Fallon had something he needed to get off his chest.

"When I went to college, I was still a virgin. I'd kissed a few guys, fooled around a little, nothing serious. But when I turned twenty-one, I decided that was gonna change. I was gonna go find a guy, have sex, and get it done."

I winced at his matter-of-fact attitude, spoken in a monotone, as if he were reciting his grocery list. "Shit, that's not right. First times should be with someone you care about." I'd lost my cherry with Betty Waterson, after our team won the state championship. We'd been dating for a year, and we'd thought we were in love. She'd wanted to get married right after graduation and for me to stay in Kansas, but I was being recruited by multiple colleges at the time and I'd known I was going to leave. We broke up, and she'd started dating Cory Stone, the sheriff's son. Last I'd heard from my mother, Betty and Cory had five kids.

"Maybe for straight people, but we gays usually don't have that heteronormative luxury. And knowing that, Dev was worried about me being alone and meeting someone who might hurt me or worse."

The thought of a young and vulnerable Fallon, all alone, ready and willing to give his body up for a moment of pleasure, made me see red. "Dev was right. Jesus, Fallon. A stranger could've killed you or given you a disease. Shit," I swore. "I'm sorry. I didn't mean to bite your head off."

"Dev said the same thing. So he made sure that didn't happen."

"What'd he do? Hire you an escort?" I joked.

"Not exactly." Fallon returned to where I sat and stood over me. "He bought me a membership at an exclusive club where people could have sex. Anonymously." His gaze captured mine, and my stomach dove into free fall.

"A sex club?" I whispered. It couldn't be.

"Yeah. In LA. Everyone wore a mask, and the vetting was intense."

*Ho-ly fuck. It could. It was.*

"Did you...did you go?" I had to ask.

"Yeah."

I licked my lips, my body fighting with itself. One side was filled with dread and fear, while the other tingled with anticipation.

"What was the name of the club?"

"Intensity."

I blinked and released a *whoosh* of air. "I see."

"I met a guy, and we had an incredible night. After that we met for almost six months, at least twice a week. It was the best time of my life. I've never forgotten him." He sat next to me. "Or how he made me feel."

I raked a shaking hand through my hair. "How so?"

"Like I counted. Like I mattered. Like he cared. I fell hard for him. Maybe even loved him. But I got scared and ran away."

*Fallon. Fallon was my first guy.* The passion of that affair had been the gold standard I'd measured every single lover–male or female–against, and they'd always come up lacking. Maybe this was why I'd felt that strange attraction to him from the very first. My heart knew what my brain hadn't. Seeing Fallon so broken yet beautiful, confessing his innermost fears, unlocked the secret I'd buried in my heart.

"He did care," I whispered. "He still does. And you do matter."

Fallon's gaze locked on to mine. "That last time, I woke up in the middle of night, and the mask had slipped off your face. Of course I recognized you. I pushed it on halfway and left. I was freaked out, but I also knew that whatever we had growing between us couldn't last. You were going to be a football player, and that would take precedence. It had to. I knew what Dev and Brody were going through. I understood how it had to be."

Still reeling from the news, I was taken back all those years, to the days I'd returned to Intensity, looking for him, days that had turned to weeks until I'd accepted the brutal finality that he was gone forever.

"And that's why you didn't want to work for me initially."

"I was afraid."

"Of me?"

"No," he answered, the honesty in his eyes leaving me breathless. "Of me. Because I never forgot you, and I was concerned it would keep me from doing my job. And I was right."

"How?" My brow furrowed. "You're the best. There hasn't been a single problem since you began working for me."

"Oh, yeah. There was. You're going to Intensity in the city."

Like a barrel of ice water dumped over me, I knew exactly what he was talking about. "It's you. The dark-haired man. I..."

"We kissed. Yeah. I saw the envelope on your bed that first day, and I knew it was wrong, but I had to see if you would go to the club. I wore a wig and contacts so you wouldn't recognize me. And when you showed up, I thought I could deal with it, but I was mistaken. I didn't know how to handle being so close to you. You kissed me, and the years slipped away like nothing had changed. We were in California again, and I wanted you as much as I did a decade ago."

This was fucking unbelievable. Fallon. My mystery man here in New York. My first lover in California. One and the same.

"I am such a fool. I've never forgotten you either." As soon as the words left my mouth, Fallon rolled his eyes.

"Please don't think you have to say that to make me feel better."

"Fuck that," I growled, my heart pounding so hard I could barely hear. "It was my first time with a man. Do you think I could forget that? Forget you?"

Fallon paled. "I-I didn't know."

"Of course you didn't. How could you? I dug this hole I put myself in all by myself. But how could I do what I loved and be with a man? So I played the game on and off the field." I stared off into the distance, my vision blurring. "Maybe that's why my marriages failed. I wasn't done looking."

"Have you been with other guys since...me?"

I couldn't lie to him. "A couple. It wasn't great. I kept comparing them to you."

"Patrick, come on." Fallon made a face. "It was years ago. We were each other's firsts. You're romanticizing it."

This might be my only chance to shoot my shot if Fallon planned to leave me again.

"Screw that. Consider it a false start."

"What?" His face screwed up in confusion.

"Time for me to call a new play." Before Fallon could move, I slid my fingers through that shining mass of golden hair and pulled him to me. "I want to kiss you, Fallon. May I? Please? Now that I know it's you? I've wanted this from that very first time I saw you at that dinner, when I had no idea who you were except the most gorgeous man I'd ever seen."

Blue eyes wide with shock, Fallon's hot cheek rested on mine. "Patrick, this isn't a good idea."

"Why?"

"Because I can't say no."

"Then it sounds like it's absolutely the right thing. I can't believe I didn't recognize what was in front of me. You. I won't lose you a second time. I can't." I brushed my lips to his, my body clamoring for more, and Fallon's breath hitched. "Say yes. Please. I have you now, and I'm not letting you go. Please, please don't run away from me a second time."

"I work for you. You're in the NFL. Do you know how dangerous this could be for your career?"

It wasn't my career I was thinking about at the moment. The clear danger would be to my heart. But none of that mattered. I had Fallon here with me.

"I don't give a damn. Do you really want me to stop?"

A war raged in his eyes, and heart pounding, I held still, wondering which side would win. Then Fallon's lips touched mine. "No."

# CHAPTER THIRTEEN

## Fallon

This couldn't be happening to me. It couldn't be my mouth Patrick was kissing with those firm, demanding lips that caused my center of gravity to evaporate into thin air. Was it really his tongue, so warm, soft and sweet, licking and sucking mine until my head spun and I floated in a haze of lust and desire? We ravaged each other's mouths, and I'd never craved to be dominated by anyone's kiss the way I did Patrick's.

His hands settled on my face, holding me steady as he stole my breath, moving across my jaw, his scruff rubbing my cheek. I loved every fucking second of that burn.

"You smell fantastic," he rasped, and that sexy fucking growl left me melting. "Goddamn, I want to rub myself all over you." Long, rough fingers roamed my body, leaving my skin burning in their wake. My heart hammered, and I couldn't stop kissing him, afraid I'd wake up and all this would be a dream and once again it would be me in my lonely bed.

"I want it. Do it, come on."

Those big, firm hands, steady every Sunday on the football, slid with that same assurance beneath my sweats and cupped my ass. A moan escaped me, deep and loud, when one thick finger slid along my cleft to tease my hole.

"How the fuck are you so perfect? I can't keep my hands off you." He bent to kiss the pulse jumping at the base of my throat while I ran my hands across his shoulders, then tugged at the hem of his hoodie.

"Off," I panted, and he yanked it up and tossed it aside, immediately returning to sliding that damn wicked finger along my ass. His chest hair scraped mine, and I licked and nipped his arm and shoulder. "Tastes so good."

My dick leaked, dripping on my sweats, and the smell of it swirled in the air between us. Patrick eased my pants past my hips completely, freeing me to his eyes.

"Jesus, Fallon, I need you in my mouth." His hand wrapped around my throbbing cock, and I almost whimpered from the pure pleasure. "Please?" I nodded and he pushed me onto the bed, hovering over me. "I want this to be good for you."

I reached up to touch his swollen lips and traced them with my fingertips. "How could it not? You're good for me."

His dark head bent between my thighs, and at the first touch of his wet mouth sucking my shaft, I cried out.

"Patrick, please, oh fuck." It was my fantasy come to life, and I was lost in a world spinning between reality and dreams.

"*Mmm*," he hummed. "Tastes like fucking heaven." He took me fully, that tongue of his lethal to my sanity as it flicked and teased me. I writhed beneath him, and he rose and fell on my aching dick until I exploded into a million pieces, jerking endlessly down his throat. His tongue licked up every last drop, his wicked smile sending my heart tumbling.

"Come here," I whispered, and those big, muscular arms caged me under him. "Kiss me."

His mouth covered mine, and I tasted myself, salty-sweet on his tongue. I reached up, traced the thick, heavy bulge of his erection, then undid the button of his jeans. "Take them off."

His blazing eyes never left mine as he got naked, and my head spun at his heavy cock rising between us. He was beautiful, a sculpted god, and I was ready to worship him.

"Is this what you want? It has to be on your terms. I didn't come here to get sex from you, Fallon. I hope you know that."

My climax had left me woozy, and all I wanted was to give him that same pleasure. "My desire is you. In my mouth." At my words, his cock jumped, shooting out a stream of precome, and I licked my lips in anticipation of all that power and heat. "Lie down."

I got to my knees and kissed the length of his dick, licking the big vein that ran from top to bottom. I sucked the head, filling my senses with his scent. He lay still, the only sound his gasps in the still air. I wrapped my hand around his thick shaft and took him in fully.

"Oh my fucking God," he groaned, his fingers twitching on the sheets. That large body trembled beneath me. "Fal, I don't want to hurt you."

I released Patrick to fist his stiff erection, watching him grow impossibly bigger. He shifted, tense and shaking, and I leaned in close, our noses rubbing. "Fucking wreck me. Don't hold back."

At my harsh words, his dick throbbed in my hand, and I dove on him again. He bucked his hips, slowly at first, but I urged him on. My throat ached, and I gagged a few times, but I didn't care. I felt goddamn alive for the first time in years, and I wanted everything Patrick could give me. This wasn't boyish Patrick, slightly unsure and hesitant. This Patrick was all muscle and man, and I wanted him with every cell in my body.

My teeth scraped his rock-hard shaft, and he cursed and moved faster. I moaned, frantically swallowing as much of him as I could.

"Fuck, Fallon, I'm there. Oh, God."

Warm, sticky liquid filled my mouth to overflowing, and when he was finished and lay still, I sat on my heels and wiped my lips and face. Hanks of sweaty hair were plastered to his brow, and his chest rose and fell. It took me a second to catch my breath, still in disbelief he was here. With me. I traced his cheeks and the outline of his lips. He patted the space next to him, and I snuggled close, my head on his shoulder.

"How do you feel?" I asked, still unsure about Patrick, me, or anything in my life anymore. Everything had been turned inside out the moment Patrick stepped through my door.

"That's the answer right there. I feel. For the first time. No going through the motions for show, no pushing through to get it done. I'm alive. Dammit, Fallon. What the hell was that?"

I pressed my nose and lips to his damp skin, licking the salty tang, inhaling his smell. Forget football—if he could bottle that scent, Patrick would be a billionaire. He tightened his hold, and I nuzzled into his neck. "I don't know."

"You're no help." He chuckled and kissed my head. "Seriously. You blew me apart. I'm not even sure I can walk."

"I'm not kicking you out. Yet." I smiled against his shoulder.

We remained quiet, his fingers threading through my hair, rubbing it over his cheeks. I knew he loved its length, and it was pretty much close to heaven to be by his side and have him touch me. Everywhere his fingers brushed left threads of fire.

Patrick wound my hair around his fingers and tugged gently to kiss the corner of my mouth. His lips moved on mine, tantalizing and slow. "I can't let you go. I don't want this to end with a quickie on a sofa bed. You deserve more than that." He rolled to his side and frowned. "And what the hell is this place anyway? I've seen closets bigger than this."

I knew it was pretty much a dump, but Patrick's tone got my pride up. "It's called a studio apartment in New York City. I needed to be close to Dev, this was all I could afford in Tribeca, even with the salary he paid me."

"No fucking way Dev thought it was okay for you to live here." He scanned the ugly little space. "I don't believe it."

"You're right," I admitted. "He never came here—why would he? And frankly, I'm here to sleep and change my clothes. Other than that, I'm always at yours."

"I don't like it."

I busted out laughing. "Well, sorry, but this is all I've got." I watched as he found his briefs and jeans and slipped them on. "Are you leaving right now?"

"Not unless you want me to." Those penetrating eyes raked over me, rendering me breathless. I shook my head. "I can't stay the night because of my parents, but I meant what I said. We have to discuss what happened here. I don't want this to be a one-off."

Patrick could say whatever he wanted, but I knew the score. "It would be nice, but you have to be careful. Remember, I've already lived through this with Dev and Brody. They spent more than a decade worrying they'd be outed—half the time I had to find out-of-the-way hotels for them to meet when they played near each other or during the Super Bowl. It was hell for them, Patrick. Always looking over their shoulders, waiting for someone to discover their secret. Trust me, you have eyes on you at all times. If people think you're seeing someone, they can be relentless in trying to find out who it is."

His brow puckered, his lips drooping. "We can be discreet. Unless you don't want to..."

"Of course I do." Frustrated, I tied my hair with an elastic from my wrist. "But I'm trying to be smart and think of you and your profession, not only myself. You can't lose your entire career because of sex. Everything you worked so hard for. I won't let you. Is that what you want if they think you're in a secret relationship—people stalking your every move? You'll end up hating me for it."

He crawled onto the bed and cupped my cheek. "I won't. And this isn't just sex. You know that as much as I do. All these years, I never stopped thinking about you. It's not a lie. At Intensity, I was drawn to you. Our conversations, the fire in your eyes...sex is only the physical. I want to know all of you. Everything." He brushed our lips together, and I couldn't help sighing. "We'll make it work." He kissed me again. "I'd better go. I'll see you in the morning, okay?"

I nodded, watching him dress, then left the bed to pull on my sweats. He put his arm around me, and I walked him to the door. "Bye."

"See you tomorrow. Come for breakfast." His warm mouth met mine, and I clung to him for a moment, pressing against his stubbled jaw.

"I'm happy to. I ordered bagels and lox for your parents." I snickered.

He pinched my ass and opened the door. I watched him walk away until he disappeared from sight. I shut the door and leaned against it. My body hummed from Patrick's touch, and I knew sleep would be a long time coming. The rumpled bed waited, and like a kid with a crush, I lay in it, sniffing the pillow deeply for a whiff of his sweat and faint cologne.

*"We'll make it work."*

I doubted it, but if Patrick was willing to try, I was too. All I knew was, walking away from him this time might prove impossible.

******

"Can I gain ten pounds in two days? Because it sure feels like it," Lori joked, rubbing her slim middle. "Guess I'll be spending time with my treadmill when I get home. These bagels are the best, Fallon, and I'm so glad you had a chance to join us so we could say good-bye. We really didn't have enough time to spend together on this trip, but we'll be back."

"I have a goodie bag for you to take home with you of some New York mementos. And whenever you're ready to come visit again, let me know and I'll make the arrangements. I'll give you my cell phone number so you can call me. In case you want to surprise Patrick sometime."

She laughed. "That would be fun." She put my contact information in her phone. "And we'd better finish packing. Patrick, I know you can't come with us to the airport, so we'll say good-bye here."

I met Patrick's eyes over Lori's head. "I'll come with you. Make sure you get off okay." He brightened.

"Thanks. I'd appreciate that."

They disappeared into the second bedroom, and I began to clear the kitchen island of the plates, stacking them in the dishwasher. When I opened the refrigerator, I sensed Patrick's large presence behind me. He put his hand on mine, resting them both on the handle. "How'd you sleep?" he murmured in my ear.

That deep, husky voice sent a shiver of anticipatory lust through me, and I struggled to catch my breath. "Okay." I shut the door. "Had some pretty awesome dreams."

A teasing grin curved his lips. "I bet they weren't as good as mine. Thanks for the send-off breakfast for my parents. And I appreciate you going with them to the airport."

"I like your parents. I'm happy to go with them. After dropping them off–"

"Come here. Please? We'll have dinner. I should be home from camp around six thirty."

"If that's what you want."
"You. That's all I want."

# CHAPTER FOURTEEN

Patrick

"Sloane, we're gonna do shotgun. The Mavericks like to blitz, but they're weak on the line of scrimmage with two tackles injured, so we're gonna see what we can get."

"You got it, Coach." I jogged to the field, where the rest of the team had gathered. "Shotgun. Let's do it."

I bent over behind the center and called out the play. "Blue 42, Blue 42, hut, hut." I took the snap and faded from the line of scrimmage a few steps, yelling, "Where the hell's my offensive line?" Downfield I saw Rio, who'd become my favorite wide receiver. He was open, so I sent the ball sailing toward him.

"What's the matter, Trick? Worried about your pretty face?" Lincoln King, star tackle and built like a damn refrigerator, cackled and made kissy noises my way.

Troy grabbed my butt. "Nah. More like his ass, I'm thinkin'. That's what the ladies see most on the field."

"And they love it." I smacked his hand away. "So don't bruise the merchandise."

I played along with them, though it bugged the shit out of me that we could all joke like this only because they thought I was straight. What would they think of their leader if they knew I'd spent the night sucking a man's dick, swallowing his come, and loving every damn second of it?

"Let's go, let's go," Coach yelled. "Moore, King, stop slacking off and hit the tires. Durant, nice catch. Do some sprints downfield. Sloane, practice with Harte. Snaps and throws. Move it. Just 'cause the Mavericks suck this year don't mean they won't come to kick our butts. They're gonna be gunning for us, especially you, Sloane. You haven't played against them in years."

"You got it, Coach. Hey, Harte," I yelled to my backup, who was tossing the ball to one of the offensive coaches. "Let's go. See you jokers later."

I met Harte McKinney at centerfield. "Coach wants us to practice snaps and throws."

"Yeah, sure."

I approached him tentatively. We hadn't talked much since I joined the team, more my fault than his. I figured he resented me coming in and taking a job he'd hoped to get. Being second string was ordinarily not a job most people wanted, but in the NFL, a player could make upward of three million a year—more if he was a veteran with the league.

"How're you liking being part of the Kings?" he asked as he caught my throw and tossed it to me.

"I'm liking it. You've been here a while." We were about ten yards apart, so we could easily converse.

"Yeah, about five years. Came a little after Luke Fontaine was traded." I threw a perfect spiral to him, and he repeated one to me. "But I know they're scouting for a younger backup for you, especially since I strained my arm when I filled in before you started. Look, let's get it out in the open. I'm not interested in being the starting quarterback."

About to return the throw, I stopped and stared at him. "Uh, okay. I guess I should say thanks. But isn't that a little unusual? Don't you want playing time? On my old team, JC was hoping for me to get sacked on every play, just so he could get a chance."

I'd heard from the guys that JC Downs would cheer whenever I had a rough outing and had actively campaigned to get more playing time. It was one of the reasons I'd been eager to get away from the team—I'd never had a feeling of camaraderie with the other players. And the fact that they were struggling with one of the worst records in the league, with JC as their starter, did give me a bit of satisfaction.

"Yeah, sure. But I'm not a rookie. I've got fifteen years in, and I have a ring already. Come on, let's do some snaps." He motioned to the ball in my hands. "Give it to me, and I'll do it for you. See, I'm not looking for glory or to get my name in the record books. I'm happy to be your second and earn my bank." He bent, I took the snap, and then he ran out and I threw to him. Harte McKinney was quick, with fast hands, and I knew from watching him play over the years that he was a steady but not flashy player. A guy who came to get the job done.

"I got to admit, that's not what I thought I'd hear, but I'm glad."

We repeated the snaps with Harte doing five more, then me giving him the chance six times. We continued to throw the ball to each other while talking. Or rather, Harte talked and I listened. "I was never the superstar, but all I wanted was to play football and win games. I'm planning on retiring after this season anyway. My contract is up, and Coach told me that with my salary and age, they aren't planning to re-sign me. They need younger backups for you."

"Damn, man. I'm sorry."

He shrugged and threw the football to me. "Is what it is, but maybe it's for the best."

"Your family will be happy to have you home, I'm sure."

Even at the ten-yard distance, I could see the downward tick of Harte's lips and his shoulders sag beneath the padding. "Nah, my wife bailed about three years ago. Said she wasn't about to stay with a second-stringer." His next throw to me was a hard one, with the weight of anger behind it, but I couldn't fault him. "So much for true love, huh? What about you? Enjoying the playground of the city?"

Coach blew the whistle, and I motioned to Harte. "Better go see what he's got to say." We jogged over to him and joined our teammates gathered around him and the other coaches.

"All right. Time to call it a day. Tomorrow we'll do a couple of hours here, watch some films, and go over plays. Hit the showers, and I'll see you in the morning."

Harte and I walked off the field together, and our offensive coach joined us on our way to the locker room.

"Nice teamwork out there today, Sloane, but a little less talking and a lot more throwing next time, got it?"

My face heated. "Understood, Coach."

"You need to work on getting out of the pocket as fast as possible. Like we said, they're gonna be on your ass. Make sure you have an alternate receiver if the one you planned for gets jammed up. You can't throw to Durant all the time. Anticipation is the key to winning."

I gave him a sharp nod. "Got it."

"Good. We don't want a repeat of what happened with Dev Summers. You need to stay healthy. Harte, good job. How's the shoulder?"

"Fine, Coach. It was just a simple strain. With the PT and rest, it's back to one hundred percent."

"Good, good. See you tomorrow."

He left us to the organized chaos, and I was happy to strip off my uniform and get into the shower. Still early, I was hoping to get home and have a little one-on-one time with Fallon. Anticipation crawled through my veins at the thought of a whole night together. I reentered the locker room and was getting dressed when my phone rang. Seeing it was Dev, I picked it up.

"Hey, what's up? Just getting out of practice."

"Good, then you're free. Can you do us a big favor?"

I sat on the bench. "If I can, sure."

"You know Riley Carson, tight end for the Sparks? He was scheduled to be on *The Huddle* but had to cancel last-minute. He forgot his kid has a school play. Could you fill in for him? Please?"

As much as I wanted to say no, I couldn't. Not to Dev and Brody. They'd been nothing but good to me since I came to the city.

"Yeah, sure. When and where?"

"Oh, thank fuck. You really saved our asses. You can do it from home—it's a video podcast. I'll text Fallon and have him get the computer set up. I'm sure you've done them before."

"Yeah. I'm familiar with it. I'm finishing up here, and I should be home in about an hour."

"Perfect timing. You'll have enough time to relax for a few and settle in. Thanks again, Trick."

"Not a problem. Catch you later."

I pulled on my hoodie, laced up my sneakers, and picked up my bag. "See you tomorrow, boys. Be good."

"Or at least careful, right?" Troy cackled. "Where you rushing off to, my man? Got a hot date?"

My grin was big and bright. "Maybe so." Without another word, I left to the catcalls of my fellow players.

An hour and half later, I clicked on the link Dev sent me, and he and Brody popped up on my screen. Both had on blue T-shirts and ball caps with *The Huddle* on them, and I laughed.

"Nice merch, fellas."

Dev waved. "Hey, Trick. Don't worry. We've sent you over some. Thanks for joining us on *The Huddle*. To our viewers and listeners who were hoping to hear running back Riley Carson, he's been rescheduled due to a personal conflict, but we were lucky enough to snag our good friend and star quarterback of the Brooklyn Kings, Patrick Sloane. Patrick is new to the Kings, having come in only this year. Tell us, how are you liking it here in the Big Apple?"

"I'm loving it," I responded with a big smile. "Everyone's been welcoming and friendly—"

"That'll change once you lose the first game," Brody interrupted with a laugh. "Trust me."

"Who said we're going to lose?" I smirked.

"Oh, damn! I love it." Dev slapped his knee and howled. "There's that confidence you bring on the field every week. Some call it arrogance, don't they?"

I arched a brow. "They can call it whatever they want. I come every week with the intention of winning. It's up to the other team to take that away from me. And I know my teammates feel the same. We're fired up for a winning season."

"I know that adrenaline rush every Sunday. How's the transition been with your team?"

I leaned back in my chair. This podcast wasn't such a bad gig after all. "My teammates are terrific. And as you know, the Kings are a great organization. They've been great every step of the way, even making a very generous donation to my charity—shoutout to Hearts and Hands. They provide services to families with terminally ill children. I spend time in the off-season visiting hospitals to see the kids. They inspire me every day."

"A very worthy cause that Brody and I donate to as well. Anytime you want us to come with you, give a holler." Dev leaned into the mic. "Now that we've got the professional part of the program out of the way..." His grin widened, and I groaned and shook my head. Brody pointed and cackled.

"You knew it was coming, man. Don't pretend you're surprised the listeners want to hear about your personal life."

Covering my eyes with my hands, I hung my head. "Damn, guys. I've only been here a hot minute, and my concentration's been on the game. Give a guy some time."

But Dev had always been a persistent fucker. "I bet the ladies are chomping at the bit now that you're single again. We heard you had some fun on the recent road trip."

"If they are, I'm not paying attention. And that was just me being friendly to the local fans. You remember how it was. We're in the heart of the season, and my only goal is to bring another Super Bowl to the fans and the Kings. Besides, I've only just moved into my new apartment. I barely know where my towels are."

"How do you like living in the city?" Brody asked. "I remember moving here and not being able to believe the size of the crowds everywhere. Sometimes I still can't."

"Yeah, I'm from a small Kansas town, and I think I see more people here walking down the street in one morning than I ever did in a week at home. But there's an energy and vitality...I didn't think I would, but I love it."

"A big difference from San Diego and the West Coast, I'm thinking?" Brody questioned. "Do you miss the weather?"

"Well, yeah. But I'm looking forward to the change of seasons."

"Okay, let's talk about the game. What do you anticipate from the Mavericks on Sunday?"

I breathed a sigh of relief that we'd returned to discussing football. "The Mavs are a tough team. They've had a hard schedule this year, and we anticipate a fight. I don't believe their record reflects the talent on their team—Orion Woods might be a rookie quarterback, but he's fast and quick. Juno Walters is one of the best tight ends now that you've retired, Brody. And they have a bunch of tackles and guards who are built like tanks."

There. That was playing nice. I didn't want to shit-talk the opponent and give them any more reason to gun for our asses other than the fact that we were the best team in the league and had a target on our backs. Everyone hated a winner.

"I agree. I see Orion having a great future in the league." Dev gave me a nod. "We'd better let you go, Trick, but I wanna thank you for being such a good sport and stepping in at the last minute. Good luck on Sunday, and we'll be at the game. Eyes on you, my brother."

"Just call me Stunt Double Sloane. It was my pleasure—anytime. And I'll do my best. Talk to you soon, guys." I gave them a salute and tapped out of the podcast. I removed my headphones and spun in my chair to see Fallon on the couch, staring intently at the computer screen. I doubted he even knew I was finished with the podcast, and I crept over behind him and pressed a kiss to his neck.

"Hi," I whispered, and he shivered under my lips.

"H-hi. I didn't know you were finished."

"Yeah. A minute ago. What're you so wrapped up in? Must be important."

He shut the computer and turned around, kneeling on the couch to face me. Big blue eyes hazy with desire, cheeks flushed and mouth slightly parted, he was everything perfect, and my bones went weak.

"Not at all."

"Good. Because I need to do this right now." I slid my hands through his hair, anchoring him, and settled my mouth over his. Like the other night, I lost myself in the silky, sweet taste of Fallon's tongue. I sucked hard, and he moaned.

"More. Everything." His tongue met mine, teasing and dancing.

The absolute abandon with which he gave himself to me was a fucking turn-on. "Come on. I can't do what I want to you on the couch. I need room."

His hand in mine, we almost ran to the bedroom and stripped until we were both naked. His dick rose out stiff and proud, and I needed to put my mouth on it. On my knees, I took him all the way to the back of my throat, and Fallon's eyes fell shut, mouth open and gasping for air.

"Fuck me, oh God, Patrick, I need you."

Hearing those words set my blood on fire, and I let him go. "Bed," I rasped, going to the nightstand drawer for the lube and condom. Fallon lay with all that glorious hair spread across my pillow, and I dove into its silky beauty, my cock dragging along his rigid length. "Feels so good." I kissed his ear, shoving my tongue into the tiny canal, and his dick spurted out precome. "You're everything."

"Don't stop," he whispered.

"I gotta be inside you, or I'll explode." My mouth caught his, our kisses sloppy and wet, growing more demanding.

"So do it." Fallon dug his fingers into my shoulders, his hips bucking hard against mine. "I told you last night to wreck me. Do it now. Fuck me hard. Shove it up in me. I wanna feel you for days."

His dirty mouth was more of a turn-on than I'd imagined, and a red haze descended over my eyes. All I could think of was my dick in Fallon while his tongue played in my mouth. Rolling on the condom physically hurt, but I managed and lubed myself up. Fallon raised his legs, and I rubbed the head of my dick around his hole, loosening him up.

"Baby, I'm so fucking hot for you, I might not last."

"I don't care." Eyes wild, a sheen of perspiration on his face, Fallon clawed at the sheets. "Please, please."

Inch by inch I sank into him, caught between watching Fallon's face turn pink with pleasure and the sight of my dick disappearing in his twitching body. "Holy fuck. You are the sexiest thing I've ever seen."

A half smile tipped up the corner of Fallon's mouth. "Yeah?"

Lust curled in my belly as he stroked his flushed cock, the slick sound of it moving in his fist my new favorite music. My head spun as, like a spider, he drew me into his web of lust and passion. And like a fly, I tangled myself into the glittering threads of Fallon's silk, knowing full well I'd never escape.

And didn't want to.

"Oh God, fuck, fuck me," Fallon cried out and came, arching against me, hot come making our sweaty skin slippery. The bed banged, our pace hard and punishing. My heart thundered in my ears, and I barely felt the sting of his fingernails digging into my shoulders. The air between us shimmered golden, and under me, Fallon stilled.

"Patrick," he whispered, sounding dazed.

"Yeah." Still buried deep within his body, I ran my lips along the bridge of his nose, coming to rest on the softness of his mouth. "I feel it too."

I began to move again, slowly this time, pulling out almost completely, then slamming in on return. Fallon moaned and trembled—I knew he was sensitive, but I was too far gone and continued to hammer into his almost limp body. A tingling started in my legs, traveling upward to my groin, and I thrust hard, once, twice, until I exploded and collapsed.

"Patrick," Fallon choked out, but I couldn't move except to open one eye. "Please. I can't breathe."

"Sorry," I grunted. With effort, I managed to pull out and get rid of the condom before falling back into bed. "I feel like I've been sacked a hundred times in a row. There's no way I can get out of bed."

Fallon rolled to his side and laid his head on my chest. "I can't either. Not yet."

I managed to tuck my arm around him, holding him close. "Not at all. Stay with me tonight. Please. Don't go home to that place. I'll be here by myself, and you'll be there alone. It makes no sense."

"I don't know."

His hesitancy upset me. Why didn't he want to stay?

"Come on, Fal, please? No one has to know."

His eyes grew stormy. "Somehow, people always find out."

I tightened my grip on him. "I promise we'll be okay."

# CHAPTER FIFTEEN

## Fallon

Each morning I swore I'd muster my self-control to be strong and not let the physical overtake my common sense, but nothing made sense when it came to Patrick. It was as if my brain had switched off and only my emotions were left to rule my body.

From that first night I'd stayed with him, I hadn't left—every night I'd gather my things to go home, Patrick would kiss me, and weak with desire, I'd capitulate. "One more day" had turned into a week, and now it was time for him to go on the road. Tuesdays after game days were mandatory for the players to rest and recuperate from the battering they took on the field. And Patrick had been a target for the Mavericks, who'd come after the Kings with every weapon in their arsenal. Penalties galore, shit-talking between the teams, and despite massages, whirlpools, and icings, Patrick was hurting. His focus during the day had been on practice, but at night he was all mine. Aware that our time together was limited, I took care of him from the moment he came home, giving him the physical comfort we craved from each other.

It wasn't only sex between us. Curled up together at night, Patrick would tell me his fears of not being good enough to replace someone like Dev.

"Every time I step on the field, I'm in his footsteps, and it's hard not to make the comparison."

I rubbed his shoulders. "You have to walk outside his lines and make your own path. Your goal shouldn't be to remake yourself in Dev's image. You need to be the best Patrick Sloane you can be."

"Thanks. It's hard, but having you here helps."

I hugged him. "I'm glad. Because from where I sit, you're my number one."

That night, I waited for him to come home, already missing him, as he was leaving the following day. I made sure his travel bag was packed, and media appointments were scheduled while he was in San Diego. Patrick's appearance on *The Huddle* had been a success but had also sparked renewed interest in his personal life, and his social media was on fire.

The elevator opened, and Patrick walked in. Our eyes locked as he strode across the room to where I sat at the kitchen island. Warm lips grazed my neck, and I shivered.

"Hi. Have I told you I like coming home and finding you here?"

A thrill shot through me at his possessive, growly tone. His still-damp hair tickled my nose as I slipped off the barstool to meet his mouth in a heated kiss. He smelled clean, like body wash, but I wished one day I could have him sweaty and fresh from the field.

"Only a dozen times this past week." I smiled and ran my fingers over his stubbled cheeks. "I have everything ready for you to leave in the morning." A forlorn expression darkened his eyes, and I tried to lighten his mood. "Hey, at least you're going to the West Coast, where the sun is shining. They said on the news the temperature here is about to drop twenty degrees."

"Wouldn't matter. I'd have you to keep me warm." He put his arms around me, resting his chin on my shoulder. "Come with me to San Diego."

Startled, I laughed, even as my body buzzed from his touch. "That's not happening."

"Why? Other guys bring their wives or personal assistants. It wouldn't look out of place."

"Because...because...I don't know. It would be tempting fate. We couldn't spend the night together, anyway. You're busy with training from morning to night and have to stay in the hotel with the team." He continued to press his lips on my cheek and jaw while he pulled off my hair tie. My halfhearted attempt to wiggle away did nothing to stop Patrick from winding his fingers through my hair. "And you're not playing fair," I protested as he slid his hands inside my jeans and kneaded my ass.

"I play to win. And you as the prize is extra incentive." He kissed me fully on my mouth, and I sighed, desire flooding my bloodstream like a drug.

"Doesn't the coach have a no-sex rule before games?"

"No, there's no rule for regular games. Only the Super Bowl. Please? I'll put you up at a hotel nearby. You can go to the beach and work on your tan if you want."

I couldn't help laughing. "Wow, you're really grasping for excuses."

He stopped touching and kissing me and took my face between his palms. "It's not an excuse. I want you with me. Period. This week has been pretty damn amazing, hasn't it?"

I'd be a liar to deny it. "Yeah, it has been."

"We make a good team." He continued to play with my hair, twirling the ends through his fingers. I loved how much he enjoyed that. Once I came home from college, I'd decided to grow it. Maybe it had been part of my rebellion, knowing my parents wouldn't approve as it didn't conform with their old-school values.

"Team?" I repeated, the intensity of his eyes piercing through my attempt to stay lighthearted.

"Yeah. You have no idea how hard it is to find someone you can trust. Almost every friend, wife, or casual acquaintance has wanted something from me. Not you."

That was where Patrick was so very wrong. Because I wanted what he couldn't give me. But I couldn't say that. I'd gone into this arrangement eyes wide open, knowing he couldn't come out, that we'd never have an overt relationship while he was actively playing. If we even lasted. Stress could do terrible things to a couple.

"You make it sound so simple. Trust me, it's not. Even my staying here this week is a risk for you. I've got nothing to lose. You're the one who's putting every-thing on the line."

His smile was sweet. "I play the line every Sunday. And I'm used to risks. Shouldn't I be the one to decide if I'm willing to take them?"

"I don't want you to end up resenting me."

"Fal, you've made my transition here seamless. I couldn't have done it without you handling every detail. Any obstacle that popped up, you've smoothed over so I didn't have to think twice or worry. You're the best damn assistant ever. And you've become my best friend as well."

"I told you—I'm just doing my job." God, I sounded so weak, but hearing him say those words was a balm for my wounded heart and soul.

"And then there's this." He kissed me. "This isn't your job. It's separate and apart. I don't want you to think for a second that I'm confusing one with the other, because you're the ultimate professional. But you can't deny this connection. I feel it, and so do you. When we first met, it was special between us. And noth-ing's changed since. Whatever we started in California all those years ago isn't finished yet. Not by a long shot."

I kept silent because to say otherwise would be lying. After our time together, I hadn't had many lovers, but I couldn't deny that what I'd shared with Patrick was special. The night we'd kissed at Intensity, the years had fallen away and I'd become that virgin again, giving myself up to the man who'd managed to steal my heart and hold the key. Now he was here, in front of me, offering to unlock it.

"You've had much more experience in the relation-ship department," I teased.

But Patrick didn't take the bait. "It was all bullshit. Half the time they were models using me for exposure for their own careers. Everyone using everyone. Except you." He captured my mouth in a fierce kiss. "Never you."

I should be stronger, less submissive, but all I could do was return his kiss with the same fervor and wish it could last forever.

Breathing heavily, Patrick held on to me. "Maybe I was trying to recreate what we had with everyone else, thinking if I gave it time, or tried hard enough..." He shook his head. "But you can't force something that never existed in the first place. And nothing and no one has ever replaced you."

Knowledge without true insight was a facade. It was apparent in how they presented Patrick's off-field persona, Trick Sloane, who the press claimed wildcatted around with models and starlets. They stressed his love life as much as his football prowess—at times even more. But that wasn't real. He was a dedicated professional. A son who loved his parents and was grateful for all they did for him. And a lover unparalleled, who left me in a puddle of pleasure every time we kissed.

"Are you saying you never loved your exes?" We hadn't ever delved deep into Patrick's past relationships, but maybe now was as good a time as any.

"I thought I did." He released me, frowning, and leaned against the kitchen island. "We laughed a lot, had fun together, and I wanted to be with them. The sex was good, and I liked having someone to come home to." He folded those powerful arms and cast his gaze to the floor. "But playing football was just as important. It didn't come second. My personal life melted into the professional until it was impossible to separate the two."

"And no one likes to be second best. Especially to a football." I appreciated how he didn't lay the blame totally on his ex-wives.

"No. But that didn't mean they had to lie, cheat, or spend my money like I owed it to them. That's where it all broke down." He ran a hand through his hair. "It's hard to learn to trust after you've been burned. But not with you. I trust you with my business, but more importantly, my biggest secret."

"I'll never do anything to jeopardize your life, but we hardly know each other."

His face hardened, dark eyes glittering with anger. "Hardly know each other? What don't you know? My favorite pizza topping? What my favorite song is? That doesn't make us closer." Two long strides brought him nose to nose with me. "I know you, Fallon. How you always make sure I have everything I need without me asking or even knowing what I want. You took care of my parents and gave my mother the best birthday ever—she's still talking about it to her friends—because you know how important she is to me. I know how you watch out for your friends, even to your detriment."

I trembled at his fierceness, captivated by his words and passion. "I do it because I care."

Patrick skimmed his fingers along my jaw. "Yeah. But if you think I don't know you, you're wrong. You have a little frown line that pops up on your brow whenever you're concentrating. I know how you love when I play with your hair. You turn pink all over right before you come, and your lashes flutter." He nuzzled into my cheek. "You love to suck my dick in the shower."

Face burning, I wrapped my arms around him and hugged him tight. "Patrick, stop."

He continued, stroking my back. "But I also discovered sometimes you cry out at night like the devil is chasing you, and it makes me so damn mad that you were hurt and had no one to help you."

Shocked, I stared at him. "I-I what? Cry in my sleep?"

He kissed my cheek. "Yeah. I figured if you needed to talk about it, eventually you would. Because I know you miss your brother, and I wish I could make it better for you."

"There's nothing to talk about. You know all my secrets."

"Fal," he said gently. "Don't be ashamed. Everyone lives with nightmares."

"Oh, yeah?" I challenged him. "Even you? What's yours? What're you afraid of?"

"Being alone forever."

His honesty hit me like a punch to the stomach, and I met his eyes. "Sometimes you can be surrounded by people and still be invisible. I understand." More than he knew. I'd grown up with parents who didn't know me and never cared to try.

"Toward the end of both my marriages, we'd sit across the table from each other, resentful, in dead silence. It was hard to believe there was ever love between us, and I couldn't think of a single word to make them stay." He paused. "When I discovered the cheating, I realized I didn't want to work on something irrevocably broken, and I filed for divorce. In the end, all I felt was relief when my marriages were over."

The breakdown of anything that was once a significant part of your life was hard. And marriage, no matter how short, was as significant a relationship as one could get.

"That's sad. I'm sorry. Even if you knew it wasn't working out, it's still hard."

"I should've known it wouldn't last. I wanted love like my parents have. You saw them together. They're not like that. I grew up with them very involved in my life—we talked about everything."

"Not everything," I said pointedly, and he flushed.

"Yeah, well…there's that."

"Why haven't you told them? Are you afraid of how they'll react?"

He nibbled on his bottom lip. "I want to say no, but I'd be lying. And before you ask, no, my parents aren't homophobic. But I also know it's easy to say you're liberal and support gay rights when it doesn't personally affect you. I can't be sure how they'll feel if I tell them I'm bisexual and that I have a male lover."

While he did have a point, I usually had a good sense of people and didn't get that vibe from Lori or Don. But I certainly wasn't the right person to discuss proper parenting.

"I understand. But you've had years of a healthy relationship with them. Even if they were surprised or shocked, I bet they'd come around eventually. They love you very much."

Holding me tight, Patrick steered me toward the couch, which overlooked the river. "I'm sorry your parents let you down. I can't and won't even begin to understand how they could treat you differently from your brother. But that's their problem, not yours. You don't need to look for validation from them. You're a wonderful person, a fantastic worker, and the perfect lover."

I opened my mouth to deny his words, but he placed his large hand over my mouth.

"Stop it, Fallon. Stop telling me everything wrong with you, when all I see is everything right."

I had no idea how to respond to that, so I remained quiet, and Patrick set his hands on my shoulders, gazing directly into my eyes.

"You don't believe me, do you? How can you not know how great you are?"

All this truth and barrier-breaking was way too intense for me, and I thought to lighten the mood, hoping Patrick would drop it. "You're just saying that–"

He cut me off with an angry growl and a hard shake. "Don't you fucking dare finish that sentence by saying *because I work for you*. You know it's more than that."

My heart swooped, and I couldn't catch my breath. "What're you talking about?"

"I'm crazy about you. I can't stop thinking about you and me. Us. And all that time we wasted not being together." He framed my face and kissed me. "Now we have the chance to do it right."

# CHAPTER SIXTEEN

## Patrick

My family had always called me impulsive. Maybe they were right, considering that at the age of thirty-one, I had two failed marriages behind me. But having been through those experiences, I believed myself to be wiser and capable of making better decisions now that I was older. And everything in me screamed that Fallon was as special as I'd thought the first time we were together.

When we met, I'd had no idea who he was. Our brief time together had remained, not a dirty secret, but one I'd realized had shaped my life. And now that Fallon had reappeared, I had no intention of letting him go again.

"Please, Fal. Come with me to San Diego. I've been meaning to have my training stats tracked, and you're the person I want to keep those records."

His face revealed nothing but skepticism. "I'm sure your coaches monitor all that."

"Yeah, of course. But they keep those records. I want them for my own. Plus...dammit, I want a friend there. Please?" I brushed the hair off his face. "You traveled with Dev plenty of times. Why not with me?"

He chewed the inside of his cheek. "Because I wasn't sleeping with Dev. It was strictly business."

I grinned. "I promise to be good. And you won't stay in the same hotel. Find one out of the area. I would just feel better knowing you're close by."

He rolled his eyes. "Oh, for God's sake. All right. I'll come."

My heart gave a happy jump. "Let's celebrate." I pounced on him, and soon we were making love, Fallon riding my dick, his head thrown back, hair wild and messy round his face.

"Oh fuck, you're splitting me in two," he moaned, eyes bright with lust. "Harder. Fuck me harder."

Fallon's unbridled desire was always a massive turn-on, and as he clawed at my shoulders, I held his hips and thrust up, deep and hard. His ass squeezed my shaft, and I wrapped my hand around his dick, rubbing him with vigor.

"Goddamn, your face," I panted, the beginnings of a spectacular orgasm spinning through my blood. He moved faster and faster, and I thumbed the sticky crown of his dick. "Come on, Fal, give it up for me."

I slammed into him while jerking his dick and he came, splattering all over our stomachs while I blew up inside him and filled the condom. Fallon fell onto my chest, and I held him close, not caring we were a sticky mess.

"You're mine," I whispered, and he sighed and kissed my neck.

"And you're mine," he answered.

**

"Ready to face your old team, Trick?" Harte sat across from me on the flight to California. I accepted a glass of orange juice from the flight attendant with a smile, which he returned.

"Yeah, should be interesting. I'm more curious to see how the fans will react than facing my old team. I know they'll be gunning for me."

It was a nice perk that players didn't have to fly commercial—it meant no waiting in line for security. Most NFL teams owned private jets to fly the players, the coaches, and all the equipment. Fallon had taken an earlier flight, and as I had the bye week coming up, we'd decided to take a few extra days after the game for a little R&R. He was staying at a hotel less than ten minutes away from mine.

"Most likely. So you're not gonna be meeting anyone tonight for old times' sake to shoot the shit?"

Sitting behind me, Rio snickered. "Why? You wanna ask him out on a date, McKinney?"

Anger darkened Harte's face for a brief second. "Don't be stupid. Just making conversation." He met my eyes, and my heart stuttered. Was Harte interested in me? He looked away, out the window.

"Would you like something else, Mr. Sloane?" the flight attendant asked me with a flirty smile.

"No, I'm fine, thank you."

"Let me know if you need anything."

"Damn, Trick. Bet he'd initiate you into the mile-high club if you wanted," Rio cackled when the attendant was out of earshot.

"Rio, shut up. You gotta make everything seem dirty."

"Just callin' it as I see it, brother."

I tuned him out and thought about the days ahead. Having the extra night in town was a bonus. First, dinner with the team, and later meeting Fallon at his hotel. Tomorrow would be training and dinner with the team, then bed check. After the game on Sunday, I planned a surprise—we were going to my little house on the beach for the bye week. Just the two of us.

I slept a little on the plane, and once I was settled in my room, I texted Fallon.

*Here at the hotel. Gonna do a walk-through of the stadium, have dinner with the guys before coming to you.*

I got an immediate response.

*I'll be waiting. Just picking up something quick for dinner.*

Grinning to myself, I took a shower.

**

Only about two months since I'd left the Sharks and the field felt like foreign territory. No longer home. My transition to the Kings was now complete. I started jogging around the perimeter to get the feel and stood at midfield, gazing at the stands, while my teammates picked out their spots to familiarize themselves. Harte joined me, tossing a football from one hand to the other.

"Feels weird, right? I remember when I got traded from the Stallions, and we played them less than a month later. The fans were cool, but my old teammates were less than kind, calling me washed up, old man...shit like that."

"Fuck that. You're what, thirty-six?"

"Thirty-seven, but yeah. I'll admit I'm getting up there in age, but plenty of quarterbacks play until they're older." That same darkness I spied on the plane re-entered his eyes. "Only I don't feel like putting my life on hold anymore."

"So you've got plans?" I did some stretches and lunges. Travel, even in first class, wasn't fun when you were my size. Sitting on a plane for five hours plus was enough to stiffen me up.

"Professionally? I'm not sure. But personally, I'd like to meet someone. My divorce was hard—Maya and I had been together since college, and I'm used to living with someone. I don't want to be alone."

Harte was a good-looking guy, with thick blond hair and big blue eyes. A little shorter than me, he was muscular without being bulky, which kept him fast on his feet.

"I get that. Probably why I rushed to get married out of college and again after my divorce. I don't like it either."

His eyes twinkled. "I noticed. But you're not dating anyone now, are you? I saw you broke up with the swimsuit model."

I'd almost forgotten about Mimi—Fallon occupied every corner of my mind. "No. I'm not dating anyone.

My focus is on the game and getting us to the Super Bowl. You might have one of those rings, but I don't, and I intend to change that."

We bumped fists and rejoined the team, listening to Coach's instructions. He pointed to me.

"Trick. Let's go through the Sharks' weaknesses one more time, and then you all should go for dinner."

"Okay. So my guess is JC's gonna wanna throw big 'cause he's a hot dog and he also wants to show me up. He's got something to prove, so look for a lot of play action. Coach Morris loves screens, fakes...all that smoke-and-mirrors stuff. Plan for their defense to come at me at any and all times. I know their wide receiver Dale Carson likes to run to his right to catch a pass. If you break free of Andre Holbrook's tackle, he just kind of gives up—he's a diva and hates running hard—and you'll have a good chance to score."

"Sure you don't want to be a coach, Trick?" Jack O'Malley, our defensive head coach, joked.

"See me in six or seven years," I teased.

Coach Jackson clapped his hands. "All right, fellas. That's it. Dinner together, and you're on your own for the evening. I know it's Friday night, but stay out of the clubs. Be in your rooms by eleven—I'll be knockin'. See you tomorrow at breakfast, eight sharp, and we'll go for practice."

On the way to the hotel, Harte asked, "Wanna go out after dinner? Have a beer?"

I'd been getting vibes all day from Harte—interested ones, I believed—and I needed to stay friendly but distant. As well as we were getting along, I wasn't ready to reveal any part of my personal life.

"I can't. I'm meeting a friend. Sorry."

He shrugged. "No worries." We pulled into the hotel driveway and exited the bus. "I'm hungry. I hope the food is good."

They'd set up a buffet for us in one of the larger conference rooms, and I filled my plate and joined Rio, Troy, and Lincoln. They were talking about going out, and I mentioned Harte wanted to hang out.

"I'm going to visit a friend." I wiped my mouth and tossed the napkin. "See you in the morning."

"A friend. Is that what you're calling it now? Remember, Coach said bedtime was eleven, so get in and out quickly, my brother." Rio laughed and elbowed Troy.

"Very funny." But I smirked and flipped them off. I was anxious to get to Fallon. I'd had enough of being with my teammates all day. I needed some alone time with my guy.

In the car, I texted him I was on my way over, and he sent me his room number. At my first knock he opened the door. His hair was loose, and he stood barefoot. I stepped inside and reached for him, but he ducked me.

"Don't give those sexy eyes. I'm afraid I'll have to disappoint you."

"Why? What's wrong?"

"I have the stomach virus from hell. Something I ate for dinner must've done a number on me." Now that he mentioned it, he did look a little pale. A strange gurgling noise emanated from his midsection, and alarm rose in his eyes. "Oh, God. Here it goes again." He took off running, and I was about to follow him when I heard the door to the bathroom slam shut and his moans and groans.

"Think I'll stay right out here." I called room service. "Could you send up some tea with honey and toast?"

"Yes, sir."

Ten minutes later, I answered the door, and a young man walked in with a tray. "Here you go...oh." His eyes bugged out. "You're Patrick Sloane."

"Yeah. Thanks." I handed him two twenties.

"Yeah, wow, sure." He chewed his lip. "Would you mind..."

"Not at all." I stood, he took some selfies, and I signed the napkin for him. He left, and I shut the door and locked it.

White and shaky on his feet, Fallon emerged from the bedroom.

"What's that?"

"Tea and toast. I figured it might be good to settle your stomach." To my surprise, his eyes grew shiny, and I crossed the room in two long strides. "Fal, what's wrong? Are you really sick? Do you need me to call a doctor?"

He shook his head, his hair hiding his face. "No," he whispered. "Thank you for doing this for me."

"Come on and sit, and I'll pour the hot water. Maybe it's time someone looked after you, the way you're always solving everyone else's problems." I steered him toward the sofa and helped settle him with a pillow, then made his tea with a little honey. "Here. This is what my mother always gave me if I had a stomachache."

Fallon blew on it and took a sip before setting it on the coffee table. "My mother would send me to the doctor. As a child, I used to get sick every winter–that's one of the many reasons my father thought of me as weaker than Rory. He was stronger, better in school, played sports—that's how he met Dev—and all around the better son."

I'd read and heard the stories about families that showed favoritism for one child—lucky me for being an only—yet I couldn't conceive of loving one child more than another. As a child, I used to wish for a brother I could play with, but when I grew older, I appreciated the undivided attention from my parents. I'd only known unconditional love.

"You're a terrific person, and I'm sure you were a wonderful son. You don't need their approval anymore."

"I don't know why I feel like I still do."

That was something so deeply engrained in Fallon's psyche, and it left scars that even time could never heal. Fallon still suffered, and I felt powerless to help him.

He took another sip of his tea, his gaze frank and open. "You say I don't need my parents' approval, but you still want it from yours, which is why you've never told them you're bi, I think."

"Is that what you want? Me to come out?" Funny how the idea didn't seem as scary as it once had. Perhaps because I had someone by my side.

"No, I'd never force you to do that."

"Well, we don't have to think about it now. How're you feeling? Any better?"

Fallon nodded. "Much." His grin was wry. "Most likely because I have nothing left in my stomach."

"Have the toast. It'll help."

"I don't know..." He hesitated, and I joined him on the couch, where I picked up a piece of toast, buttered it lightly, and held it out to him.

"Eat."

His lips kicked up in a smile. "Come on, you don't have to do this."

"I know. I want to." I wiggled the toast. "Open up for me, or do I have to play airplane?" I swooped my hand holding the piece of bread. "*Zoom, zoom.* Coming in for a landing." I brought it to his lips, and this time he ate it, plus two other pieces.

"I feel better, thank you." He rested his head on my shoulder. "What time is it?"

I checked my watch. "Shit. It's ten thirty. I need to leave. Coach said to be at the hotel by eleven."

He kissed my neck. "I'll get dressed and ride down with you."

"Are you sure?"

"Yeah. The toast and tea helped, and I need to get out of this room." I could see his face had a bit more color. "I'll just put on a sweat shirt."

The night might not've turned out the way I wanted, but it was nice to simply relax with someone I felt comfortable with. Fallon returned, hair brushed, hanging loose around his neck, and I grinned.

"My sweat shirt?"

Red blossomed on his cheeks. "I grabbed it instead of mine when I packed. It's a little big."

I chuckled. "Yeah. You're a large, and I'm a 2X." I winked at him. "You look cute."

We left the suite and rode down in the elevator. Fallon pressed a kiss to my cheek. "Thanks for coming and making me feel better."

Eyeing the elevator panel, we still had ten floors to go before we hit the lobby. "How about something else to make you feel better?"

Back to the doors, he tipped his face up. "Whatcha got in mind, big guy?"

I leaned in for a kiss and cupped his ass. He tasted slightly sweet from the tea and salty from the butter. It was only meant to be a brief kiss but as usual, the moment my mouth touched his, all sense of time and place went straight to hell. I heard a sound and pushed Fallon off me.

"There he is. Patrick Sloane," I heard someone call out. "Hey, Patrick!"

With his back to the doors, Fallon froze, and my heart dropped. Over his shoulder, I spied people with their phones out filming me. Holding Fallon. That damn waiter must've told people I was here, and they were waiting for me. Instinctively, I thrust him behind me, shielding him from prying eyes.

*Shit.*

# CHAPTER SEVENTEEN

## Fallon

"Get out quick and distract them." I frantically wracked my brain for a way out of this mess. "I'm going to stay facing the wall. With my long hair and big sweat shirt, they'll think I'm a woman."

He met my eyes and nodded. Without another word, he strode off and engaged the crowd. I remained huddled in the corner while the people chased him.

"Trick, who is she?"

"Trick, can I have your autograph?"

Luckily, the doors closed before anyone transferred their attention to me, and I let out my breath in a *whoosh*. At my floor, I kept my head down and ran to my suite. Heart pounding, I locked the door behind me and leaned on it. My phone buzzed with a text, and seeing it was from Patrick, I closed my eyes for a second, imagining what he'd written.

*I can't do this anymore*, or, *Sorry, but I'm done.*

"You're an idiot," I stated out loud and opened the message.

*Are you ok? Sorry you had to go through that. Tomorrow is practice and an early night. I have your access set up for the suite on Sunday. I hate that we have to sneak around, but I'll see you at the game.*

This dream I'd had of Patrick telling me he was ready to come out was nothing if not foolish. He had everything to risk and nothing to gain. I wasn't ready to give him up, but I sensed this inevitability about what was to come, and darkness spread through me.

As a naïve kid, I'd always pictured the perfect boyfriend. He'd be sweet, kind, and thoughtful. An incredible lover. Close with his family and not afraid to show me affection in front of them. Patrick possessed all those qualities, except he couldn't come out.

**

I slept fitfully and wasn't completely rested upon awakening. One good thing was that my stomach bug had worked its way through, and deciding it made no sense for me to sit in my room all day, I gathered some things and headed to the beach. This was California, after all. If the sun, sand, and ocean couldn't cure my mood, nothing could.

The car dropped me off, and I picked a spot that wasn't near little kids running, kicking sand, or groups of teenagers blaring their music. I spread my blanket, sprayed on my sunscreen, and took a swig of my iced coffee. It was busy but not crowded, and I people-watched. A gay couple caught my eye—one man lovingly massaging lotion onto the other's back and shoulders. Their deep-brown skin, covered with tattoos, gleamed in the sun, and I spotted gold wedding bands on their hands. My guess was they hadn't been married for too long.

My phone rang, and I smiled. Speaking of married couples...

"Hey, Dev. What's up?"

"Me," he grumbled. "Way too fucking early. I hate traveling for these damn West Coast games."

I laughed, remembering how hard he'd bitched about them when he was playing. "Poor baby."

"Listen. What're you doing tonight? We're arriving this morning about eleven thirty, and though I'll proba-bly need a nap, let's meet for dinner and drinks."

No matter what would happen between Patrick and me, I knew I'd always have Dev and Brody in my corner.

"Sounds good. I won't be seeing Patrick since it's the day before the game."

"Yeah. Besides, it's Saturday. A day to relax."

Seagulls swooped and soared, and I squinted at the ocean. A few dolphins played far out among the waves.

"You know it. I'm at the beach."

"Good for you. Get that tan on. Okay. I'll text you the deets on when and where later on."

"Sounds like a plan. Can't wait to see you."

"Same, dude."

Cross-legged, I watched people swimming and boogie-boarding and drank my iced coffee. The couple next to me held hands and jumped the waves, the water glistening off their bodies. They stopped on the shoreline and kissed, hands at each other's waists. It made me miss Patrick even more. I sighed.

*You are so fucked.*

As I continued to watch the couple loving it up, touching and kissing in between each crash of the waves around them, I had to admit what I'd been trying to deny for a while. Against my better judgment, I'd fallen in love with Patrick. It might've started with sex, but when he'd come and taken care of me, not pressing me for anything more than comfort and companionship, it had further cemented what had been swirling in my head and heart.

I loved Patrick, but I needed to let him go.

The sun dipped, and I shivered. Three thirty. Time to return to the hotel. I gathered my things and called for a car. Once in the back seat, I checked my messages and saw Dev had set up dinner for six o'clock at a steak house not far from my hotel.

I showered and changed and left for the restaurant. I arrived at six exactly and laughed to myself that Dev and Brody weren't there yet. Forty minutes later they appeared and I wagged my finger at them.

"See? This is why you still need an assistant. You wouldn't be so late."

Dev's smile was quick and didn't reach his eyes, and my heart began to pound. "What's wrong?"

"Let's sit. I need a drink."

Considering Dev wasn't much of a drinker, I grew more concerned, and Brody's stoic face didn't help. The server approached us, gushed over Dev and Brody, and took our orders. Dev ordered whiskey, and Brody a beer, like me.

"The day at the beach did wonders. Last night I got laid low by a stomach virus. The absolute worst."

Dev drummed his fingers on the table. "A stomach virus? From what?"

"I dunno, but I don't want a repeat. Glad it only lasted a day."

"So you didn't go out last night?"

I wet my lips, wondering what the hell was going on. "No, I stayed in my room. Why are you asking?"

Our orders came, and though Dev had stated he needed the drink, he merely held the tumbler. We sat in silence for a minute, and then Dev pushed the glass aside and leaned in close.

"You know I love you. But I need you to tell me the truth."

My brows drew together, and I laughed. "Okay, I love you too. What's going on? Of course I'm going to tell you the truth. I always have. The truth about what?"

He huffed out a breath and pulled out his phone, scrolling for a second before stopping on a picture. He handed me the phone, and my stomach went into free fall. It was a picture of Patrick from the elevator. His hands were on my ass, and it was obvious he was kissing me. I met Dev's eyes.

"Why are you showing me a picture of Patrick kissing some girl?"

His eyes narrowed. "So you're saying that's not you? Because that sure as hell looks like the back of your head and your beautiful blond hair."

I folded my arms. "Right, Dev. Because in Southern California there are no women with shoulder-length blond hair." Our gazes clashed. As much as I hated lying to Dev, I couldn't out Patrick. "And why are you getting photos of Patrick? That's so creepy—someone taking pictures of him."

"He's a celebrity, and his former girlfriend was on the cover of the last swimsuit edition of *Sports Beautiful*. Patrick has always surrounded himself with beautiful women—his ex-wives were both top models for that famous underwear chain. Someone probably got a tip he was at a hotel and waited to see whom he was with. This was on some local gossip site, but you know how it goes—things can blow up and become big in the blink of an eye."

Brody finally spoke. "We're concerned only because we don't want to see you taken advantage of."

Irritated, I took a swig of my beer. "Last I checked, I was over thirty years old and living on my own since I went to college. I think I can take care of myself."

"I know, but—"

"No, Dev," I snapped. "No buts. There's nothing going on, and I resent you trying to get me to say there is. Did you invite me to dinner to interrogate me or to catch up? Because if it's the former, I'm leaving."

"All right, all right. Stop being so touchy. It's only because if you *are* in a relationship, I want it to be healthy and with someone who can acknowledge the special man you are." He took a sip of his drink and grimaced. "*Ugh*. Why did I order this? I hate whiskey."

Despite my annoyance, my lips twitched. "I guess that's your serious-lecture drink. And I know you're concerned, but I'm fine. You have to stop thinking of me as that helpless little kid who had no place to go. I'm an adult, and I make my own choices, and whether they're good or bad in your opinion is just that. Your opinion." Seeing him readying to open his mouth, I put up my hand. "But that doesn't mean what you think. I work for Patrick, and his personal life is private."

It physically hurt to deny my feelings for Patrick, but I'd have to get used to it. This conversation with Dev and Brody proved it. No way could Patrick make this work without ramifications from all sides, and I'd never be the one to jeopardize his livelihood.

Skeptical still, Dev's shrewd eyes studied me. "I still think you're not telling me the whole story, but I won't get into an argument. Let's order dinner."

"Good. Because I'm hungry," I stated. "And I want a steak."

It ended up being a nice evening, and I caught up on Dev and Brody's charity work and the summer football camp they'd started in Brody's hometown.

"How's my ex, Kelsie, doing?" Dev laughed as he finished his coffee. "I heard they're expecting a baby?" My cousin Kelsie had once played the part of Dev's girl of the moment to throw an overcurious teammate off the scent of gossip.

"Yep. In January." Kelsie had married one of their old teammates and moved to North Carolina to be close to his family. When it came to lousy parenting, my uncle was no different from my father and wanted nothing to do with Kelsie once she'd married a Black man. Marlon's parents welcomed her with open arms, especially now that they were going to be grandparents.

"I'm happy for her."

"So am I. She wanted a family really badly."

Brody handed his credit card to the server. "We all do. Sometimes we have to work harder at it to make it happen."

We waited outside for our cars, and Dev put his arm around me. "I miss you. Don't be such a stranger. Let's try and do dinner at least once a month at home."

My eyes burned. "I'd like that."

Being with the two of them again brought me back to the years they'd spent hiding who they were for the sake of their career. A decade of their lives spent in the shadows. If Patrick and I did make it, that would be us—maybe a little simpler because I worked for him, and as his assistant, I'd have easier access to him. But I wasn't sure I could handle the stress of hiding my emotions. One slip, like last night, and it would all come crashing down.

My car pulled up, but Dev held on to me. "If anything is bothering you, please come to us. We'd never judge you. I know you tend to keep everything inside, but at some point you have to let it out."

I forced a smile. "You're so dramatic. Thanks for dinner, and I'll see you soon." I got into my car and saw a text from Patrick.

*Hope you're feeling better. Don't worry about the picture. Everyone thinks I hooked up with some hot blond. They're right.*

I couldn't help laughing at the winky emoji.

*Went to the beach and had dinner with Dev and Brody. They said someone sent them the picture. Dev thought it was me and asked if we were together. I told him no.*

My phone rang. "He really asked you that? Why would he think I was with a guy?"

"He said he recognized my hair, but I brushed him off. Don't worry about it."

"I'm not. It's just weird that he immediately suspected you." Patrick's voice dropped to a sexy growl. "I wish you were here with me."

I sidestepped that. "Did you have a good practice? Ready to face your old teammates?"

"Yeah. I'm looking forward to it, but not as much as the few days after. The bye week couldn't have come at a better time. I've got a place set up where no one will bother us."

It all sounded wonderful. Perfect. If only…

"First get that win."

"Are you sure you're all right? Dev didn't say anything to upset you, did he?"

"No. I'm good. Just getting to the hotel. Gonna get into bed."

"See you tomorrow. Night."

"Night."

In my room, I showered and packed, then opened my laptop and changed my reservation. I could get a red-eye leaving later that night at eleven thirty. I hesitated only a moment, knowing how upset Patrick would be, but I was doing this because it was the best for both of us. Because I loved him. That close call had brought it all into perspective. He'd understand when he stopped being angry with me.

I checked out on the television, grabbed my bags, called for a car, and headed to the airport. I might be going home, but I had no idea what the future held.

# CHAPTER EIGHTEEN

## Patrick

I'd expected my former teammates to come after me and prepared for it, but this was next level. Every defensive player was on the attack, and it seemed they didn't care about a flag on the play. They wanted a piece of my ass. But I met each of them with equal ferocity, and by the end of the game—which we won in a blowout, 35-3—I was beaten up and ready for a massage, a hot bath, and most of all, Fallon.

First, though, I had to do a few interviews, and Dev and Brody were my broadcasters of choice. Brody caught me first.

"Tough game out there, but looks like you showed them who's boss."

"Yeah. We came to win, and I think we showed that we're on track for the postseason."

"Looks like it to me. You made some good throws, especially to your favorite receivers, Rio Durant and Troy Watkins. You clicked right away on the field after you came to the Kings."

"Yeah, we've gotten into a good groove, but it's a team effort and everyone contributes."

"Thanks, Patrick."

"You got it."

Dev was waiting with the microphone. "Well, Trick, you certainly lived up to your name. You came with a bag full of them today. Massive win against your former team. Did you feel like you had anything to prove?"

"I don't know about that, but I did want to have a good showing. I love the fans here in San Diego, and it was great getting to play in front of them again."

"I'm sure. And you've certainly gained lots of Kings fans as well. What're you looking forward to? You play the West Virginia Wildcats next, don't you? That's a division rival."

"Yeah, and it's been a couple of years since I've played them. They're tough—their quarterback is quick, and they have a young, strong offensive line. It'll be a tough battle for sure."

"Thanks, Patrick, and enjoy the bye week."

"You know it." Dev shut off his mic, and it was several yards before I realized he was following me. I waited until we passed the crush of reporters and players and stopped. "What's up, Dev? Did you want to talk?" I was curious if he'd bring up the picture.

"We had dinner with Fallon yesterday."

"That's nice."

His eyes narrowed. "I'm gonna put it right out there. Fallon is like my little brother. He's had it shitty his whole life, and I've always tried to watch out for him."

I wasn't about to take his bait. "I'm glad he has a good friend."

"I don't know what game you're playing, but whatever it is, don't. Not with Fallon."

Nose to nose, I glared at him. "I don't play games on or off the field. I don't know what the fuck you're getting at, so I'm done talking." With those words, I walked away, and this time he didn't follow.

It didn't feel good to lie to Dev—he was my friend, but more importantly, it ate at me that I had to keep denying my relationship with Fallon. He was worth more than hidden elevator kisses and secret hideaways.

In the locker room, Rio patted my shoulder. "Yo, Trick. Those bastards really came after you. I'm glad we buried their asses."

Since that first time I'd set the tone about shit-talking, things had settled down somewhat in the locker room. The blow-by-blow of Rio's sex life often had me cringing, but I kept out of it. He was a beast on the field, and that was what mattered. In this game alone, he'd run for over two hundred yards and made two touchdown catches.

"Thanks, man. Yeah, they had it in for me, but you were like the wind, blowing past their tackles."

Milo chuckled. "They didn't know what hit them."

"Candyman, you were cool as ice even being double-teamed every damn time. How many catches? Seven?" They knocked their fists together.

This was what I loved about the game—the camaraderie and single-minded focus on getting the job done. Who someone had in their bed in the evening shouldn't have any bearing on how he played the game. Listening to Rio and Milo praise their glory on the field, I couldn't help wondering if they'd turn on me if I came out as bisexual. The endorsements and money didn't mean shit to me—I had enough invested to last me a lifetime, and if a company dumped me for loving a man, did I really want my name on their product?

It was something I contemplated on the ride to the hotel, getting so lost in my head, Rio had to nudge my shoulder twice to leave the bus when we arrived.

"Dude, what's goin' on? You're all spaced out."

I blinked to come out of my brain fog. "Nah, just thinkin'. Can't wait for the bye week and some time in the sun. What're you doin'?"

"Gonna go see my mama. Gonna get me some home cooking." We walked off the bus together. "You gonna hook up with your blond hottie again?"

My gut twisted, and my lips thinned. "Damn, a guy can't even take a piss without it being news. Nothing's going on."

Rio's grin was all sorts of wicked. "*Mmmhmm.*"

"Go on, get outta here." I sought to lighten the mood and gave him a friendly shove.

"Nah, c'mon. Help a fella out. See if she's got a friend." Figuring Rio wasn't about to let it go, I shrugged.

"Sure. I'll let you know, but don't count on it."

In my room, I texted Fallon to let him know I was coming over, then spoke to my parents.

"Hey, Mom."

"Patrick. What a great game. They didn't hit you too hard, did they?"

Even at my age, she was always worried about me taking care of myself. "Thanks, and yeah, don't worry. I'm fine. We're happy with the win. How's Dad?"

"Good. Just finished cleaning up from dinner. Have you eaten yet?"

"Not yet. We just got back. I'm gonna get something now, so I wanted to check in with you first before I left."

"That's sweet. You have a nice dinner and say hi to Fallon. I hope you're not working him too hard."

With any luck, his magic mouth would be working on me in a matter of hours. "No, he's good. I'd better go. I'll call you in a few days. Love you."

"Love you too."

I slid the phone into my pocket and hurried out of the room, hoping I wouldn't meet anyone else to delay my escape. I caught sight of Milo and his wife in the restaurant, having a drink together, and a pang of longing hit me to be able to do the same—sit with the person I cared about and have a simple drink.

In the car, I checked my texts but didn't see any response from Fallon. Probably sleeping. Preparing for our night together. I grinned, anticipation thrumming through my veins.

I entered the hotel, and several people recognized me. Of course I had to take pictures and sign autographs, which took close to half an hour, until I begged off.

"Guys, it's been great, but I have to meet my assistant. Poor guy's been waiting for me, and he's gonna get on my case for making him wait. Take care." I took the elevator up to Fallon's suite and knocked. The door opened, and a woman about my mother's age answered.

"May I help you?" She seemed confused and a bit wary.

"Uh, I thought this was someone else's room. I'm sorry to have bothered you."

"That's all right. I just checked in. Perhaps they were here before me."

I forced a smile. "Yeah. Thanks. I apologize." She closed the door, and I checked my phone, which remained quiet. Worry trickled through me, and on the way down I sent Fallon another text.

*Where are you? I'm at the hotel.*

In the lobby again, I waited to speak to someone from reception. A clerk with the name tag *Gustavo* pinned to his navy-blue suit greeted me.

"Mr. Sloane, welcome. How can we help you?"

"I'm trying to locate my assistant, Fallon McKenzie. He was in room 1102, but I just went up, and a lady was in that room."

"Let me check." His fingers clicked over the keyboard. "Ah. Yes, I see that Mr. McKenzie checked out around nine o'clock last night."

I blinked at him, uncertain I heard him correctly. "What? He checked out?"

"Yes, sir. Is there anything else I can help you with?"

"No, thanks." A bit dazed at the news, I wandered away to sit on a chair. Fallon had left without telling me. *What the fuck?* I pulled out my phone, and this time I called him.

"Hi." He sounded quiet and wary.

"Fal, what the hell is going on? Where are you?"

"Home."

I stared at the phone screen then put it back to my ear. "What? Like, New York, home? Why? Did some-thing happen? Are you all right?"

"I'm fine. But after what happened with the picture and everything, I got to thinking that it wasn't fair to put you through all that."

"All that? What the fuck does that mean, all that?" I hadn't realized I was raising my voice until I caught several people eyeing me, one even filming my conversation. "Listen. I'm coming back, and we'll talk."

"No, don't. I'm happy to keep working with you until you find another PA, but I can't do this anymore."

"Do what? Fal, please."

"Bye, Patrick."

The call ended, leaving me frustrated and furious, but being in a public place, I had to keep my cool. I called for a car, and on the way to the hotel, got a plane ticket home. I quickly packed my things and got to the airport, breezing through security and boarding the plane with minutes to spare. Panic welled in my chest at the thought of losing Fallon. It choked me. I couldn't imagine not having him with me, by my side. Us. Together. The way I looked forward to seeing his face every morning on the pillow next to mine. How he lay tucked into my side while we slept, as if he knew I'd always be there to protect him. I loved his hair in my face and his breath against my cheek. His sweet, sleepy smile and the fierce possessiveness of his grip when we made love.

He and I, we had unfinished business, and when I got home, we were damn well going to talk.

**

Eight a.m. might have been too early, but I didn't care. I went straight from the airport to Fallon's apartment. I couldn't get to him without being buzzed in by someone, and on a hunch, I buzzed Josh the dog walker, hoping he'd be home. Luck was with me because a moment later his voice came through the tin box.

"Yeah?"

"Josh, my man, it's Patrick Sloane again. Can you buzz me in?"

"What? No shit? Yeah, sure."

I pushed the door, and Josh stood in his doorway, pants on and shirt untucked, tie slung around the collar. Obviously getting ready for work. His dog circled between his legs, then sat. "Thanks, buddy. I hope you got those tickets and enjoyed the game."

"Hell to the yeah. Right on the fifty-yard line? It was sick. My buddy and I had a blast. Thanks so much."

"For all your trouble, I'll make sure to have my PA hook you up whenever we're home. For postseason, too."

"Are you kidding me?" His eyes bugged out. "Damn. Wow. Thanks so much. That's so cool."

"No problem." I started climbing the stairs.

"Who's your friend living here?" Josh called out. "I can tell you if he's home."

"Uh, Fallon McKenzie. He's my personal assistant."

The dog barked, and Josh shushed him. "Oh, the blond guy on the third floor? I saw him come in."

Eager to get away, I raised my hand. "Great. I should ask him for a key." Not wanting to get caught up in conversation, I took the stairs two at a time and stood in front of Fallon's door, my nerves making it hard to catch my breath.

I knocked twice before I heard footsteps. The door opened with him grumbling, "I hate when people just let anyone in. Oh...shit. Patrick. What the hell." He tried to close the door, but I stuck my size thirteen foot in it and pushed.

"Yeah, me. Let's talk."

"There's nothing to say," he responded with a mulish thrust of that stubborn jaw.

"Says you."

"Yeah, I think that's how it goes." He gave me his back and walked away, but I slammed the door shut and followed him, which didn't take long, considering how tiny his place was. At the window, he faced me with a grim expression.

"You shouldn't have come."

"I disagree." I reached out to touch him, but he shook his head, and my hand fell away. This couldn't be solved with a kiss. "Talk to me. What made you run away?" I thought for a second. "It was Dev, wasn't it? You freaked out after dinner with them. Did he say something? What didn't you tell me?"

"Nothing." He held up his hands, then let them fall. "Don't you see how this was never going to end well? That near miss in the elevator woke me up to how impossible us being together was from the start. Just getting to the postseason means every step you take will be scrutinized, and if you win the Super Bowl, it's ten time worse. You have no idea the hoops I jumped through for Dev and Brody so they could have their privacy."

"But they stuck it out. Together. They're the ulti-mate goal—a couple who fought hard and won their right to be happy."

"Of course." He stared at me as if I'd said something outrageous. "They love each other. They deserve to be happy."

"Doesn't everyone?"

Nonplussed, he stammered. "I guess...I mean, yeah, but—"

"No buts, Fal. You're still stuck under a mountain of uncertainty left by your parents' miserable treatment of you. I know it's hard to let go, but you're strong, smart, and independent. A wonderful person who deserves only good things. You have friends who care about you. Love you. Me included." The words tumbled out, momentous and shocking.

Pale-faced and trembling, Fallon hung his head. "You don't mean that."

"The hell I don't." I grabbed his arm and hauled him to me. "Since that first time in California, you've never really left me. Those months were the best times of my life. I'm beginning to understand that it was the only part of my life where I was able to be free. To be myself."

"We never had a chance—still don't. You're in the public eye, playing a sport that's the most macho of them all. There's no place for me. Why can't you see that?"

"I do see it." I smoothed his hair off his face, its silky strands reminding me of the endless Kansas wheat fields, the golden heads nodding in the breeze. "But who says I have to accept it?"

"Be-because you're...you. Trick Sloane, star quarterback and heading to the Super Bowl."

"And?" With Fallon back in my orbit, the disquiet in my chest settled, which reenforced what I'd suspected. "That's an awful lot of pressure on me. I'm going to need the people I care about most in the world to be by my side."

Lips close, our breaths mingled, but Fallon still radiated fear. "You have your parents. They love you and will always be there for you."

I caught him by the nape. "What about you?"

"Me?"

I was beyond caring and ran my nose down his cheek, feeling his full-body shudder at my touch. "You. Are you going to be there for me?"

"I don't think—"

"Yeah, you do. Too much. That's your problem. You're turning what we have into a negative when it's everything positive."

With surprising force, Fallon twisted out of my grasp. "Goddammit, Patrick, can't you see I'm trying to protect you? You'll lose it all. Everything you worked so hard for all your life. You do this now, and you might not even get to play in the Super Bowl if the Kings make it. Is that what you want? To have that dream turn into a nightmare?"

"I'm trying to do what's right for me. And that's you."

A tear fell from his eye. "And I'm trying to do what I think is best for your career. I can't let you lose everything." He squared his shoulders. "You're better off without me."

Time to make the biggest play of my life, something not even a Super Bowl touchdown could eclipse. If I didn't have by my side the one person who made my heart happy, all the glory meant nothing in the end. Because when the dust settled and the cameras were gone, it would be me standing alone. My name merely an entry in a record book. No one to laugh with. No one to touch at night.

And I didn't want that.

"I'm only good when I have you with me. You're everything important in my life." I grabbed him again, capturing his gaze. "I've never said this before, knowing the full weight of its meaning. I love you, Fallon, and we will make this work. Just tell me you love me too."

Crystal blue eyes bright with tears met mine. "You're not being fair," he complained, blinking furiously.

I allowed myself a smile. "I already told you, when it comes to you, I'm not interested in fairness. I'm here to win."

"How can you? How do you think you can be with me and play pro ball?"

The more questions he asked, the better, as he'd stopped being negative. "I don't know," I replied honestly but hopeful. "But I'm not going to wait as long as Dev and Brody. It's not fair to make you hide."

He lifted his chin. "Maybe I-I'm willing to."

"I'm not," I growled, exasperated. "This lasts until the Super Bowl. After that, I'm coming out."

"Patrick," Fallon began, but I cut him off with a kiss.

He hesitated only a moment, then met my mouth with a hunger I hadn't yet seen. We virtually ripped the clothes off our bodies, and I tossed him onto the bed, jumping on top of him, claiming his mouth.

"I want you. All of you. Your heart as well as your body. Say it. Say you love me."

"Yes," he moaned. "I love you. I've always loved you."

Joy surged through me, and I cupped his face. "We're going to make this work. I can't lose you now."

Our tongues played and danced. Fallon's cheeks flushed red, his golden hair spread on the sheets, body hard and anxious beneath me. His harsh breath drove every thought from my mind aside from the need to possess. Take. Slightly unsteady, my hands glided over his naked body, tracing the swell of muscle and the hardness of bone. The rough hair of his thighs rasped against mine, and my heart thundered, causing my vision to blur.

I grabbed the lube from the end table and poured some on my fingers. I pierced his hole with my thumb and moved in and out, preparing him for me.

"Oh God, more," he begged. "Everything. Fuck me raw. Hard. I need it now. Please."

I slathered my dick with the lube and inched inside him. Hot muscled walls throbbed and clenched around my aching dick. "Fallon," I groaned. "I can't stop."

"Don't. I need you. Want you so bad."

He writhed on my cock, and I tried to take it slow, but Fallon locked his ankles round my waist, and I drove in deep. Again and again.

"More, Patrick. I need it all...every inch of you in me."

I was lost, a pulsing, quivering ball of need that could only be sated by the man under me. Fallon was in his own world, eyes squeezed shut, stroking his leaking cock with short tugs. His mouth fell open, and I knew he was ready. I increased my thrusts, hips snapping until I fell apart and came. We lay holding each other for who knew how long. I slipped out, but made no move to leave, and he held me tight, lips pressed to my shoulder.

"I've never gotten carried away like that. Outside of my marriages, I've never had sex without a condom," I murmured. "If you're worried–"

"I'm not," Fallon cut me off with a shake of his head, his hair stuck to his cheeks, dark with sweat. "I know I'm safe with you."

I slung my arm around Fallon and pulled him close. "You always will be. I promise. You'll see."

# CHAPTER NINETEEN

## Fallon

At some point we'd gotten under the covers, and when we woke, Patrick was spooning me, his large body molded to mine. The sun had crossed the sky from the morning to noon. I sighed and shifted, but Patrick held me firm.

"Still worrying?" he rumbled against my nape. He pushed my hair away and began to press kisses to my neck and shoulder.

"It's my job. Professional worrier. I have to think about your public face." I scooted away, knowing if he continued, we'd end up having sex again, but my organizational brain needed to work through all the obstacles first. "How do you plan to handle this?" At his snicker, I rolled my eyes. "Not funny, Patrick. I'm trying to be serious and figure us out."

Propped up by a few pillows, Patrick folded his arms behind his head. "Far as I'm concerned, there's nothing to figure out. We're together, and that's it. As I said, we'll wait until the season is over, and then I'll make the announcement." As if sensing I'd have something to say, he put out a hand. "Hear me out. I'd tell everyone right now, but we're in the middle of a run at the postseason, and I want all the attention on that. Not me and my love life, because you know if I do say something, after that, no one's going to be interested in anything I do on the field. I think that's only fair to my teammates."

"I agree."

Those generous lips kicked up in a grin. "See? We're already in sync."

"About that, at least." I tied my hair back. "So we'll go on as we have been and revisit this after the Super Bowl."

He swung his legs off the sofa bed. "Yeah. Except one thing has to change." With a pained expression, he rose to his feet and stretched, giving me a chance to admire—okay, ogle—his muscled torso. Damn, he was so incredibly fine. I had to look away before I jumped him. I retreated to the kitchen area to get a cold glass of water.

"What's that?" I asked, cracking out ice cubes from the tray.

"You can't live in this shithole anymore. Come stay with me."

My snort at that sent me into a choking fit of laughter. "Didn't we just have a conversation about waiting to tell people? If I move into your place, that's gonna be somewhat conspicuous, don't you think?"

"You're my PA. I'm sure it wouldn't raise any suspicions."

His nonchalance made me want to bonk him over the head. "Patrick. What the hell excuse would we have to come up with to make that sound plausible? Why would I need to move in with you?"

His brow furrowed in thought, and I couldn't believe I was sitting there waiting for him to answer me, instead of telling him it was wishful thinking and to forget about it.

"Say you have mold and the landlord is taking forever to fix the problem, and you can't live here because it's a mess. Instead of me putting you up in a hotel, you're staying in my second bedroom." He shrugged and grinned. "See? Problem solved. Now come here."

"Not so fast, big guy." In theory, his idea wasn't the worst, but there were so many ways it could go wrong, the least of which was that damn picture. "Don't you think the gossips will be all over the fact that you were caught kissing some blond in an elevator, and then all of a sudden I'm there in your apartment, a long-haired blond guy? Something tells me they can put two and two together."

A puzzled expression settled on his face. "Why would you be doing anything different now than you have been? We won't start going out holding hands or kissing in public." He paused. "Yet."

"I hate when your arguments make sense," I grumbled, and he snickered and caught me around the waist.

"Everything I say makes sense." He kissed my neck. "Say it again."

"What? That you were right? It happens occasionally," I teased, growing weaker by the second as his lips skimmed across my cheek.

"No. You know." He caught my mouth in a hungry, possessive kiss. "Tell me, please."

It left me breathless that this big, tough guy, so feared on the field by his peers, was standing in my crummy little kitchen, begging for three little words.

"I love you. I fell in love with you all those years ago, but I told myself it could never work because of who you are."

"And I promise you, nothing—not football or anything else—will stop us from being together. Not now. We're getting our chance, and this time we'll go the distance."

I let him drag me off to the bed, but in the back of my mind I had a feeling nothing would be as easy as he believed.

**

I sent Patrick home after lunch, claiming I needed time to sort through what to pack and what to leave. Frowning, he leaned against the door.

"Leave it all. Whatever you need, you can buy once you get to my place."

I chuckled. "Oh, the lifestyles of the rich and oblivious. With what money do you suggest I purchase an entire new wardrobe and still have funds for living?"

"Fuck that. I can afford whatever you need, ten times over."

Having grown up with money, then losing it all, I'd had to learn the value of a dollar. Patrick, who didn't come from money, no longer needed to worry about how much things cost, but he'd better learn quickly that the macho attitude of him paying for everything wasn't going to fly with me.

"I'm sure you can. And I appreciate your offer, but it's not happening. I refuse to let you pay for my things. I still have to figure out how we're going to work out this situation."

"What situation?"

*Better to have this talk now than later*, I thought as I zipped up a duffel bag. "Look. I'm not gonna move in and live off you. And before you start yelling about how much money you have and all that jazz—which I already know—I have a salary, and that's it. Period. I also have a lease here, and I'm not giving it up. So when I come tonight, we'll sit down and figure out how much I'll contribute to household expenses."

"Spreadsheet king," he grumbled. "I swear you get off on all those charts."

"Part of my charm. It's what you hired me for, remember?"

"Okay, okay. We'll work it out. I promise." He arched a dark brow. "And yeah, it was. You being hot as fuck was a bonus."

My face grew warm, and I raised my gaze to the ceiling. "God help me." I pointed. "Out. I have stuff to finish. And your lawyer called. He wants a meeting. He knows it's the bye week."

"Yeah, yeah. We've never met in person, only on video. With these new endorsements I signed once I moved to New York City, and more coming in all the time, he wants to go through them, plus foreign ones as well." He paused and narrowed his eyes.

"What? I can see you're thinking about something."

"I want to tell him about us. And before you object, he can help us deal with media and get NDAs in place, things like that."

"I'm not sure that's a good idea."

"He's my attorney, Fal. There's attorney-client privilege."

"I guess. And in the same vein...I'd like to be able to talk to Dev about us. I don't keep things from him, and this is something no one else has insight into like him and Brody. Would it be okay if I spoke with him?"

Fear and doubt played in Patrick's beautiful, blue-green eyes. "He's gonna be really angry with me."

"Until I explain everything, yeah, probably. And if you say no, I won't. You should have a say in when you come out and to whom." I bit my lip. "But Dev...he's the only one who's always been there for me. He saved my life. And I know he blusters, but it's because he loves me and wants me to be happy. I think he'll come around once he knows the whole story of how we first met." I couldn't help grinning. "After all, if he hadn't given me that membership, you and I would've never met."

Patrick pulled me close. "Don't even say it." He rested his chin on my head, and it was times like this that I was reminded just how big he was. "All right. Maybe it's better if I'm not there when you tell him. That way, by the time I see him, he'll have calmed down." With his lips buried in my hair, he murmured, "I'd better go. I haven't even been home since my plane landed. But I'll see you later, right?"

I nodded. "Yeah."

With one final kiss, he left, sucking all the energy out of the room. Patrick was such a presence that no matter where he went, he drew attention. If we were going to keep our relationship quiet, we'd have to be careful. I reached for my phone.

"Dev? You busy?"

"Never for you. What's up?"

"Can we talk?"

"Okay," he said, sounding guarded. "Everything okay?"

"Yeah. Can I come over?"

"Of course. I'm here all day, catching up on stuff. Brody's got a doctor's appointment, but he should be back soon. Come when you want."

I was glad to hear that, as Brody would be able to keep Dev calm when I broke the news about Patrick and me.

"Be there soon."

Showered and dressed, I left my apartment for the five-minute walk to Dev and Brody's place. After all the years I'd worked for Dev, the doorman greeted me and let me up without announcing me.

Dev opened the door, his face wary. "That was quick."

"I do live in the neighborhood, you know," I joked. "It's not a far walk."

"Let's sit in the living room. Do you want a drink?"

*A bottle of tequila would help right now...*

"No, I'm good."

We sat facing each other on the couch, and I tried to ease the obvious tension. "You look like you had a good time in San Diego. Did you and Brody get to go to the beach at all?"

"No. We came right home after we wrapped up our network obligations. Not to be rude or anything, but can we discuss what you came here for?" My heart hiccupped at his steady gaze. "What advice do you need?"

The door opened, and Brody walked in. Seeing me sitting there, his face brightened. "Fal, great to see you again. How's it goin'?" His soft, Southern lilt played in direct contrast to Dev's steel-edged rumble.

"Fallon called and asked to come by for some advice. We were just getting to that part when you walked in. All good, by the way?"

Brody joined us and kissed Dev on the cheek before taking the chair across from us. They were way too big to share the couch with me there as well.

"Fine and dandy." He and Dev smiled into each other's eyes, and it made me realize...what the hell was I so worried for? If Patrick and I could have this, it was worth whatever storm might blow my way. At the end of it all, I knew that Dev, who loved me, would only want me to be happy.

"Getting back to you"–Dev refocused on me–"what's going on? Are you okay? That's my only concern."

"I'm fine. There's no need to worry about me. I just...I need to tell someone, and there's no one else I can share this with who'd understand. At least, I hope you will."

Dev's lips pressed together, and he nodded. "Go ahead."

"I think you already know, don't you? Patrick and I...we're together."

Dev smacked his large hand on his thigh. "I knew it. I told Brody, Fallon is lying to us. That picture was you, wasn't it?"

"Yeah." I raised my chin.

"Dammit, Fal. Of all the people to let yourself get seduced by...Patrick Sloane? He's too busy to go out and find a woman, so he set his sights on the easiest target? I swear I'm gonna—"

Time for me to shut this down. "Dev, listen for a minute. Patrick's bi."

"Is that what he told you?" he growled. "He'll say anything."

I wouldn't take the bait because I knew it was coming from a place of caring. "Dev. Please. You have to listen to me, because it's not what you think. Patrick didn't seduce me. As a matter of fact, we're together because of you."

"Yeah, and I shouldn't have asked him to hire you. I should've kept you on like you wanted me to."

"Dev," Brody interrupted, "I'm thinkin' Fallon has more to say. How 'bout you let him?"

*Thank God for Brody's calm presence.* I sent him a grateful smile.

Always the more emotional of the two, Dev huffed out a breath. "Fine. Go ahead."

"Do you remember when I turned twenty-one, and you gave me a membership to Intensity in LA?"

In addition to being a star football player, Dev was also one of the smartest people I'd ever met. It took less than five seconds for the information to click in his brain.

"You met Patrick at Intensity? Both of you went to school out West...son of a bitch. But wait...identities are hidden. Don't members have to wear masks?"

"Yeah. And for the almost six months we were together, I didn't know who he was. We were very close, talked about everything...I know it sounds unbelievable, but I was in love with him even though I didn't know who he was. One time...after...when I woke up before him, his mask had slipped off, and I recognized him. Knowing it was impossible for him to be a pro-football player and be in a relationship with a man, I ran away. And seeing how you and Brody suffered all those years, I knew I made the right choice."

"For him," Brody said softly, shooting an arrow through my heart. "But what about you?"

"Fallon." Stricken, Dev turned pale under his dark stubble, and next thing I knew, he was hugging me. "I am so damn sorry."

"I tried to forget him, and I kind of did—to the extent that I wasn't pining away whenever his name came up on a Sunday. Plus, I figured he'd forgotten about me. After all, he'd married twice and hadn't exactly kept his name out of the gossip magazines with his swimsuit model girlfriends."

"And then he turned up in the city, and I forced you to go work for him. Fal, I'm sorry. I didn't know." His big arms tightened around me, and much as I loved Dev, I didn't want cracked ribs.

"Ouch, Dev. Let go." I pushed him away. "And no one forced me. Remember, he had no idea who I was. But we both showed up at Intensity here in the city and...-surprise!" I faced him with a wry smile. "We found each other again. But this time I couldn't let it go."

"Whoa." Dev's eyes blew wide. "Wait a minute. Is that who you were talking about that time we had lunch? The guy you once knew...so you ended up telling him after that?"

It was a relief to finally be able to talk about it. "Not at that time, but yeah. And things have been really good, until that picture. And I freaked and ran because I refused to let Patrick jeopardize his career for me."

"It's his life too, you know," Brody pointed out. "From everything you've said, I'm gathering this is more than a fling."

"Ten years ago, it started out as just sex. We were each other's firsts. But then we began to see each other steadily, two or three times a week, for months, and it became way more than that. We were each other's anchors in the storm of life's uncertainties. He wasn't sure who would draft him, and I was still unsure what to do with my life. We shared our dreams and hopes. Everything." My words ended on a quiver, yet strength flowed through my blood saying the words out loud.

Brody met Dev's eyes. "You remember how it was when we realized we loved each other."

For the first time, Dev smiled. "Like there was no one else in the world."

And from their tender expressions, nothing had changed. Dev and Brody had loved each other for so long. They were the gold standard I measured relationships against.

"So you understand. Seeing Patrick again now...it was like we picked up where we left off." I met Brody's blue eyes, then Dev's green ones, both wet with unshed tears. My vision turned blurry as well. "I love him. And he loves me. Somehow, we'll try and make it work and be together."

# CHAPTER TWENTY

Patrick

"C'mon, Ethan. Have a drink. It's five o'clock somewhere." Without waiting for an answer, I poured him a hefty slug in a tumbler and added ice. "I'll join you."

Laughing, he accepted the Scotch. "I see you're enjoying the bye week."

I lifted my glass. "Cheers."

"*L'chaim.*" He took a healthy swallow, and then his sharp, light-blue eyes traveled around the space. "Nice place. Two or three bedrooms? I can't remember even though I scanned the mortgage documents only a month or so ago."

"Two bedrooms with an office. I like my space, and I need a place for my parents when they come visit." I felt a little guilty not flying to see them during my week off, but I couldn't leave Fallon. Maybe we could take a quick flight over. I should really tell them sooner rather than later.

"And you're happy with the contracts we negotiated? All the extras for postseason appearances?" A line bisected Ethan's smooth brow. "Or are you having an issue with one of your endorsements? Not that I don't enjoy meeting you out of my office–the Scotch is a hell of a lot better, as is the scenery–but I'm trying to figure out why I'm here. Is everything okay?"

I'd asked him to meet at my apartment, instead of at his firm, to ensure no one would overhear us, even turning off my phone to prevent distractions. Coming out was proving more nerve-wracking than I thought.

I was about to answer, but the door to the elevator slid open and Fallon walked in with his duffel bag. He saw me and smiled, but then his attention shifted to Ethan, and his eyes widened.

"Oh, sorry, I didn't realize your meeting would be here." Keeping his distance, he set his bag on the floor. I noticed Ethan had risen and set his glass on the table, a curious expression on his face.

"Fallon, come on in. You haven't met my attorney, Ethan Phillips. Ethan, this is my personal assistant, Fallon McKenzie." An awkward silence reigned between them, and my unease grew. "Okay, what's going on?"

Ethan's lips kicked up. "Fallon and I have already met."

My brows shot up. "That's so funny. When and how?"

Red-cheeked, Fallon shrugged. "It was at a club. I, ah, went after work when you were playing an away game. I was about to leave when I met Ethan."

Jealousy surged through me, but I remained calm. "Did you–"

"No, of course not," Fallon rushed to answer, and I swore my heart skipped a beat. "We went for a cup of coffee."

"I recognized Fallon because I'd seen him at plenty of Kings celebrations. Why do I feel like I'm missing something here? No offense, Patrick, but Fallon can go to a club and meet whomever he wants."

An imperceptible nod from Fallon gave me the courage and strength to say out loud what I'd kept hidden all my life.

"No. He can't. We're together. In love."

Shocked didn't begin to describe Ethan's face, and he looked from me to Fallon as if to confirm.

"I'm bisexual. I wanted you here to tell you because as my lawyer, I figured you'd be the best person to help me with privacy issues, plus I know you wouldn't say anything to anyone else. But I didn't know *you* were gay, Ethan...or bi. Sorry."

"No, I'm gay, and it's fine, you can say it. I keep my sexuality to myself because, as you can understand, whom I sleep with is no one's business. But damn, Patrick." He shook his head. "Talk about coming out of left field."

The weight of this secret I'd held my whole life lifted slightly, and a grin kicked up my lips. "Wrong sport, dude."

We all laughed, and Ethan approached the two of us with less reserve. "To clear the record, nothing happened between Fallon and me. We had a cup of coffee and discussed our jobs, but I had no idea he was working for you."

"When Dev didn't have enough work to keep me full-time, he introduced me to Patrick," Fallon explained.

"Makes sense. So what do you need from me, Patrick?"

I sat on a barstool at the kitchen island. "I'm not sure. It's not as if there are any out active players."

Friendly Ethan shifted to Lawyer Ethan, and I could see his brain working. "Are you thinking of coming out? Making a statement to the press?"

"Not now, but after the Super Bowl, yeah. It's not fair to Fallon to hide him, and I don't want to."

Ethan leaned against the island. "I'm glad we're having this conversation now. Thanks for trusting me, and you know I'll keep anything you tell me in confidence. I'm sure you'll get backlash, and some sponsors might want to pull their contracts, but if they do, we'll fight it. Of course, there are morality clauses that allow them to scrub a campaign, but you being bisexual isn't immoral. I'd relish a chance to argue that one in court."

From the cocky grin and the sparkle in his eyes, I had no doubt he meant it. "But do you think it would happen? I know it's not the same, but Dev and Brody seemed to have come through it all right."

"They're not my clients, but from what I know, it was easier because they waited until their retirement. You're not in that position."

"No. And I'm not willing to wait."

Ethan's attention shifted to Fallon. "What do you have to say in all this? You're going to come under pretty intense scrutiny yourself."

"I told Patrick I was willing to wait before he made any announcements."

"Why? Is there a reason?" Ethan was in full lawyer mode now.

"Yeah, there is," Fallon responded quietly. "I love him, and I don't want him to lose what he loves doing. I can wait if this is going to hurt him in any way."

"And I said no. I'm tired of hiding. I believe the Kings will support me—after all, how would it look for their organization to come out against one of their players when the owner is gay and in a relationship? The right time is now."

Ethan's sharp eyes raked me up and down, and though I'd never been on a witness stand, I could imagine how forceful he'd be in court. I held my ground, meeting his probing gaze steadily.

"You'll have to be prepared for a media onslaught," Ethan said, "especially if you win the Super Bowl. The public's eyes will be on you nonstop."

I reached for Fallon's hand, and he took it, his palm warm and comforting in mine. "I can deal with it."

"And what about you, Fallon?" Ethan asked. "You didn't answer my question earlier. Do you think you'll be able to deal with the pressure?"

What I loved most about Fallon was the calm and deliberate way he handled questions or any challenge thrown at him. It's what made him such a superior assistant, but it was easy to see how it transferred to his private life.

"I do. I spoke with Dev and Brody today." He squeezed my hand, and his grin turned mischievous. "After picking their jaws up off the floor, they were completely supportive of our relationship and offered any help they can."

That was a conversation I needed to hear about, but not until Ethan left. "So what do you think? I'll need to have security for me, but I'll want it on Fallon as well." When he opened his mouth, I glared at him. "Not your choice. There are too many people with ugly views who aren't afraid to show how low they can go."

"He's right, Fallon. And frankly, Patrick, I don't know why you don't have security right now. I want you to arrange that as soon as possible." He smirked at me. "And you don't have a choice, either. It's happening. If I find out you haven't, I'll call the Kings and have it done."

At Fallon's snicker, I huffed. "Fine, whatever. My concern is Fallon."

His blue eyes shot daggers at me. "Why? You think I can't take care of myself?"

"No, I know you can, but it would make me feel better, when I'm not here and you're out, to know there's an extra set of eyes."

Ethan checked his phone. "I'd better go. I have another client meeting at six. I'll arrange the details and send them to you to read. Meanwhile, I'll go through your endorsement contracts with a fine-toothed comb so we can anticipate any potential trouble. And don't worry. I won't be passing this off to a junior attorney. No one but me will have their eyes on it."

"Thanks, Ethan. Appreciate it."

"No problem. I take care of my clients. That's why I'm the best." He grinned, and we clasped hands. "Fallon, good to see you again. Glad it's working out for you." They shook, and then the elevator whisked Ethan away, leaving Fallon and me alone.

"Finally," I said, and settled my mouth over his. After the long day I'd had, this connection was what I needed. We kissed and held each other for several minutes. "It felt good to tell him. And funny that you'd meet Ethan of all people. Let's go sit, and you can tell me about that and your conversation with Dev."

Hand in hand, we walked to the couch. Fallon stretched out and put his head in my lap. "There isn't much more to tell you about my meeting Ethan. When you were in Austin and I saw those pictures of you with those girls, I went to a club."

"I'm sorry. Nothing ever happened. It was all for show."

"I know that now, but at that point I didn't, so yeah, I was a little depressed and decided to hit up a club. When it was obvious it wasn't my scene and I was about to leave, I met Ethan, and we talked for a few minutes. He asked if I wanted a cup of coffee, and I said sure. I made it clear from the start I wasn't planning on going home with him." Fallon smiled. "He said he hadn't planned on asking but that it was good to know."

I chuckled. "He's pretty sharp. And I had no idea he was gay."

"Why should you? It's no one's business. When a man and woman start dating, no one thinks twice and says, 'Wow, I didn't know they were straight.' " Fallon made a face. "Anyway, he confessed he recognized me and said he appreciated that I was circumspect where my employer was concerned. Of course, neither of us had any idea you were the connection."

"Who said New York City was an anonymous place?" I joked. "More importantly, how did it go with Dev?"

"As I expected, he was upset at first. He thought you took advantage of me and were just dicking around."

I couldn't get angry with Dev. He'd had no reason to suspect I wasn't straight, and Fallon and I had a past he knew nothing about. "That couldn't have been pleasant for you."

Fallon lifted a shoulder and sat up. "Can't blame him. You have a reputation, and he's always considered me vulnerable. I might be older than thirty, but he still sees me as the little kid brother who needs rescuing."

"You're strong as hell. And everyone needs a little help occasionally."

"Even you?"

I bent to kiss him. "Especially me. Without you, I couldn't do this." As I spoke, I tugged his shirt off, and did the same with mine.

"So you're not the hard-ass everyone thinks, huh?" His blue eyes twinkled, and I threaded my fingers through his hair and kissed him until we were both breathless.

"My ass isn't what's hard right now."

He pulled me to him, and our kisses turned hot and frantic. "Let's go to the bedroom so I can take care of this beast." Fallon's hand slid inside my sweats—when I heard my name.

"Patrick?"

Still holding a half-naked Fallon, I blinked to clear the fog of lust from my brain and saw my parents standing in front of the elevator. Slack-jawed, they were pale under their tans and frozen in place.

"Shit," Fallon choked out and scrambled off my lap. He grabbed his shirt and pulled it on.

"Mom, Dad, what're you doing here?" On my feet, I took the shirt Fallon handed me, and with slightly shaky hands, slipped it on.

Dad cleared his throat. "W-we tried calling you for the past two days, and when you didn't answer us, we got worried. Your mother thought we should come, in case there was a problem."

Mom walked into the kitchen area and set her purse on the counter. "I tried calling Fallon, but he didn't answer either."

*Shit.* We'd both been so wrapped up in our personal issues.

"Maybe we should all sit." I gestured to the couch, but Fallon jumped aside.

"I should leave so you can talk." Red-faced and uncomfortable, Fallon looked ready to run.

"No." I grabbed his arm. "I'd like you to stay. Please?"

Fallon cast his eyes downward but nodded, his hair swinging to hide his face, so I couldn't see his face.

My parents took one side of the large couch, and I sat on the other. Fallon chose the chair farthest from me and stared straight ahead, not looking at anyone. My guy was so fucking hurt from life kicking him down all the time that he expected me to bail on him.

"Mom, Dad, this is a conversation I've been putting off way too long—like fifteen years."

"You're gay?" Mom asked, her voice giving nothing away, and my heart dropped, unsure if she was hurt, disappointed, or puzzled.

"I'm bisexual. I'm attracted to men and women."

They seemed confused but not upset, which gave me hope.

Dad's brow furrowed. "Both? I don't understand how that can be."

"Probably because you're not bi." I smiled in an attempt to lighten the mood. "But I've known since I was a teenager. When I'd go to the movies, I was equally attracted to James Bond as I was to the Bond girls."

"B-but you've only had girlfriends...you were married." Mom didn't grasp the concept, and I struggled to find the words to help her understand.

"Twice, yeah, I know." At this point, Fallon had to become part of the conversation. "In college I met Fallon and...without getting into details, we fell hard for each other, but Fallon selflessly stepped aside, knowing I was on my way to a professional football career and that coming out would kill that opportunity." There was no need for my parents to know about anonymous sex clubs. Hearing my news was enough for them to handle.

"Fallon? You did that for Patrick?"

He nodded but still didn't speak.

"When I hired him, I hate to admit it, but I didn't recognize him. Trust me, the explanation for that is far too confusing to get into. Fallon knew right away, and it took a while, but we decided to try to be together again. I don't want to put my life on hold anymore. I think I deserve to be happy, like everyone else."

"Of course you do." Mom sniffled. "And I'm sorry you didn't feel you could tell us. It's a shock, but only because we had no idea." She wiped her eyes. "I want you to have the life you deserve. I don't want you to have to pretend."

"And I don't want to play the grinch," Dad added, more somber than I'd ever seen him, "but what is this going to mean for your career? Are you planning on telling people? Your teammates?"

I'd never wanted to sink into the floor and disappear more.

"You don't think I should? You want me to keep it a secret? Keep Fallon hidden?" The words tasted bitter on my tongue.

"Maybe it's for the best," Fallon stated, quiet and sad.

Fallon's shocking words hurt my heart as much as my father's question.

"What the hell does that mean? For the best?" I whipped around and was met with the tragedy in his eyes.

"I don't want to come between you and your family. Football—"

"Is just a game," Mom cried out. "But love is everything. Whatever you choose to do—tell everyone or stay silent—we'll be right by your side."

My throat tightened. "Thank you," I whispered, dangerously close to tears. "I was worried."

"You're our son. We're always going to be in your corner." Dad's words broke me, and I couldn't believe I was crying. Big ugly tears of relief and joy. Mom and Dad hugged me, and I spied Fallon, his cheeks wet. My heart twisted with the pain he still carried from his family's rejection. I had been lucky enough to be accepted, but in his mind, he was still alone.

"We're Fallon's family now," I told them. "Not everyone is as loving and accepting as you."

Mom met my eyes, and I could see she understood. But in a night filled with surprises, the biggest came when Dad left his chair and put his hand on Fallon's shoulder.

"When you told us at dinner that you and your parents don't get along, is it because you're gay?"

A rush of something deep and visceral swept through me, and I wanted to protect Fallon from having to relive the terrible rejection, but he surprised me by answering.

"Yes, partly. Even before I told them, I was never the favored son. Telling them I was gay was the final nail in my coffin, and they could bury me and forget I ever existed. If they couldn't have the son they truly loved, then they'd rather have no son at all."

"Oh, honey." Overwrought, Mom ran to Fallon and put her arms around him. "I can't imagine what that must've been like, but you have us now. Maybe we can't heal all your hurts, but we can try."

Knowing Fallon's pain had become part of his psyche, it wouldn't be easy, but if anyone could help Fallon, it would be my parents. Now I had to hope my own path of acceptance would hold the same unconditional caring.

# CHAPTER TWENTY-ONE

Fallon

Surprisingly, it took Dev four days to reach out. Not to me, as I'd thought and prepared for. Instead, he'd called Patrick, asking for us to get together. We'd gotten home from taking Lori and Don to the airport when his name flashed on Patrick's phone. Patrick had paled, not wanting to answer, but I'd told him to stop being an idiot. The conversation had been brief, and afterward Patrick had set the phone on the couch.

"He wants to have dinner tomorrow night. The four of us." He ran his fingers through his hair and licked his lips. "What do you think that means?"

I laughed and kissed him.

"That he's hungry and wants us to eat with him. You're cute. It'll be fine. Dev's bark is worse than his bite. You'll see."

I honestly didn't believe Dev would have a problem with us, but if he activated his big-brother mode, Brody and I would make sure he kept his cool.

"I need to get ready." Patrick sprang up and grabbed his wallet and keys. "Let's go shopping."

Whooping with laughter, I held my stomach. "It's nine at night. The stores are closed. Besides, you have a huge wardrobe. You have plenty to wear."

Sheepish, he sat on a barstool. "I just...I want Dev to know I'm the right one for you."

I reveled in his sweetness, and no matter what Dev or anyone else thought, I had no intention of letting Patrick go again.

"You don't have to worry about that. I don't need anyone's approval for whom I love. No matter how close we are. Dev will understand."

"That's all fine for you. He's like your family. I'm nobody to him."

"Then work on that. Because you're right—Dev is like my family, and I want you to be friends. But as I said, as far as I'm concerned, you have nothing to prove to anyone. You're the man I want to be with. My anchor in this fucked-up world, grounding me, and we belong together." I tugged his hand. "Let's go to bed. Much as I loved having your parents here, no sex for three days has been a killer. I'm dying for you."

Patrick allowed me to pull him to his feet and wrapped his arm around my shoulders. "We both get noisy. No way could I be inside you and not let loose." He squeezed my ass, rocking his pelvis against mine, his rapidly thickening cock dragging along mine.

"Isn't this better than shopping?" I nuzzled his ear, and he growled, his hot breath gusting over my cheek.

We almost tripped in our rush to get to the bedroom. I ripped off my sweats and pulled off my shirt. Patrick's eyes glowed when I stood naked in front of him.

"Oh, yeah. It's gonna get very noisy in here."

We rolled on the bed, my legs tangled with Patrick's, my heart lost to him. Eyes brimming with lust and longing, he kissed me repeatedly, leaving me trembling with love.

"I wish we could go back. I'd have chosen you over it all."

"Don't wish for what can't be changed. Dream about the possibilities of what can."

"You. Me. Us. I love you. I've always loved you." Giving me no chance to answer, he covered my mouth with his, sliding his tongue to meet mine, and I sucked it hungrily. He broke the kiss, moving lower and lower, leaving no part of me untouched and unloved. At the first wet press of his lips, my hips bucked, and he licked and sucked.

"Fuck, Patrick, oh God." I clutched the sheets, my head thrashing on the pillow. Sweat poured down my face, and I tasted salt in my mouth. Every time he touched me, I lost control. "Fuck me. Goddammit. Fuck me." My cries rose in the air, and his eyes turned feral.

"That's right. Tell me how much you want me." With his gaze locked on to mine, he licked three fingers and slipped them into me one by one, working them in and out.

At one point in my lonely life that had been enough, but no longer. I needed his body filling mine, pushing me into the bed, thrusting harder.

"Not...enough...please," I panted, and the wicked grin that always turned my heart over curved his generous lips.

"You want this?" He stroked his heavy dick, and I swore my ass could feel the burn without him even touching me. I craved him like an addict, only my drug was Patrick Sloane.

"Yeah." I watched as he slicked himself up. "Oh, yeah. Every perfect inch."

With a husky chuckle, Patrick slid into me, tantalizingly slow, but stopped. My heart banged in anticipation. His smile broadened, and then he drove in.

"Fal, Fal," he grunted and snapped his hips, pumping fast. That stiff, probing shaft pierced me to my core, and I moaned, my ass clenching as he continued to drive into me.

"Patrick. More, fuck me, more."

He increased his pace, the bed creaking with each movement. My dick ached, and I'd barely touched it before I exploded, my come coating our bellies and chest.

"Fuck, you're so gorgeous. You love this, don't you?" He pulled out fully, leaving only the tip, then sank in and hovered above me, eyes boring into mine. "You love me?" Picking up the pace, he pounded me through my climax, and I couldn't respond. Body twitching, I hung on to his muscled biceps and watched as his lips pulled back in a snarl. "Say it."

"I love you," I managed. "So damn much."

At my words, he dug his fingers into my shoulders, and my ass filled with heat. His dick pulsed, and Patrick buried his face in my neck.

"You're mine."

We hung on to each other and slept.

**

"Stop being so nervous." I rested on the bed and watched Patrick change his shirt for the third, no, fourth time. "You've known them for years. It'll be okay."

Patrick finished buttoning up the new turquoise shirt he'd purchased from Dior. That was after he'd gotten a haircut, a facial, and a manicure.

"Not like this." He tucked the shirt into his slacks. "Not as your boyfriend."

Hearing Patrick call himself that sent a thrill through me. I'd awakened in the middle of the night and stared at his bulk next to me in bed, unable to believe this was my life and that we were finally together.

"Dev invited us to dinner. He's not going to cause a scene."

Patrick reached into his pocket, and pulled out a small blue box. "This is for you. I picked it up today."

Shock ran through me. "What is it?"

"Maybe you should open it." He held it out. "Go ahead. It won't bite."

I took the box from him, hesitating only a second before opening it. Hanging off a silver chain was an anchor. "Last night when you called me your anchor, I started to think about how I'd never really felt at home anywhere. No roots to keep me grounded. Until here. With you."

I picked it up by the chain, and it dangled in front of me. "It's beautiful."

His smile was sweet. "Can I put it on you?"

"Yes, please." I pulled my hair off my neck and waited for his warm hands to touch my skin. Soft lips kissed the spot where the clasp rested. "Turn around and let me see."

Touched he'd remembered what I said, I traced the curve of cool metal with my finger. "I love it. And you."

His hand rested on top of mine, and he grinned. "Your heart's pounding so fast."

"Better to fall in love with you all over again." I smirked, and he pulled me closer.

"You're sure it's going to be all right?"

I kissed his cheek. "I promise."

**

Inside the crowded restaurant, I spotted Dev and Brody at a table in the far corner. Carbone was one of those upscale but casual places where million-dollar deals were celebrated alongside a couple's twenty-fifth anniversary party. The hostess led us to them, and Dev and Brody hugged me while giving Patrick handshakes.

"I asked them for their most private table since we're having a personal conversation," Dev explained. His penetrating gaze searched me up and down, coming to rest on my necklace. I'd worn an open-collar dress shirt, figuring Dev would comment, and he didn't disappoint. "That's new." He tipped his head toward me. "The necklace."

Instinctively, my fingers touched the heavy piece of silver. "It is. Patrick gave it to me."

"That's nice." Dev's words didn't thaw the chill in his eyes. "Maybe Patrick would like to start with why he lied to me when we talked in California."

Brody nudged Dev's shoulder. "Server's comin'." We all turned quiet and waited.

The server took our drink order and left. Under the table, I gave Patrick's thigh a squeeze for support.

"Look, Dev," Patrick began. "I didn't lie. We talked around the subject. Plus, you can't think I'd come out to you, or anyone for that matter, fresh off the field after a game with a million eyes on us. Anyone could be listening, recording. But also, I had to talk to Fallon first, make sure he was all right with it." He clasped his hands. "I know you understand what it's like to have to hide who you are. I've lived with being bisexual for so long, it's second nature to keep quiet about it. When Fallon and I first got together in college, we were kids. It was our first time, and I fell for him."

Dev opened his mouth, but I rushed in. "Let Patrick have his say, please. You'll have your chance to speak."

Dev nodded and remained quiet.

Taking the opportunity, Patrick took a sip of his drink. "I know what you're gonna say. *You didn't know who he was. You never even saw his face, so how could you love him?* You know what I say to that? So fucking what? I fell for his heart and who he is as a person. I would think that made our connection more real because it didn't matter to me what he looked like. I've never met anyone so innately good, caring, and thoughtful. He makes me feel like I'm the only man in the world, and I want to be better. For him."

"That sounds familiar, don't you think?" Brody nudged Dev, who hadn't taken his eyes off Patrick. "I kinda remember you sayin' that about me."

My lips twitched.

"You know how much I hate it when you throw my words back in my face," Dev grumbled, and Brody didn't even try to hide his laughter, cackling out loud.

"I know. That's why I love doing it."

Unused to their banter, Patrick turned to me. "Is he still mad?"

Dev, of course, didn't allow me to answer. "I was never mad. I'm concerned. I know how hot the spotlight shines on you now. I'm thinking of the future—for both of you. You've been to the Super Bowl once already, so you know how intense it gets. Now you're in New York, where the media coverage always ramps up to the nth degree. That picture they took of you shopping the other day? Man, you won't be able to take a piss without worrying if a camera's on you."

"All kidding aside, Dev's right," Brody said. "You'll be hounded everywhere. Especially you, with your reputation."

Patrick scowled. "That's bullshit."

Dev's dark brows rose high. "Is it? You're thirty-one and have two ex-wives."

Red-cheeked, Patrick ducked his head. "Who were only interested in being football WAGs with all the perks. It wasn't me they loved. It was the lifestyle. And maybe I never gave them a hundred percent of myself because I wasn't complete after losing Fallon. Yeah, over the years I had love affairs, but never like what he and I had. I don't expect you to understand. You were lucky enough to meet each other and managed to be together."

"I wouldn't call hiding who we are and that we were in love lucky, but I understand." The tenor of Dev's voice changed, and knowing him so well, I could see how affected he was by Patrick's story. "All I want is for Fallon to be safe and happy. He deserves it."

"Then we want the same things."

"If I'm allowed to speak," I joked, "you know, since it's also my life we're talking about? I want Patrick to have the career he's worked so hard for. I'm willing to wait for the time to be right."

"What if it's never the right time? Or it's a year, or two, or five?" Dev turned the full force of that famous, fierce gaze on me. The one that once made the opposition quake in their cleats. I remained unfazed.

"Turn it down a notch, killer. I'm not the defensive line."

A snort escaped Patrick, and his shoulders shook with laughter, but I held Dev's stare.

"It's my decision, though. Mine and Patrick's. Much as I love you, Dev, and I know you love me, I'm not that eighteen-year-old kid you saved anymore. I can handle my own life."

Softy that he was, Dev's green eyes grew shiny. "No, you're not, and I know you can. You're a hell of a man and the best friend. And Rory would've been damn proud of you."

At the mention of Rory, tears flooded my eyes. "I wish he were still here to see. My parents don't give a damn, but Rory always said I'd find someone."

Patrick shifted, waves of frustration rolling off him. "I hate that we're here, in public, and I can't make you feel better. This is what I'm talking about. It's not fair that I can't give my boyfriend comfort because someone might see."

Gathering my composure, I drew in a deep breath. "It's okay. I know how you feel. I just hope, Dev, that you and Brody see that this isn't a phase for either of us. I'm not being exploited, and Patrick isn't waiting for someone better to come along."

"There is no one better." Patrick's husky rasp melted me into a gooey mess, and Dev's expression softened.

"You're really in love with him."

Hidden by the flowing, white tablecloth, Patrick took my hand and squeezed it. "Yeah. I really am."

The server approached, and we all put on our game faces and ordered. A seafood tower for the table, and I ordered the lobster ravioli, while Patrick had the double lambchops. Dev ordered chicken *scarpariello*, and Brody had the *linguine alle vongole*. The food was delicious, and the talk turned to the Kings and their chances to win the Super Bowl. In his element, Patrick grew animated, and I sat back, listening to the three of them hash out the possible competition. I gazed around the restaurant, and of course people had their phones out, snapping pictures of our table. Having spent years in Dev's high-profile orbit, I was used to this lifestyle, but if Patrick and I ever did come out as a couple, the media coverage would be ten times worse.

"Ready for dessert?" The server removed our plates, and I answered automatically.

"I'm good. Just a cappuccino, please."

Patrick's eyes narrowed. "Carrot cake, please, and a cappuccino."

"Same for the two of us, please," Brody ordered.

"What's wrong?" Patrick murmured. "You got awfully quiet."

"Nothing." My smile was quick, and I could tell it didn't fool him. "I don't know anything about football. Only my favorite players."

"Uh-huh."

When dessert had been consumed and the bill taken care of, we exited the restaurant, where they were approached by fans. I stood to the side, watching women cozy up to Patrick and asking for pictures and autographs with all three. After about fifteen minutes the crowd waned, and Patrick approached me.

"Ready to go? I'll get a car."

"Yeah, sure."

Dev and Brody had already called for theirs, and it pulled up to the curb.

Dev hugged me. "I'm glad you're happy. That's all I've ever wanted."

"I know. Thank you for being my friend."

"Always." Those bright-green eyes twinkled. "He's really into you. Guess your dry spell is over."

I grew warm. "Shut up." But I couldn't help it. "I have no complaints, even if I can't walk the next day."

"Good for you." Dev busted out laughing, and still snickering, I said good-bye to Brody. By then our car was waiting, and Patrick and I climbed inside.

We arrived at Patrick's apartment, undressed, and lay on the couch together. His long fingers twirled in my hair, and he asked, "What's really bothering you?"

"It's all been great, but I'm still worried. As happy as I am that you've worked it out with Dev, I'm wondering what the future holds, if you do come out about us."

"Not if. When. Tonight solidified it for me. I have no desire to hide us for the next five, six...ten years. However many years I might have left to play. I can't do it, Fal. It's not right that just because I fell in love with you, I have to hide it. Fuck that. Ethan's reviewing all my contracts, but he doesn't think there can be any fallout legally."

While I understood what Patrick was saying, I knew it couldn't be as simple as he wished. I could only love him and hope for the best, whatever that might be.

# CHAPTER TWENTY-TWO

Patrick

This was not a position I wanted to be in. First our defense moved as though trudging through mud, and the Bisons slipped past our front line like a hot knife through butter. Then my pass was picked off and run back forty-six yards for their second touchdown in the first half. We only managed a lousy field goal, and it made me want to punch something.

Halftime, and to the sounds of boos, we pounded feet into the locker room and sat in stony silence as Coach ripped into our asses.

"What the fuck am I seeing out there? We're at the end of the season, and you're playing like a goddamn team of rookies. Interceptions, sluggish snap retrievals, broken tackles, and your ends ain't tight. They're loose like a fucking untied rope. You got a problem? Someone didn't give you a good-night kiss or you didn't have enough milk for your cookies?"

I might've only been with the Kings for part of the season, but damn. I'd never seen Coach go off like this. And looking at the rest of the team, it seemed neither had they. It seemed even Rio knew enough to keep his wise-ass mouth shut, and he stood the same as us, wide-eyed and shamed.

"Sloane, you're not going to get that Super Bowl ring and impress your new girlfriend if you don't move quicker and anticipate. Got that? You know their plays, right? You watched tapes on the bye week, or were you too busy shopping and having dinners with Dev and Brody?"

My cheeks grew hot as he called me out. "Yeah, Coach. I did. And I'll step it up to a hundred and fifty percent."

"Make that two hundred. Rio, Troy, move those asses, push harder. Candyman, you looked like you were moving backward. I expect some touchdowns this second half, hear me?"

"Yes, Coach," we all shouted, loud enough to make the walls ring.

I turned to face the team. "Let's do this. They're weak on their left side, and I thought I saw Logan favoring his right ankle. Let's capitalize on all that and crush this second half. Am I right?"

"Yeah, dude. We're gonna kill it." Rio clapped his hands. "We're gonna crush their asses."

With fire in our eyes, we took the field in the second half and ripped the Bisons' defense to shreds. We scored a touchdown, and after the extra point, our special teams kicked off. The Bisons' kickoff return player caught the ball and started his run, but then tripped over his own feet. The ball went flying, right into the hands of Monty Wilson. Small and speedy, Monty motored upfield to the end zone, and with the crowd screaming almost as loudly as us, scored a touchdown. After the extra point, we were now ahead by three, but that wasn't enough.

"Back at it, Trick." Coach went head-to-head with me. "Play it like it's first and goal at the Super Bowl."

"You got it, Coach."

Offense jogged on the field after the kick return. Kings Stadium was rocking, and I bet they could hear us over the Marine Parkway Bridge in Queens. I could barely hear my own play calls, but it didn't matter. Our spark had reignited. I threw a ten-yard pass for a first down, then a thirty yard. Next play, I faked a pass, then handed off to a receiver who was wide open, and he spun around, eluded a few tackles, and made it to the four-yard line before he was stopped.

We huddled, and I got the play from Coach in my earpiece. "All right. Rio, Troy, you split up to each side of the end zone. I'll see who's got less coverage. Let's gooooo!"

We split and formed the line. The Bisons weren't going to make it easy for us, and it was third and one. I knew they were expecting me to pass, so I ran it in, busting past their line of scrimmage. They piled on me, but I refused to be denied. I summoned up my strength and thought of Fallon, waiting for me at home, and charged inside the end zone. My teammates pushed me forward and I fell, stretching every inch of my six-foot-five frame to make sure I was well past the goal line.

"Touchdown, touchdown." Troy and Rio danced and pulled me to my feet. I held the ball up to the crowd, pumping my fist. To the screams of the crowd, I jogged to the sidelines, where Coach and the rest of the staff smacked me on the back.

"Ow. Careful of the merchandise," I joked.

Instantly wary, Coach called the team doctor. "Mike, take a look at him. McKinney, you're going in. Get ready." Harte shot me a quick look before beginning to stretch and loosen up.

"What? No way, Coach," I sputtered as the crowd cheered the extra point. "I was kidding."

"Save it, Sloane. We need you healthy for the division playoffs. Take the rest."

Mike ran a rapid assessment. "You look fine, but I want to check for any bruising or swelling, especially around that ankle."

I knew better than to argue. "Can it at least wait until after the game? I want to see it to the end. I promise to sit on the bench like a good boy."

Mike nodded. "I'm okay with that. But no jumping up and down or sudden movements, just in case."

"You got it."

The defense was holding the line, and I was getting hoarse cheering them on.

"Great plays," Harte remarked. "You really lit a fire under everyone's asses."

"Including my own," I joked.

"You've got that quality, Patrick. You're gonna go all the way this year. I feel it. There's something different about you now than when you first joined the team."

I ran a hand through my sweaty hair. "You think? I was just as hungry then as I am now. Even more now that we're so damn close."

"Yeah, but that's not it. I see you're not into the party scene—I remember the stories of you going out during bye weeks and partying."

"Yeah, well, I've got more important things on my mind," I mumbled, focusing on the turf beneath my feet.

"Or someone?" Harte asked, and I jerked my head up.

"What're you talking about?"

But he couldn't answer me because the Bisons failed to score and weren't in range for a field goal. I watched as Harte took the team downfield and we scored again. When the whistle blew at game's end, we'd won 31-14. The Bisons had been completely shut out in the second half.

I gave a few on-field interviews, then sat at the postgame media circus, as I called it, with Coach.

"Trick, how's the ankle? Any problems?"

I frowned. "No, of course not. Coach was just making sure I'm completely rested for the postseason because we know it's gonna be a fight."

"So you're ready for the division playoffs?" a reporter called out. "Does it matter who you face?"

"Nope," I responded with a grin I knew was cocky as fuck. "I'm ready for it all. It's what I've been waiting for since I was signed by the Kings."

"Are you feeling any pressure from the New York fans?"

"No more than I put on myself. The fans want another Super Bowl, and so do I. Devlin Summers set a high bar, and I mean to keep up the winning tradition of the Kings."

"Have you spoken with Devlin and Brody? Have they been helpful?"

"Nothing but. I couldn't ask for better friends."

Coach put up his hands. "All right, everyone. Thank you."

I couldn't wait to get out of my uniform and into a whirlpool. By the time I got to the locker room, most of the guys had gone to get their own treatments, and I undressed, showered, and went to find Enzo, who waited for me patiently.

"Ah, there he is. The man of the hour. Come lie down and let me work on you."

With a groan, I crawled onto the bed and lay face-down, sighing as the warm oil spread over my skin. Enzo's hands moved firm and strong as they kneaded my sore muscles.

"You have no idea how much I looked forward to this."

"I'm sure. You were giving it your all." He stopped a moment. "You have some scratches on your back, and some bruising, but it doesn't look fresh, like from today."

"Uh, I don't know. Maybe practice?" My cheeks burned, and I was glad not to be lying right side up.

"I don't think so. They're pretty symmetrical." Enzo chuckled. "I'm guessing she's a wildcat, *hmm*? Someone new?" I grunted, not answering, and he moved carefully over the area. "She must not have long nails. The fingers are larger. More square-shaped..." His voice dwindled until he stopped speaking, and I grew cold with fear. I sat up, facing Enzo, who busied himself with the heating pads, not meeting my gaze. "It will be fine. I have special creams and oils to fade the marks."

"Enzo," I murmured. "Those marks...you know they're not from a woman."

Instead of answering, he left me to lock the door and returned to where I still sat on the table. "What you are telling me, you know I'd never repeat anything."

Funny enough, I did. And the relief of saying the words out loud sent tears to my eyes. "I'm with someone and...well, obviously, I haven't said anything. I've known I'm bisexual since I was a teenager, but with me playing pro ball..." I paused, my throat dry and aching. "We first got together when we were younger, but it was complicated, and we separated. We met again only recently, and I don't want to have regrets about what might have been. I want what everyone else has. I've decided I can't keep silent anymore."

Enzo's eyes grew wide. "You're going to come out now? During the season?"

"No. We talked, and he's willing to wait longer, but I'm not. It's not fair to him or me to have to hide. We're not doing anything wrong. After the Super Bowl, I'll make an announcement."

"Years ago, Dev sat on this table and told me his story, and my heart broke." Enzo laid the heating pad on my shoulders, and it felt so damn good, I groaned. "You spoke with him and Brody about this? They can give you good advice."

"Yeah, I did. And they helped, but in the end, it's up to me. If I don't make the decision to show people that I can be a bisexual athlete, what kind of message am I sending? That I'm ashamed or afraid? Screw that."

Enzo spread the cream on my back, and I rolled my shoulders to allow it to sink in. Enzo went to work on my calves and ankles, his nimble, strong fingers digging deep into the muscles. After ten minutes, he wrapped my ankle, and I raised a brow.

"What's that for?"

"It's feeling a little bit different than the other, and I want to make sure you don't overdo it. Better to be safe."

I nodded. "Okay, but it feels fine. Not a twinge."

"Good. We will keep it that way."

I dressed and held out my hand to Enzo. "Thank you. I appreciate your friendship and your discretion."

"I thought when you first came to the team that you were just going to be another pretty-faced quarterback with a big reputation. But you've proved me wrong."

I laughed. "Glad to hear it."

His eyes were wise and warm. "Be safe out there."

**

I returned to the apartment to find Fallon waiting. His smile lit up all the empty spaces in my heart, and I knew I could never return to the life I had before—the aimless partying and casual hookups that left me lonelier when they were over.

"Great game, but it was like two different teams from the first half to the second." He handed me a beer.

I chuckled. "Yeah, 'cause Coach roasted our asses and told us we'd better wake up or he was gonna kick our butts." I settled on the sofa with a contented sigh.

"Why'd he take you out?" He spotted my taped ankle. "Shit. Are you injured? Does it hurt?" He ran his fingers along the bandage.

"No, Enzo just said it felt a little different, so he wanted to be careful. It's fine."

Fallon's blue eyes glowed. "You're pretty damn fine yourself." I held out an arm, and he came over to lay next to me.

"I told him. About us, I mean." Fallon grew stiff, but I held on. "I didn't mention names, and it's your fault in a way."

He sat up, brow furrowed. "My fault? What're you talking about?"

"You left scratches on my back. Enzo called you a wildcat." It was cute to watch Fallon turn red. "But he realized the bruises and marks were too big to be from a woman."

"What the hell?" he muttered. "Is he a masseur or a forensic lab tech?"

"It's his job. But I felt safe telling him. He was Dev's masseur for more than ten years, and he's gay himself. We had a good talk."

"You're still planning on coming out after the postseason?"

I frowned. "Yeah, why? You think I shouldn't?"

"I don't know what's best. I guess we'll take it one day at a time. See how it goes."

"How what goes? Fallon, I'm not sure you realize this is it for me—*you* are it. I'm not leaving you."

His head hung low. "I never wanted to force you to have to make a choice between me and your career."

I framed his face between the palms of my hands. "There is no choice. No matter what, no matter when, I choose you. First, last, and always."

# CHAPTER TWENTY-THREE

Fallon

Two months later, postseason madness had reached a fever pitch. The Kings had ended the season with only four losses out of the seventeen games and had won their division title. On Sunday they were playing for the conference championship. With the team pretty much traveling every other week, I hadn't seen Patrick for more than a quick kiss hello in the evening and another good-bye in the morning. Practices were intense and long, and the media coverage was chaotic.

Conference championships were in Portland, and Patrick had asked me to come. My automatic response was to decline, but he continued to push me to change my mind. That morning, I watched as he was getting ready to leave . It was early, six a.m., and the car was coming to pick him up and take him to Teterboro, from where the Kings' jet would fly them across the country. For a regular game, the team would normally fly out a day or so early, but there was nothing normal about the NFL postseason. Years ago, I'd learned that was a whole separate animal, and Patrick had been tapped to make commercials for the games and some of his sponsors. It did give me a bit of a thrill every time I saw him on television, knowing he was mine.

"It's not like you're going to be the only assistant there. Lots of the guys have their close friends, families, and my parents will be there too." He stood in his briefs and no shirt, his travel outfit waiting for him on the valet, where I'd hung it the night before.

That made me smile. "I know. Your mom's been texting me. I figured you put her up to it."

His brows drew together. "No, I swear I didn't. They really care about you."

It was tempting. I did enjoy spending time with Lori and Don and learning more about a younger Patrick. I never got the feeling they were putting up with me for Patrick's sake.

"Make sure you have everything. Take one last look."

"The only thing missing will be you."

He knew saying things like that would get to me. Sensing my weakening, Patrick put his arm around me. "It would mean a lot to me to have you there, supporting me." His demanding lips met mine. "Knowing you're there helps me. It's like I can feel your good vibes. I'm going to let you know I'm thinking about you when I take the field. So you can feel me with you. Like an invisible string connecting us."

God, how could I say no to that? "Okay," I whispered and kissed him back, hungry, but understanding this was as close as we'd get to be for the next few weeks. Not all coaches believed in no sex prior to big games, but Coach Jackson was one of those who did, and being this close to Patrick, smelling and tasting him without being able to do anything more, was torture.

"Good." He pinched my ass, then cupped it and held me close, and I could feel how hard he was.

"Patrick, don't you have to go soon?" But my words sounded weak even to me.

"Not being able to have you for two weeks? I'm ready to go right now." He wet his thumb and slipped his hands past the waistband of my sweats. I gasped as his finger entered me and moaned as he worked it in and out.

"Patrick, God." The thick bulge of his cock dragged against mine, and we bucked our hips. Through the fire of lust building up inside me, I decided to try something new and pushed his briefs down, giving me access to tease his hole with the tip of my finger.

"What the—oh, fuck," he groaned, and with his finger buried deep in my ass, he came, his cock jerking and spurting. Seeing him so lost in his climax sent me over the edge, and I hung on to him as my orgasm crashed through me.

"What the hell was that?" he murmured once we were both able to catch our breath and speak.

"I figured I'd give you something to think about on the plane ride. Looks like you enjoyed it."

"Yeah. I did." He kissed me. "Now I have to shower again," he grumbled.

"Hey, it's your fault. You started it. Besides," I added as we stripped out of our sticky clothes. "We can do it together. Save water and all that jazz."

"I love having an environmentally conscious boyfriend."

**

"Fallon, Fallon, we're here." From the corner of the luxury suite, Lori waved to me. The Kings had a private box that could hold up to thirty people, and Patrick had asked for us to be included with some of the other team families as well as Kings management. At the Kings' stadium, Dev had bought his own box, and I made a note to ask him if he wanted to sell it to Patrick.

"Hi, how are you?" I bent to kiss Lori, then shook Don's hand. "Exciting, isn't it?"

"Yes, and I'm so glad you decided to come. It's been a long time since we were at a postseason game."

Don handed me a beer. "They're looking strong, and Patrick has settled in with the team."

I scanned the stadium, spotting Dev's and Brody's media boxes. I'd have to go over at some point during halftime to say hello and made a mental note to text them.

"He has. Most of the players I knew from working with Dev have also retired or were traded, so this is a pretty new team to me as well. But the management has stayed the same, and I always heard they're great to work with."

"Glad to hear that," a voice said from behind me, and when I turned, I recognized Armand Winters, the team's owner. At his side was his personal assistant and boyfriend, Hayden. My cheeks grew warm.

"Oh, hi, Mr. Winters, Hayden."

Armand Winters's smile was sweet, and I knew from Dev, he was the force behind Dev not being traded after he'd suffered a bad concussion. "Please, call me Armi. Good to see you again, Fallon. From what I've heard, Dev and Brody are doing well in their new careers."

"We all know how much Dev loves to talk about the game. Or simply talk in general," I joked, and everyone laughed. "But he and Brody have been a great help to Patrick. I know they've met to discuss strategy. They really love being part of the Kings franchise."

"They are the face of the franchise no matter what, but I'm confident Patrick is going to leave a huge mark of his own on the team. Mr. and Mrs. Sloane, nice to see you."

"You too. Patrick loves being part of the Kings, and we've loved visiting him in New York," Don assured him.

"Here's hoping we'll be in the same position in two weeks for the Super Bowl." Hayden lifted his glass, and we all toasted to his words. "You've become an honorary member of the Kings too, haven't you, Fallon? Us PAs need to stick together."

The teams had taken the field, and I immediately found Patrick, who, hot dog that he was, played up to the crowd by pumping his fists to cheers. He pounded his heart and pointed up to the box where we were gathered.

"That's so sweet." Armi, standing beside Lori and Don at the window, smiled at them. "He's letting you know he's playing for you."

"He's a wonderful son. All we want is for him to be happy." Lori turned to me. "Fallon, can you see?"

"Yep. I'm good." Because I knew Patrick had included me in his gesture as well, even if I couldn't say anything.

The game proved to be nerve-wracking with the lead see-sawing between the two teams. By the end of the fourth quarter, with only a minute and ten seconds left, the Kings were behind a field goal, but they had possession of the ball. The crowd was on its feet, and my attention was riveted. Patrick was on his toes, intensity vibrating off him in waves.

"I'm so nervous," Lori whispered, but I couldn't answer. All my energy was focused on Patrick.

*Come on. Come on. You can do it. Throw that pass. You got this. I love you.*

Almost as if he'd heard me, he glanced in our direction, and they lined up. He faded back and threw a long pass, well over thirty yards, that was caught by the receiver, who was wide open. He raced upfield and into the end zone.

"Holy shit. Did you see that?" Hayden yelled, pulling at Armi's hand.

"Oh, my God. That was incredible," Lori screamed.

I watched as Patrick celebrated with his teammates. He turned and made the same gesture—hand over his heart—and pointed up to our box. Lori's hand found mine and squeezed it tight.

"That was for you, I know it," she whispered.

"We're going to the Super Bowl." I hugged her and Don. "Let the games begin."

And I wasn't kidding. If the postseason was a party, the two weeks leading up to the Super Bowl were a circus. On the closed-circuit television, we watched Patrick's postgame Q&A session, and I was impressed by his calm demeanor when one reporter questioned him on the close score.

"At this point in the season, we're playing the best teams in the league. Why would you expect any team to blow out the other?"

"Patrick," a female reporter from *Football Daily* called out. "You made a gesture before the game started and again after you threw the winning pass that won the game. Was that directed to anyone in particular?"

I held my breath.

"They know who they are." He nodded to Coach Jackson. "I'm gonna go join my team now for a little celebration."

I hadn't expected to see Patrick that evening, but he showed up at our hotel, predictably mobbed by fans. After spending close to half an hour signing autographs and taking pictures, he begged off in his usual, good-natured way.

"Hey, everyone, I'm thrilled to see you all, but I'm here to take my parents and assistant out to dinner. Make sure you tune in for the Super Bowl, though."

Lori and Don hugged him, and even I got to put my arms around him for a moment.

"Love you," he whispered in my ear, and that was all I needed.

Early the next morning, I flew home with Lori and Don, got them settled into their room in Patrick's apartment, and sat my ass down to set up Patrick's schedule for the following two weeks. There were multiple calls from Ethan Phillips that I sent directly to Patrick, and I spent the better part of the day creating spreadsheets for his interviews and public appearances. *Saturday Night Live* wanted him, as well as all the late-night talk shows and a few daytime ones, and I arranged everything as I chewed on a pastrami sandwich from the tray I'd ordered in. Lori and Don had gone out for a walk and returned, but I barely registered them, until Lori tapped me on the shoulder.

"Fallon. It's almost six and you haven't moved since we came home at ten this morning."

I gazed up at her and rubbed my eyes. "Yeah. It's chaotic once Super Bowl week hits. We're barely going to see Patrick—in the days leading up to the big game, he's either in training camp or doing publicity. He's only home for this week, and then he's off to Arizona for the game."

"Will you be going with him?"

The elevator door slid open, and a tired but jubilant Patrick walked in and dropped his duffel bag.

"It all depends on what Patrick wants," I answered, hanging back as Lori and Don greeted him with a hug and kiss.

"I can tell you what Patrick wants." He grinned, and my lips twitched.

"Behave," I murmured as he came over and gave me a kiss on the cheek. "We were talking about whether you'd want us to come to Arizona for the whole week prior to the game." I smirked. "And I have your schedule for this week set up. You're welcome." I handed him the colorful sheets I'd printed out, and he groaned and rolled his eyes.

"Stop. Let me sit for a little while." His eyes lit up. "Is that deli? Do you have corned beef? And coleslaw?"

"Yeah. On the kitchen counter. I see it didn't take you long to become a true New Yorker and fall under the spell of Second Avenue Deli."

"My mama didn't raise no fool." He took a sandwich and sat. "To answer your question, of course I want you all there. I've already talked to the Kings, and they've got rooms set aside for you. And I have your access for the stadium and the box the Kings rented." He rolled his shoulders, chewed, and swallowed. "God, I'm beat. I need to lie down. That game was way too close for comfort. Coach wants us in at ten sharp tomorrow morning."

Lori gave Don a look and took his hand. "We'll leave you two alone. There's a TV show we want to watch."

She kissed Patrick on his cheek. "You gave it your all. And I hate to say it, but it was so exciting, even though I know it was stressful. I'm sure your coach will make sure you know where you fell short."

Patrick snorted. "No kidding. My ears are still ringing. Thanks, Mom, Dad. I'll see you in the morning."

They passed by me, and Lori gave me a kiss as well. "We had a wonderful time with you. I can't wait until next week. We're going to have so much fun together."

Their door closed, and with a gleam in his eye, Patrick left his seat, slipped his arms around my neck, and kissed me. "I'd like to have some fun with you right now."

"Cool your jets, big guy. You know you're not supposed to have sex before the game." He thrust out his bottom lip, and I busted out laughing at his expression. "You're cute when you pout. Plus, remember, your parents are here. And you get noisy."

"We could go to your place. For old times' sake." He waggled his brows.

"Stop being a dog." I patted his cheek. "But we can take a shower together, and I'll make sure you're nice and clean for practice tomorrow."

His grin broadened, and those gorgeous eyes twinkled. "What're you waiting for?"

# CHAPTER TWENTY-FOUR

Patrick

*Super Bowl Sunday*

After two nonstop weeks, it was almost a relief to step onto the field to play the game. Even knowing that close to a billion eyes were watching, I wasn't nervous. I was fucking ready. I wanted this win with a hunger that would not be denied.

And no lie, I could feel Fallon's vibes flowing through me. As I had every postseason game, I pounded my chest and pointed to the box where he and my parents were sitting. He was my good-luck charm, the talisman I carried with me next to my heart.

The sold-out stadium cheered, and I wondered if they knew what was coming because win or lose today, I was telling the world who I was. Maybe that was what had lent a fire to my soul—even my fingertips tingled with energy.

I bent to take the snap. This was it. The moment I'd been waiting for since I was a kid and Dad took me to my first game. I called the play and could see from the twitchiness of the opposing team that they were as ready for this as we were.

"White 84, White 84, hut, hut." The ball in my hands, I scrambled away from the line. My tackles and guards jammed up their players, and I spotted Troy twenty yards downfield and wide open. I spiraled that ball right into his arms, and he took off like he had a rocket up his ass. The crowd went wild at our thirty-five-yard gain.

"All right, let's not get ahead of ourselves. We're only at midfield. They won't expect this again, so let's try it. If it doesn't work, Denny, I'm gonna want you to stay open."

"You got it, Trick."

And so it went. We marched down that field like a conquering army and scored first. On the bench, with the defense taking the field, Harte nudged me.

"You've got this. I can see it in your face. You're gonna win this today."

I laughed. "I'm sure the Lonestars said the same to Luke Fontaine. And he actually played with you guys, so he knows how you operate."

"You think Coach don't know that? Once the Lonestars advanced, he pulled out every old play starting from ten years ago, and the team turned around before Luke was drafted. Milo told me there are still a few tricks up Coach's sleeve."

"I don't doubt it." I searched the sidelines for a moment and found Coach, pacing and shouting instructions, more intent than I'd ever seen him. When I heard the roar, I shifted my attention to the field to see that Fontaine had been sacked for a loss of twelve yards. It was now third and twenty. "But it's still gonna be a hell of a fight."

My prediction came true. At halftime we were ahead by a touchdown, 17-10, and Coach was giving us our instructions.

"Quicker off the snap. Break through those holes." His eyes burned. "Eat their balls for dinner. This isn't fourth-grade square dancing. It's the fucking Super Bowl. Get up in their faces. Tear their asses up. We're gonna win this because we are the Kings."

"Yes, Coach," we yelled.

It was foolish to think the Lonestars hadn't received the same talk from their coach, and when we faced off in the third quarter, both lines were out for blood. I stepped back to make a pass and somehow ended up facedown in the turf. Furious at being sacked, I sprang up immediately and got our line together. The guys were pissed at themselves and at how the Lonestars were congratulating themselves.

*Fuck that.* Rio slipped past a tackle, and I laid that ball in his arms like a mama holding her newborn baby. He motored down the field like a fucking race car and scored. A forty-three-yard touchdown pass.

"That's what I'm talking about," I yelled along with the crowd's wild cheering. They got even louder after we faked the kick for the extra point and threw for the two-point conversion, scoring on the surprise play.

"Yeah, yeah!" I screamed myself hoarse and hugged each and every guy on special teams as they returned to the sideline. "You guys are fucking beasts."

Picking up on the energy, the defense went out on a mission and sacked Fontaine twice. On third and twenty-three, we knew he'd have to pass, and it was a beautiful thing to see his throw get intercepted and run to the Lonestars' forty-yard line.

Back on the field, we dominated, and with only five minutes left in the fourth quarter, we led 30-14. I didn't let up on the guys, knowing it wasn't a win until the whistle blew.

"Play it safe. I'm not passing unless I have to, but make sure you superglue the fucking ball to your hands if you get it."

"That's right. I'm ready to taste that champagne, baby," Rio said, and I shot him a look.

"No celebrating yet. We lose this, and I will personally beat your asses."

We huddled for a moment, then joined hands. "One-two-three, the Kingdom is here!"

I took the snap and handed it to a wide receiver, who plowed through the Lonestars' line and gained a couple of yards. In no rush, we took the full forty seconds allowed before the next play. That was the plan. Get tackled on the field so the clock kept running. We repeated and gained another two yards. It didn't matter if we didn't get close enough for a field goal. My goal was not to turn the ball over. The Lonestars knew that, and on this last play, with less than three minutes left, they sent everyone toward me to try and force a fumble. I had to scramble, but my guys were ready and blocked them, giving me the opportunity to run four yards and make the first down.

Tempers flared, and some pushing broke out between Rio and a Lonestars tackle. Benches emptied, and one of their tackles, a big moose, slapped Rio's head. Flags were thrown, and I ran into the middle of it to talk to them.

"Stay cool. We're almost there. Don't wanna get tossed out right before we win this. Coach'll have your dicks for dinner."

Milo and Rio pushed past me but nodded.

The ref stood and made the call.

"Defense. Penalty, unsportsmanlike conduct. Fifteen-yard penalty. First down."

The crowd booed, but I didn't care. We had this game, and I wasn't going to let some dumbass fight lose it for us.

"All we need is one more play. Troy, I'm gonna fake hand it to you. Run to the left, and I'm gonna go to the right."

"You got it, Trick."

"Let's do this."

The crowd was on their feet, and I looked up at the Kings' box, knowing, even without being able to see, that everyone was screaming their hearts out for us.

*This one's for you, Fal.*

The play went off beautifully, and I ran toward midfield as the clock ran out. I held the ball up high, screaming my lungs out while the team mobbed me.

"We did it. We did it." Rio jumped me, and we all hugged Coach, then dumped the obligatory barrel of energy drink over him.

After getting rid of our pads and equipment and congratulating the opposing team, Super Bowl Champion merchandise was flung into my hands, and I pulled on the T-shirt and stuck the ball cap on my head. I searched the crowd for my parents and Fallon. Random people came up to congratulate me and take pictures.

I spotted Dev and Brody, each with their own team of cameramen. Brody reached me first.

"Dude, you did it. How does it feel to win your first Super Bowl?"

"Awesome, amazing. I'm still shaking."

"You had a great night. Three touchdowns, and you passed for over two hundred yards. What do you think was the key to your win?"

"Just the whole team. We were hungry for it, and we decided nothing was gonna stop us."

Brody congratulated me, and Dev stepped up and hugged me.

"Trick, that was a masterplan of playing. Except for that one sack, you did everything right."

"Well, nothing is ever perfect, and the Lonestars have a great defense, but we had a mission to keep that Lombardi Trophy in New York for the fans. Go Kings!" I pumped my fist.

"Was there a turning point in the game when you said to yourself, 'It's now or never'?"

"Definitely the sack. This was what I've waited all my life for, so I had to go out and show the world how much I wanted this. And I did."

"You sure did. Great game."

"Thanks, Dev."

Finally, I spotted my parents and Fallon, surrounded by security, making their way across the field. Behind them were Armand Winters and Hayden. I rushed to my parents.

"Mommy, I did it." It was the same thing I'd said to her during my first game. I was ten years old and had thrown my first touchdown pass. She hugged me.

"You sure did, sweetheart. I love you, and I'm so proud of you."

"Dad." I was almost too choked up to speak, but he understood and put his arms around me.

"You deserve this. I'm so proud of you."

Fallon hung back, understanding the protocol.

"Armi, Hayden," I greeted them, and they shook my hand.

"Great win, Patrick," Armi congratulated me. "The Kings are on top once again. Super Bowl champs."

"Thanks, Armi. It's been a great year, and I love being part of the Kingdom."

I faced Fallon. "Hey."

"Hey yourself, champ." He hugged me tight.

"I was thinking of you, feeling your energy during the game," I murmured against his hair.

"I'm glad because I was sending everything I had to you."

We separated, and I saw all the other players hugging and kissing their wives and kids. I wanted so badly to show Fallon how much I loved him, but like always, he had that sixth sense and shook his head while taking a step away.

"Not right now. Not here."

"Trick, Trick, come on. They're gonna do the trophy." Rio pulled at me. "Hey, Fallon."

"Great game, Rio. Congratulations." He and Fallon bumped fists.

"Catch you later." I pinned Fallon with a fierce gaze. "Don't you dare leave."

"Wouldn't think of it." I watched him walk away to where Dev was on a commercial break. Happy that Fallon had a friend to hang with, I allowed myself time to enjoy the moment and stood onstage with the rest of the team to receive the trophy. All my dreams, all my hard work, had come down to this moment.

His short speech finished, the president of the NFL handed Armi the trophy.

"We did it. The Kingdom has spoken, and it said we are the Super Bowl champs. Continuing our winning ways, Patrick Sloane has proven to be a great leader and our quarterback of the future."

Armi handed me the trophy, and I didn't care that tears slid down my face. I was going to enjoy every damn second.

"Thank you, Armi, and thank you to the entire Kings organization. I gotta first thank Coach Jackson and the staff for their unrelenting push to make us better every time we step out on the field. To my parents, for always being by my side and loving me. To Devlin Summers and Brody Martin, your help put me on this stage. Most of all to the Kings fans, the greatest fans in the greatest city in the world, I love you." The stadium roared as I held up the trophy and kissed it. "And to the one who owns my heart, thank you for believing in me."

I handed the trophy off to Rio, who took it and made his speech. My teammates mobbed me when I was named MVP, and I wondered if they'd still feel the same once they learned that Fallon was the one I loved.

With the speeches finished, we hopped off the stage, and I was surrounded by media, superfans, and VIP guests. I made my way through the crowd to where Dev and Brody stood with Fallon and my parents.

"Congrats again on MVP. Totally deserved. You owned that field." Dev hugged me.

Then Mom and Dad hugged me. "We're going back to the hotel to relax for a little while. Go out and have fun with your friends, and we'll see you tomorrow."

She was so cute. "Yeah, we'll meet for breakfast. Love you both." I kissed them, and they hugged Fallon.

Several Kings security were standing on the field, and I called them over and asked if they'd escort my parents out.

"Almost ready to go?" I nudged Fallon.

"Me? I figured I'd go to the hotel while you partied with the team."

"Fuck that. You're coming with me."

Dev cocked his head. "That might cut into your face time with the ladies."

I shrugged. "That doesn't seem to matter much to me anymore." Thinking fast, I narrowed my eyes. "When's your next podcast?"

He looked toward Brody. "Tuesday. We're doing a rundown of the game."

I smiled. "You've got yourself a special guest. Your ratings are gonna go through the roof."

Dev's jaw dropped. "You're gonna do it on *The Huddle*? You're sure?"

I slung an arm around Fallon's shoulders. "Never been so sure of anything in my life."

**

Fallon's hair swung over his face as he moved on top of me. "Patrick, oh God, Patrick," he moaned as I held tight to his hips and thrust up deep.

The hot walls of his ass gripped my throbbing dick. He rode me faster, his eyes gleaming with wild passion, and I fell into their blue depths, spiraling downward.

"Fal, Fallon," I cried out as I exploded inside him, my climax almost painful in its intensity. A shower of stars burst through me, burning me from my blood to the marrow of my bones. Vaguely aware of his come splashing across my belly and chest, I pulled him on top of me, burying my lips in his hair. "I love you so damn much."

He sighed and rolled off me, staying close enough for me to feel the quivers still running under his skin. "Are you really gonna come out on the podcast?"

"*Mmm*, that's my plan." I turned on my side to meet his eyes. "You're still worried?"

"I'm always worried," he confessed. "I don't want the world to come crashing down on you and for you to end up with regrets."

I cupped his cheek. "The only regret would be never loving you the right way. Openly, proudly. I'm tired of hiding who I am and who you are."

A tiny grin ticked up his lips. "That's what Dev used to say."

"And it turned out fine for them."

"Because they waited until after they retired," Fallon pointed out.

"I'm greedy." I kissed away his objections. "I want it all. Now."

**

"Welcome to *The Huddle*. I'm Devlin Summers, and with me is my husband, Brody Martin. I'm sure you're expecting a full rundown of that exciting Super Bowl, and you're certainly not going to be disappointed because we have Patrick Sloane, quarterback of the Kings and MVP of the game. Trick, again, congratulations, and welcome back to *The Huddle*, this time not as a stand-in."

I laughed and adjusted the Super Bowl cap on my head. I'd called Dev and Brody early that morning and talked with them. They'd warned me about the repercussions of coming out while I was still an active player, but I'd brushed aside their concerns, the same way I had Fallon's.

"Thanks, guys. It's been a hell of a ride. I'm so grateful to the Kings organization for their support and also to both of you for all your help. I couldn't have done any of this without you."

"So what now?" Dev asked. "I'm sure you're looking forward to some time off. Do you have plans for the off-season?"

I took off my cap, smoothed my hair, and took a deep breath. "I do, yeah. I'm going to take a month off and go away. With my boyfriend." I clasped my hands and looked straight at the computer screen. "Yes. You heard right. I have a boyfriend. I'm bisexual, which means I'm attracted to both men and women. I've been with my current partner for months now, and I've never been in a happier, more secure relationship."

Brody smiled. "That's wonderful to hear. I know I speak for Dev as well when I say we're very happy for you."

Fallon, who was sitting out of view, held up my phone, which was exploding with texts and phone calls. I ignored it.

"Thank you. I debated discussing this and coming out, especially now after winning the Super Bowl, but I decided, what better time to prove that it doesn't matter who you love? I play professional sports, and my talent is mine—whether I'm gay, straight, or bi. I'm the same guy who threw the forty-yard TD as well as the one who got sacked. We all bleed the same."

Serious as I'd ever seen him, Dev pulled the mic closer. "What do you expect to happen now?"

I thought a moment. "Frankly? I'd hope nothing. The world continues to spin on its axis, we all still have to watch our diets, hate paying taxes, and complain about the weather. I have a boyfriend instead of a girl-friend. So what?" I may've sounded nonchalant, but my heart pounded so loudly, I thought I was going to throw up.

"Have you spoken to anyone else—anyone on the Kings?"

I winced. "No, but I plan to. I respect the owner, Armand Winters, and my coaches tremendously, and I hope nothing will change in how they view me as a player. Because frankly, shouldn't that be their main concern? My performance on the field, not off? But I do plan to talk with them soon."

Dev nodded. "Very well. Let's get into the game and what your strategy was." He and Brody peppered me with questions, and I was happy with how the rest of the podcast went. At the end of the hour, I turned off the computer and put my face in my hands. My T-shirt was soaked through with sweat, but Fallon put his arms around me anyway.

"I love you, and that was the bravest thing I've ever heard."

I grimaced. "What's my social media saying?"

Fallon glanced at my phone, which continued to buzz. "This call I think you'll want to take."

"Hello, Armi," I answered with quiet resolve.

"Can you come into the office now?"

"Sure. Do I need to bring my lawyer?"

"Only if you want to."

That sounded encouraging. "Okay, I'll be there in about forty minutes."

"See you then."

I phoned Ethan, who answered on the first ring. "Good interview. I presume you already got a call from the Kings' management?"

"You'd be correct."

"I cleared my calendar for the possibility. I'll meet you there."

Forty-five minutes later, with Ethan at my heels, I was led into Armi Winters's office. Hayden was there, as well as Coach and Felix Amaro, the Kings' legal counsel. Nausea rose again from my stomach. We sat at the conference table, facing each other. Armi began.

"While I wish you'd come to me, I understand why you decided to speak first on Dev and Brody's show. I want you to know that we have no intention of doing anything differently next season. You're our franchise quarterback, and that's not changing."

Relief flooded me, and tears stung my eyes. "Thank you. It's been very difficult, as you can imagine. I'm hoping that after the initial media circus dies down, only my play on the field will matter."

Armi's smile was a mixture of sympathy and grimness. "I'm hopeful too, but don't count on it. Just know that the Kings plan to stand by you. If you feel unsafe and need additional security, we'll provide it. We plan to put out a statement today supporting you, reiterating that you are an integral part of the Kings organization, our franchise quarterback, and that nothing's changed."

Coach spoke next. "I wish you coulda come and told me. Did you think I'd feel differently about you?"

"I wanna be honest and say I didn't know you well enough. I admire you as a coach, but those of us who've hidden such an important part of our lives learn to live with a certain amount of mistrust."

"I got your back, son," Coach stressed. "Don't ever doubt it."

"Thank you," I whispered.

With the meeting finished, Ethan and I left and stood on the sidewalk outside the building. "That went well. The Kings are a class organization." Ethan pulled out his phone. "Call you a car?"

"Yeah, sure. Fallon's waiting to hear how it went."

A sedan pulled up, and Fallon appeared at the window. "Going my way?" He grinned, and I shook Ethan's hand.

"Catch you later. Thanks for everything."

"If anyone can do this, Patrick, it's you. Give no fucks and keep winning."

I winked. "I plan to."

I joined Fallon in the car and kissed his cheek. "Hey. This is a nice surprise."

"I wanted to be sure I got here in time, so I messaged Hayden to tell me when the meeting looked as though it was about to break up. He gave me his number during the postseason and told me to keep in touch if I ever needed anything."

I took his hand. "They were great. Armi will make a statement that they stand behind me, and Coach was there too. Total support. I haven't checked my phone yet, but tell me. How bad is my social media?"

Fallon made a face. "About fifty-fifty. Some people praising your courage and grateful you came out while you're still playing. Others calling you the usual—queer, fag, all the fun stuff you expected."

I listened with half an ear as I checked my phone. Rio was the first to text.

*Guess I know now why you were so bitchy about me calling it gay shit. Sorry, bro. Not gonna lie and say it doesn't seem weird, but you do you. Hope we're still cool.*

That was better than I'd expected from him. My next message was from Milo.

*Props to you. With you all the way.*

And Troy.

*Dude, what? You fooled me. Still better be your favorite receiver.*

The rest of the messages from the team were all supportive. I clicked on the one from Harte McKinney.

*You're brave. Much braver than I could ever be. It was great playing with you. You're gonna have an amazing career.*

"Wow."

Fallon stopped checking his phone. "What?" I showed him Harte's text, and his brows rose. "Do you think he's gay or bi?"

Thinking through our conversations, I couldn't be sure. "Maybe. Not for me to speculate, but I hope he's happy no matter what. He's a good guy."

We reached the apartment, and I let out a huge sigh of relief when I sank onto the couch. Fallon joined me, and I hugged him close.

"Finally. It's all out there in the open. I wonder what the future will bring."

"Our immediate future is packing for our trip to Barbados. I have a list—"

I kissed him into silence. "Of course you do." I let him go briefly. "But first I wanna hold you."

Fallon smiled against my mouth. "No more hiding or sneaking around. We're really going to do this."

I held him tighter. "Baby, we already are."

# EPILOGUE

## Fallon

*Two years later*

"See Daddy? He's the one throwing the football, baby." I kissed little Rory's wispy dark curls and bounced him on my knee. It was Super Bowl Sunday, and we were all in the Kings' box. My cousin Kelsie, our surrogate, sat next to us. Her husband, Marlon, was in the media booth with his network, so I'd invited her to come sit with us.

Rory babbled, and I swore I heard "Dada."

Ten minutes left in the game, and the Kings were leading. Last year, they'd lost by a field goal, and the armchair Monday morning quarterbacking was vicious, with Patrick taking the brunt of the blame based solely on his sexuality. Even the press, who'd initially treated him well, had printed veiled—and in my opinion, nasty—commentary. Several rabid fans had taken it too far, and we'd received death threats, necessitating us to travel with an even larger security detail than normal.

"Fallon, let me hold him, please." Lori held out her arms and snuggled Rory into her chest. She and Don wore matching smiles, paying more attention to their grandson than the game.

After Patrick came out and the initial uproar faded, we got married before the following season's training camp started. I continued to work as Patrick's PA, but now that I could travel with him, I spent more time with the wives and girlfriends of the Kings' players. They not only accepted me, but I'd acquired a new circle of friends, which included their children. It had made me long for a baby to complete our little family. I'd mentioned it to Kelsie and she'd immediately offered to be our surrogate.

*"I've got two of my own now, and we're not having any more, but I'm happy to help you and Patrick."*

Now Rory was six months old, and Patrick and I were crazy about him. During the season, he'd come home from practice and we'd eat dinner together, taking turns feeding him, playing with him, or reading to him. Once Rory was born, Patrick had bought his parents an apartment in our building, and it was wonderful having them there, plus they were always happy to babysit when we needed a date night or if Patrick wanted me to come with him for a public appearance. Rory would grow up knowing he was wanted, loved, and protected. I had the family I'd always desired.

Armi and Hayden stood at the window, and I joined them.

"How rough has it been for Patrick?" Armi asked with a grimace. "I know he took last year's loss very hard."

"If I can be honest with you?"

"Of course, please. I need to know."

"It's been terrible. He's such a fierce competitor, and though realistically he knows he can't win the Super Bowl every year, he thinks he should. Even the press began to hint that maybe Patrick Sloane was more interested in keeping his man satisfied instead of the fans, and he almost lost it. That was cruel and unnecessary."

Armi frowned. "I remember that article. Martin Price wrote it. The same so-called journalist who wrote a nasty article about me the year I first took over the team."

"After the season ended and the Kings lost, I insisted Patrick talk to a therapist. It helped tremendously. He feels stronger and more in control now."

"That's the most important. I made sure to speak with him several times during the season to let him know he has our full support."

Patrick had mentioned Armi stopping by after home games to talk and see how he was doing. The mental struggles were all from outside sources. Every game he would tell me how much he appreciated the encouragement from his coaches and that his teammates closed ranks around him and always had his back.

A roar rose from the crowd, and we stopped talking to watch the final moments of the game. The Kings were on the Stingers' ten-yard line with less than a minute to go. Patrick took the snap, faked a handoff, and ran it into the end zone himself. With the football held high, he danced alone until the team jumped him.

The clock ran out, and we all hugged each other. I took Rory from Lori and ran out of the suite and down to the field, ignoring the calls from Armi and Hayden to wait for security. The crowd was massive, but as always, no matter where Patrick was, I could find him. I ran to him, and he was hugging his teammates and coaches, so I waited. He turned, met my eyes, and smiled. His long stride ate up the space between us, and he was by my side. Even sweaty and filthy, he was still the most beautiful man I'd ever seen, and I loved him so much, my heart hurt.

"Fal. We did it. Another Super Bowl."

"I love you."

Cameras and reporters surrounded us, but for the first time, I didn't care. I handed him Rory, and to the baby's delight, Patrick lifted him up in the air before kissing him. Patrick held out his arm, and to the sound of a thousand cameras clicking, I hugged him, and he kissed me full on the mouth.

"I'm so proud of you, babe," I whispered against his lips. "I knew you could do it."

"Only because I have you by my side."

I hugged him again, and we each smothered Rory's face with kisses as he giggled uncontrollably.

"It's always a little sad when the season ends." I watched Dev and Brody approach, happiness beaming from their faces. "I can't believe it's over."

Patrick held me tighter. "It's not, babe. It's just the beginning. We may have begun with a false start, but from now on, it's first and forever."

I hope you've enjoyed my Brooklyn Kings series! I had so much fun writing all these characters and while the series might be over, I'm not finished with these guys just yet! Make sure you join my newsletter and reader group to find out all the insider information on what's coming later in the year.

If you're my newsletter subscriber, you know I've been writing a FREE serialized story of Josh the King's receptionist and Travis, who is Candyman's cousin. It's not going to be available anywhere else but my newsletter, so join today.

**FELICE STEVENS** writes romance because what is better than people falling in love? Her favorite part of a romance novel is that first kiss...sigh. She loves creating stories of hopes and dreams and happily ever afters. Her stories are character-driven, rich with the sights, sounds, and flavors of New York City, and filled with men who are sometimes deeply flawed but always real.

Felice writes gay romance because she believes that everyone deserves a happily ever after. Having traveled all over the world, she can safely say that the universal language that unites people is love.

Felice has written in a variety of sub-genres, including contemporary and paranormal, and she has a mystery series as well. You can find all her books listed on her website.

Felice is a two-time Lambda Literary Award nominee and a Lambda Award winner in Gay Romance for her book *The Ghost and Charlie Muir*.

## BOOKBUB

https://www.bookbub.com/profile/felice-stevens

## NEWSLETTER

https://tinyurl.com/y85e69ab

## READER GROUP

https://www.facebook.com/groups/FelicesBreakfastClub/

## FACEBOOK AUTHOR PAGE

https://www.facebook.com/felicestevensauthor/

## INSTAGRAM

https://www.instagram.com/felicestevens

## GOODREADS

https://www.goodreads.com/author/show/8432880.
Felice_Stevens

## WEBSITE

felicestevens.com

## PAYHIP STORE

https://payhip.com/FeliceStevensAuthor

## TIKTOK

https://www.tiktok.com/@felicestevens